OLIVIA ELLIOTT

A Soldier and his Rules
Book Two in The Pemberton Series

First published by Olivia Elliott Romance 2024

Copyright © 2024 by Olivia Elliott

All rights reserved. No part of this publication may be reproduced, stored or transmitted in any form or by any means, electronic, mechanical, photocopying, recording, scanning, or otherwise without written permission from the publisher. It is illegal to copy this book, post it to a website, or distribute it by any other means without permission.

This novel is entirely a work of fiction. The names, characters and incidents portrayed in it are the work of the author's imagination. Any resemblance to actual persons, living or dead, events or localities is entirely coincidental.

Olivia Elliott asserts the moral right to be identified as the author of this work.

First edition

This book was professionally typeset on Reedsy. Find out more at reedsy.com

A Soldier and his Rules

begun. He watched the dust of the street blush pink in the light of a new day that would see unimaginable horrors unleashed upon the innocent, their Spanish allies within the fort.

Richard had been stabbed in the gut by one of his own men— *Charlie fucking Montgomery*— with an officer's sword bayonet no less.

Where had Charlie acquired that?

Richard answered his own question: *another officer, another dead officer.*

The men had clearly been stripped of their humanity. They had walked through the mouth of Hell the night before and emerged the following day without a shred of their former selves. They were looting the city in a drunken onslaught of depravity, the blessed order of the British army melting into complete chaos. Richard had screamed himself hoarse, and when he had seen a young Spanish woman being ill-used by his own man, he had intervened. It had not occurred to him to draw his own bayonet because it was Charlie. Charlie who always followed orders without question. Charlie who said, "Yes, Sir!" to any request he might make of him. Charlie who had volunteered with him and fifty others to form the 'forlorn hope' that led the charge up and over the wall—a suicide mission to lay the groundwork for those who followed. How had he and Charlie survived the night? It was all a blur of adrenaline and smoke, blood and pain.

Richard had watched the sun set over the fort the night before, a glorious expanse of orange light that ignited the walls of Badajoz like a blaze of fire against a sky of wispy violet clouds. The men had swallowed their fear as they waited for darkness to descend. And once the sun was safely tucked away, they had scaled the walls on ladders as the French

Prologue

April 1812, Spain

Major Richard Winter had expected he would die at Badajoz, but he had not expected to die like this. He looked down to where a dark patch of blood bloomed against his dirty crimson jacket. Most of the blood, he knew, would be collecting internally. At least there would not be too much of a mess. Shock prevented his brain from registering the pain, but he dropped to his knees in the street nonetheless, a puff of dust rising up briefly as he hit the ground. The sun rose pink above the parapets of Badajoz Fortress oblivious to the sounds of gunshots, of doors being broken down, of women screaming.

"*Rosy-fingered Dawn shone forth upon them . . .*"
Why did that line come to mind?
Richard could feel himself slipping away.
The British troops had taken the fortress the night before with more men sacrificed to the cause than in any other battle against the French. Richard estimated their casualties at three to four thousand men. And yet, the madness had only just

Contents

Prologue		1
1	Ribbons and Gossip	6
2	A Forlorn Hope	20
3	Dawn and her Rosy Fingers	33
4	Rules, Miss Pemberton	46
5	Strict	63
6	Crossing the Alps	77
7	Winsome and Amiable	93
8	The Darkness and the Light	110
9	You Burn so Bright	125
10	Grey Clouds	141
11	Broody and Unsociable	161
12	Touché	179
13	Such Fantastical Dreams	197
14	An Improper Fraction	212
15	Fireworks	228
16	The Way these Stories End	245
17	One More Rule	260
18	Caught in the Blaze	275
Epilogue		290
Thank You!		296
Also by Olivia Elliott		297

Receive a free subscribers-only steamy novella called *The Bull of Bow Street Meets his Match* when you sign up for my mailing list at oliviaelliottromance.com. This is Book 3.5 in *The Pemberton Series*.

Prologue

despite the circumstances stacked against them.

And then what had happened? How had the very fabric of their souls been rent? How could disorder be sown so quickly?

He could feel his mind cracking once more—a fissure that stretched itself forth, branching and reaching its tendrils into all the secret corners he kept hidden from view. Richard himself was a formidable man. A stone mountain of strength that stood like a human fortress against the world. But he could feel that fissure splintering the solid architecture of his mind. Stone cannot bend, so it will break. Richard found he could not take his next breath. A cold sweat broke out across his brow, and an unfamiliar panic bloomed within him. The enormous muscle of his heart began to beat so hard and so fast that it was visible through his chest. His body began to tremble.

"Juana!" Major Harry called. "I think Major Winter is having a heart attack. Fetch the physician."

One

Ribbons and Gossip

Two years later, in London...
Patience Pemberton was twenty-seven years old, and she was attending yet another ball in a series of balls that had made no difference to her life whatsoever. She was by now so clearly on the shelf that she no longer gave a fig for manners and modesty and all the nonsense she had half-heartedly engaged with over the last several years. What was the point? She always felt somewhat demeaned by the end of the evening, having simpered and batted eyelashes and spent way too much time agreeing with various gentlemen about nothing important at all. Besides, she had her artwork, and things were going well. She had been engaged to paint the portrait of the dowager Lady Winter. A portrait of someone this important was an opportunity to demonstrate her talents, to be recognised, and to raise her profile among the members of the Royal Academy. She grinned to herself as she imagined

Prologue

hurled rocks and blazing rubbish down upon their heads. Firebombs dropped from atop the walls lit up the mayhem as they exploded in the ditches below. So many British soldiers fell before reaching the parapet that the ground beneath the ladders had been thick with the dead. The soldiers who followed had to tread over the bodies of their fallen comrades to take their place in the onslaught.

The wound in Richard's abdomen was not his first in this battle. He had been slashed with French blades across the shoulder and chest, the side of the face, his left arm. Blood had been clotting since the night before gluing his clothes to his filthy, sweaty body. His face was smeared with blood and dirt, his black hair grey with the dust of the fallen fort.

Christ Almighty! Charlie Montgomery! And Dawn with her rosy fingers . . .

Charlie was gone now. The Spanish woman as well. The sounds of the chaos that surrounded Richard came to him in a haze, and he watched in helpless silence as another British soldier dragged a small Spanish boy into the street and shot him. Richard could feel his mind begin to crack as his vision went black and his body slumped forward. He fell unconscious.

When he awoke, he found himself in a large tent being tended by a beautiful Spanish girl, her dark hair pinned up, her white dress stained with smudges of dirt and blood. A larger figure loomed into view.

Green uniform. One of the rifle regiments, thought Richard.

He tried to lift himself up to seated but was shot through with a searing pain in the abdomen that forced him back down to the cot.

"Brigade Major Harry Smith," said the man in green. He

A Soldier and his Rules

gave the Spanish girl a nod and a wink and watched as she picked up her cloth and basin of water and retreated to the other side of the tent. "And you are Major Richard Winter," he said putting up a hand. "No need to speak if it pains you. The surgeon has done what he can. We expected you would die sometime in the night two days ago, but here you are! Alive, if not kicking."

He grinned at his own little joke, then followed Richard's gaze to the Spanish girl who was now folding linen bandages at the other end of the tent.

"Her name is Juana," he said to answer Richard's unspoken question. "She and her sister are under my protection. They took refuge with us when the rioting began."

Major Smith's gaze locked itself on Juana, and Richard detected more than a protective look in the man's eye. She was an extraordinarily beautiful girl, but she could not have been more than fourteen years old. Major Smith tore his gaze back to Richard once more.

"Wellington ordered a gallows be erected in the cathedral square. To threaten the men. Seems to have worked, although I dare say three days of wanton destruction, rape, and pillage would be enough to exhaust anyone. Some of our brave heroes died drowned in vats of ale if you can believe it. This is what comes from a lack of conscription. You get a handful of good-hearted volunteers, and the rest are just desperate men to whom war seems a better circumstance than their own violent and sorry lives."

Richard disagreed. These men had been human like him. He had known them well. They all knew the rules, and they had followed those rules to a man, maintaining a degree of single-minded order that had allowed them to win the battle slapping big gobs of vermilion paint across the faces of some of the smug gentlemen at the Academy.

"I don't like that smile, Patience. It's not ladylike." Patience's mother Lady Agnes Pemberton had glided up beside her. "Be on your best behaviour tonight."

"I'm always on my best behaviour," said Patience.

Lady Pemberton gave a small muffled sound that suggested she did not agree.

"Your behaviour will count this evening because that dress is not exactly—"

"Not exactly what?" asked Patience even though she knew what.

"—not exactly fashionable," finished Lady Pemberton looking down at her daughter's turquoise silk dress layered with delicate silver netting.

Several weeks ago, Patience had engaged in what her mother had subsequently referred to as "subterfuge of the highest order". She had snuck out of the house with her maid and travelled to the modiste on her own. Without Lady Pemberton clucking about her and overriding her fashion decisions, she had been able to order a number of dresses that were more to her liking. Empire waistlines were all the rage in London, but they did not suit Patience's full figure at all. She was keenly aware that these dresses dropped from beneath the shelf of her breasts like some kind of tent over her body. While this style suited a slim lady like those pictured in her mother's periodicals, it was simply not becoming on her in particular. It made her feel as if there was something wrong with her body, and she knew there was not. She had examined her naked form in the mirror quite carefully and decided that she liked what she saw. She deserved a dress that made her feel

A Soldier and his Rules

beautiful, one with a lower waistline that would accentuate her curves.

"You have an artist's eye, Miss Pemberton," the modiste had declared. "Of course you do. And the colours you have chosen will bring out your eyes as well."

"There is no point confining art to a canvas," said Patience. "What you create here in your shop is just as important."

The modiste smiled.

"You are too kind," she said before stuffing a few pins in her mouth and gesturing for Patience to step up onto a block so that she might pin up the hem of the peacock blue velvet that was draped around her.

Back in the ballroom, Patience looked at her mother.

"The dress is not fashionable, but you must agree, it does suit me, does it not?"

Lady Pemberton's answer was given reluctantly.

"It does, my dear. I just worry about you."

"There's no need for that," said Patience. "Worry about George or Grace for a change."

Lady Pemberton gave her daughter a wan smile as Patience turned her attention out towards the ballroom. She scanned the room with her iridescent blue-violet eyes, her senses registering the familiar twinkle of candlelight and scent of roses that always promised so much and delivered so little. Gentlemen were scarce tonight for some reason, and the walls were lined with young ladies chatting quietly and waiting to be chosen for a dance. She spied her friend Abigail Fernside across the room. She was fiddling nervously with her skirts and glancing about, a bit like a twitchy rabbit in a garden.

"I do believe Abigail may need a bit of emotional support tonight," said Patience.

Ribbons and Gossip

"Where is that girl's mother?" asked Lady Pemberton. "She sends her daughter to these events with no more a chaperone than that distracted older sister of hers. And where is she? Off teasing some poor gentleman on the balcony no doubt."

"I don't think 'poor' accurately characterises any of the gentlemen here," replied Patience with annoyance. "And I think it very uncharitable of you to suggest Harriet is teasing gentlemen. Is that not what we're all here for? To tease someone into proposing?" Patience had had enough. Of this conversation and of so much more. "If you'll excuse me, Mother."

She stalked off, skirting the edge of the room as she made her way towards Abigail. As she was passing a couple of gentlemen, one in a black jacket and one in a red officer's uniform, she couldn't help but overhear a snippet of conversation.

"You should enjoy a dance with one of the ladies," said the officer.

The second gentleman in the black jacket grunted in answer, then added, "These are girls, not women, Thomas. I won't dance with girls who can only converse upon the most inane frivolities—minds filled with ribbons and gossip."

Patience stopped short, her heart clenched in agitation at the words just spoken. The gentlemen were now just behind her. She hesitated but only for a moment. Turning on her heel, she brought herself face-to-face with the gentleman in the black jacket.

"You would be wise to keep your erroneous thoughts to yourself!" she said. "There is not a lady here who does not have a great deal more to be concerned about than ribbons and gossip. In fact, ribbons and gossip can make or break a lady's life. Do you think we would spend so much time over

A Soldier and his Rules

our appearance and dress if it were not for the superficial and frankly childish attentions lavished upon the most beautiful and fashionable? Do you think a lady might find a husband by ignoring her appearance? And as for gossip, I know of several young ladies who have had their lives torn apart by a mere whisper. Do you think it an irrelevant concern then to know what is being spoken and by whom?!

Patience had come to the end of her rant. She heaved her chest to take an angry breath and was suddenly aware of the gentleman in the black jacket staring down at her. He was quite large and stood like a wall of muscle and silence in front of her. His black curly hair was cut close to his head, and he had a close-cut beard as well framing a face that was neither malicious in its appearance nor particularly welcoming.

After a considerable silence, the gentleman finally spoke: "Have we been introduced?"

Patience was incensed. *Did he have nothing to say for himself? What did he care at this point for rules and manners?*

"No," she said, "and neither do I care to be introduced to you, Sir."

The gentleman in the officer's red jacket stepped forward, a look of sheer amusement painted across his face.

"*Sir* won't do, my lady. This is the Viscount Winter. You will address him as *my lord.*"

"I will do no such thing!" said Patience before properly registering the name.

Her heart froze in her chest. Patience looked from the officer to the viscount.

Lord Winter? thought Patience as she let loose a torrent of vulgar expletives inside her head. *He is the dowager Lady Winter's son!*

Her mother's words came back to her then: "Be on your best behaviour tonight."

Too late for that now. Patience had dug her own grave, and just to save anyone else the trouble of lifting her over the edge, she had jumped into the pit as well.

Patience found herself staring at the viscount as she tried to determine the best course of action from there. She found herself involuntarily studying the strong lines of his face, noticing where the light fell, the shadows under his eyes.

Could she somehow save herself at this point? Doubtful. And why should she apologise? She had done nothing wrong? Not really. Some sort of strategic retreat needed to be employed.

"If you will excuse me, gentlemen. I must greet a friend of mine. We have ribbons and gossip to discuss."

There. That should do it. No apology necessary. Perhaps he will not even mention this to his mother, thought Patience as she turned her back to the viscount and strode off. *He doesn't even know who I am. Then again, one question to almost anyone in the room would solve that mystery for him.*

Richard Winter was attending the Crampton Ball under considerable duress. His mother would not attend as she was feeling "too delicate," and as the new viscount, he could not very well snub the invitation entirely. How long did he have to stay to be polite? He supposed he would simply leave when the event became intolerable. His friend Captain Thomas Walpole was not helping matters with his boyish enthusiasm and his unwelcome encouragement.

Richard did not want to ask any lady to dance for the simple reason that he did not want to lead anyone on. If a viscount asks you to dance, it should be because he is interested, and Richard was not interested. Not in the slightest. It was enough trouble to manage his condition and keep it hidden from his family now that he was home. He certainly would not be able to hide it from a wife. And what woman would want a husband who was so weak? So broken? But he could not explain all this to Thomas, so instead he had dismissed the young ladies as being frivolous and beneath him. He had not expected to be overheard. And he had certainly not expected to receive such a dressing down from a lady to whom he had not even been introduced! *Who was she?*

Richard watched as the irate lady in the turquoise dress walked with some purpose across the room to a refreshment table, picked up a glass of champagne, and downed the entire glass in a few steady gulps. She replaced her empty glass on the table and strode off to join one of the wallflowers by the wall. It didn't matter where she stood, Richard could tell that she was no wallflower.

"Well," said Richard, "she was—"

"—voluptuous." offered Thomas with a grin.

"I was going to say 'brazen.'"

"A woman," said Thomas still grinning. "Definitely not a girl. Or perhaps she is something else entirely. She seemed more like a storm in a dress than anything else. Just imagine what she would be like in bed."

"Thomas!"

"You should ask her to dance."

"I doubt very much that she would be receptive to that idea, and anyway, one cannot approach a lady to whom one has not been introduced," said Richard.

"Oh, I think we could make an exception in this instance," said Thomas reaching for a glass of champagne from a tray as one of the wait staff passed by.

"We have these rules for a reason, Thomas."

"Well, if you won't ask her to dance, I will," said Thomas taking a swig from his glass.

"It would be unseemly if you did," said Richard. "The action is beneath you. Certainly beneath the rank of captain."

Thomas raised his eyebrows at Richard and handed him the remains of his drink. He took two steps backwards grinning while keeping his eyes on Richard, then spun around and made straight for the lady in turquoise where she was now laughing with her friend.

Now that he was on his own, Richard took the time to observe her more carefully. Her dusty blonde hair was pinned up, a few wavy tendrils falling down against her temples. He watched as she threw her head back, laughing in the most raucous fashion he had ever seen outside of a public house. Her genuine mirth lit the air around her like a sparkler flickering against the night. Richard's eyes roved over the lush curves of her body as he took in her dress properly for the first time. There was not a lady in the room wearing anything similar. The dress looked as if it were made of two separate pieces of turquoise fabric which crossed at the front to embrace her generous breasts, wrapped tightly around her waist, and then flared once more over her wide hips. Richard watched as Thomas approached her in his smart red coat, silver buttons flashing in the candlelight.

Ever since they had returned from war on the continent, Thomas seemed at pains to extract the most hedonistic pleasures from life—drinking, gambling, boxing, women. It was as if he were overwhelming himself in sensation in order to drown out the memory of war. To all outward appearances, he seemed quite fine. He was always quick to smile, quick to laugh, and quick to throw caution unceremoniously to the wind, but Richard wondered if his behaviour was not more self-destructive than anything else. Not that Richard had broached the subject with him. Talking to Thomas about his emotional wounds would be like opening Pandora's box—every last miserable evil thing would escape into the open.

And then what? thought Richard. *No. They were men. And men did not open that box. They kept it firmly shut. Under lock and key. It was weakness that opened the box. Pandora was, after all, a woman.*

Richard watched as Thomas approached the two ladies across the room. The lady in turquoise nodded and said something as she glanced over at her young friend. Even from where he stood, Richard could see the surprise on Thomas's face as he took the hand, not of the lady in turquoise, but of her shy friend, and led her out onto the dance floor. Richard smiled to himself. Captain Walpole had clearly been outmanoeuvred by a storm in a dress. This event in and of itself was enough to make up for what had been thus far a thoroughly tedious and painful evening.

The lady in turquoise watched with an air of satisfaction as her friend began to dance with Thomas. Then before Richard had a chance to look away, she directed her piercing blue gaze straight at him. He had the strangest feeling of being completely exposed, of having nowhere to hide. She didn't glance across him or pretend to have not been looking at him at all. She simply stared him down across the ballroom, and Richard for his part, remained oddly transfixed. After several

Ribbons and Gossip

awkward moments had passed, the lady in turquoise—still keeping her eyes on his—gently lifted her skirts from the floor and sank down into a deep and extravagant curtsy. It was such a strange thing to do, and Richard could not think why she did it. It made him feel . . . it made him feel . . . Richard did not know how it made him feel, but he knew he didn't like it. The evening had suddenly become intolerable. Richard made his way to the door.

After Patience had left Lord Winter and the officer, she spied her mother chatting with a group of older ladies. Patience swiftly took a step to the side and hid behind a large flower arrangement which just happened to be conveniently placed upon a refreshment table. She picked up a glass of champagne and drained it quickly. She could already feel the bubbles going to work, fizzing and popping and shimmering all the way down her throat. For the life of her, she could not rid her mind of the viscount's face, and she was still feeling exasperated not simply by his condescension, but also by his lack of reaction to the manner in which she had called him out.

He could not have been much older than thirty or so, but his eyes looked older. If she were to paint his portrait, she thought, the beard would prove troublesome. More troublesome than the beard, though, was the way he had held his face against her like some sort of shield. As a portrait artist, Patience was used to examining faces, and she thought she had seen it all, but this was something quite new. His face was like a stone wall. She received nothing from it—no hint of annoyance or amusement or boredom. Nothing at all! She had yelled in his face, and there was not a glimmer of a reaction. She knew that something must be going on behind that wall . . . but to keep his mind so concealed . . . it must take an inordinate amount of effort.

Her friend Abigail was only too glad to see her. It was Abigail's first Season, and Patience knew what that felt like. All the expectation of a life-to-be-determined weighed you down—it was not so much your own expectation but that of others. Your own disappointment was one thing. The disappointment of someone else somehow cut deeper. Patience thought of her mother, her older brother George. Not her father the baron. He was never disappointed with her. Or if he was, he did not express it.

"I don't know where Harriet has disappeared to," said Abigail who was dressed in white as girls so often were during their first Season. *Pictures of purity*, thought Patience. She didn't feel so pure herself, but it was not because she had ever touched a man.

"Never mind," said Patience, "I'm here now. Perhaps I could introduce you to some people."

"That would be lovely," said Abigail. She sounded relieved to have someone with her. "I do not think I shall be doing any dancing tonight, so conversation shall make the evening pass a little quicker."

"And why should you not be dancing tonight?" asked Patience. "That is what the introductions are for."

"I have two left feet, Patience," said Abigail in a chiding tone. "If I am to find a husband, it will be despite my dancing, not because of it."

"I think you underestimate your abilities," said Patience

Ribbons and Gossip

kindly.

"Oh no. I estimate my dancing abilities as they are," said Abigail smiling brightly at her friend. "And they are beyond dreadful. At the last ball I attended, I caused the most horrific scene when I tripped over my partner and collapsed into another couple leaving all four of us sprawled across the floor. There's not a gentleman who attended that ball who will be asking me to dance tonight."

Patience laughed at the image Abigail had conjured in her mind.

"So what you need is someone new and unsuspecting," she said taking her friend's arm conspiratorially. "Someone who will not shy away from dancing with such a menace."

It was then that Patience noticed the officer in the red jacket approaching with a wide smile and an impish look in his eye.

What, thought Patience, *is he doing?!*

It felt for all the world like some sort of ballroom ambush. She had played enough games as a child with her brother George to know that you never shrink from an ambush.

"Ah, here we are!" said Patience brightly as the officer stopped in front of her and Abigail, offering them a little bow. Patience affected to know the man—*for why would he approach her if she did not know him?* She scanned his uniform and decided he was likely a captain. *What other kind of officer was there? A major? Or a general? Or was that a major general?* Patience wished she had paid more attention when George had played toy soldiers, but she settled on captain as any sort of general she had ever heard of seemed to be much older.

"Captain, so good to see you! This is my friend Miss Fernside. You are in luck as she is available for this one dance."

Patience watched the officer's face register her familiarity with some surprise, but he recovered quickly, and to his credit, his wide smile never faltered.

"Captain Thomas Walpole at your service," he said offering his hand to Abigail with another bow. "May I have this dance?"

"Oh . . . ah . . . yes," said Abigail taking his hand and casting a wide-eyed and accusatory look at Patience.

Patience watched with some pleasure as her friend took to the floor with Captain Walpole. *That should give these other gentlemen something to think about*, she thought. *Abigail is certainly worthy of a prince let alone a captain.*

Watching the two of them begin to dance, she noticed that Abigail had not been exaggerating about her two left feet. Captain Walpole, however, quickly adjusted to her pace. He even paused their dancing to readjust her position and speak a few quiet words into her ear. Patience could see Abigail smiling shyly as the captain counted out the steps for her with great good humour. He did not look put-upon in the slightest. When they had danced for a stretch without incident, he leaned in to say something to Abigail, and she blushed. Patience couldn't help noticing that Captain Walpole was quite appealing to look upon—longish dark brown hair, dark eyes, and an open, approachable face that looked ready to laugh or burst into song at any moment.

He stands in direct opposition to his friend, she thought. *The derisive viscount in black.* Thinking this, Patience lifted her gaze out across the ballroom in Lord Winter's direction and was startled to find him staring right back at her. She thought she had caught a glimpse of a smile on his face, but if she had, it had disappeared in an instant, replaced by that same stony countenance—a shield of a face that gave nothing away. This irritated her almost more than his previous condescension, and Patience was struck through with the sudden urge to provoke some shift in his expression. Without taking her eyes from his, she gently and gracefully lifted her skirts from the floor and lowered herself into the deepest curtsy she could manage without falling over—a curtsy fit for a king.

That did it—Lord Winter's face buckled under the pressure of her strange behaviour. The wall came down, and behind it, Patience could see that he looked quite astonished. As Patience lifted herself to standing once more, the viscount broke his gaze from hers and strode quickly from the ballroom. She watched him go, instinctively following the lines of his body, his wide shoulders beneath his tailored jacket, his thick muscled thighs pulling the fabric of his trousers tight as he placed one leg in front of the other.

I don't think I'll be painting his mother's portrait after all, thought Patience. *I am, perhaps, my own worst enemy.*

Two

A Forlorn Hope

Richard had been back in England for nearly two years now. Complications with his wounds had initially left him in a weakened state, barely able to walk across a room and certainly unable to ride a horse or fence or box or do any of the activities that would have allowed him to centre himself within the crumbling edifice of his mind. What had happened to him? It was not the death or the loss or the pain that had destroyed him. No. He had been hardened against those things long ago. His father had seen to that. Rather, it had been something else, something entirely unexpected.

Was the world a fair place? Richard knew it was not, and this did not disturb him. While the world may not be fair, we could at least make it somewhat predictable. We could adhere to a structure, a framework, that would allow us to do our best, to follow the thread of what is decent and good along its path. This was what the British army had offered Richard at the outset, and it was something to which he had devoted his life. What had disturbed his mind at the Battle of Badajoz was the dissolution of order. To see his own men shake off their mantle of responsibility, to abandon all sense of loyalty and honour in order to descend into some degenerate, corrupt version of themselves... This was what had broken Richard's mind. He had not thought the line between order and chaos to be so thin.

For months upon arriving home, Richard had lived as if in a perpetual winter, completely numb to himself, to his mother, his younger brother, the quiet servants that tiptoed in and out of his room. He curled into himself, and when an episode would descend upon him—his heart ripping itself from his chest, his body trembling—it felt like death had come, and Richard only hoped it would be quick about its business. But death never came, and his days drew themselves out one in front of the other.

His episodes did not go completely unnoticed, but from the outside, they might have appeared to be a physical reaction to the broken state of his body. If anyone thought them a mental affliction, this possibility was studiously ignored. That way lay unimaginable sadness and misery and the very likelihood that recovery was not, in fact, possible.

Gradually, Richard was able to bring these attacks (for that is what they felt like) under some control. They were somewhat unpredictable, but Richard would notice that familiar feeling like a tide slowly rising within him. If he caught it early enough, he could mitigate the outcome by taking a brisk walk or making a deliberate attempt to slow his breathing. Sometimes, he would imagine his face pressed into the soft

A Soldier and his Rules

muzzle of his childhood horse Bucephalus, the scent of apples on his breath, the stable, hay, and this would often calm the tremors. If it did not, he would lock himself in his room until the fit had passed. Afterwards, he would be weakened as if having just come through a battle, but instead of the pride he might feel at having survived such an ordeal, now he felt only shame.

Sequestered for months upon months at the Winter country home—Avery House—he had taught himself to walk again, to mount a horse, to spend time in the company of others. When he was on leave, Thomas would visit frequently, humouring him with a bout of fencing, or if Thomas was being especially upbeat and bothersome, Richard would suggest a friendly boxing match. His brother James was not given to violent sports, but he would join Richard when he went out riding, and he did Richard the blessed favour of not asking him any questions about the war. They had always had a silent understanding between the two of them ever since they were little. Some things were best left unspoken.

It had been over a week since the Crampton ball, and Richard was doing his best to reacquaint himself with London society, to attend to the duties of his new position as viscount, and to be a support for his fragile mother who after nearly two years, still appeared to be suffering the grief of his father's passing—in short, Richard had been doing his best to be a man. So here he was, out with Thomas, engaging in pleasantries at his gentlemen's club. It was the sort of thing a viscount did, especially one who was fit and healthy, sound in body and mind.

The place was as he remembered it. Low lamplight and the smell of tobacco and leather. A murmur of male voices punctuated by the clink of glasses and the occasional restrained laugh.

"Did I not tell you?" asked Thomas enthusiastically, "After you abandoned me at the ball, I found out who that lady was." When Richard said nothing, Thomas added with a grin, "The storm in a dress."

"Who is she then?" asked Richard, his face completely unreadable.

"She is Lord Pemberton's daughter. A Miss Patience Pemberton. Nine Seasons. No husband. I can't think why," said Thomas, eyes twinkling merrily.

Richard grunted in response. Then realisation dawned upon him.

"Pemberton?" he asked. His mother had said something about having her portrait painted by a Miss Pemberton.

Thomas nodded.

"And there is the baron himself and his son! Come," said Thomas delightedly as if he were inviting Richard out for a game of croquet on the lawn.

Thomas approached Lord Pemberton and his son George where they sat in their leather chairs leaning in towards one another. Lord Pemberton was speaking in a grave manner, and George was listening intently.

"Good afternoon, gentlemen," said Thomas. "Captain Thomas Walpole." Addressing the baron, "I do believe we met some years ago, my lord. I hope you have been keeping well." Then taking a half turn to Richard who was standing behind him, "I have with me the new viscount, Lord Richard

A Soldier and his Rules

Winter." He proceeded to make the introductions.

Lord Pemberton and George both stood, and Richard could see a shadow of wariness descend over their expressions. It was understandable. He was, after all, his father's son. The baron looked carefully at the captain and nodded, then addressed Richard.

"I would be remiss if I did not thank you for your service, Lord Winter. Your reputation as a soldier precedes you. And I am truly sorry for the loss of your father. We did not agree on much, your father and I, but he was a stalwart figure in Parliament and shall be missed."

Richard never knew what to say when someone offered their condolences. He did not need the least bit of consolation for the death of his father. It would have been more appropriate if people had offered their condolences when he was alive— "So sorry your father is still breathing," they might have said. "We pray he doesn't live long." But the baron was merely being polite, excessively so considering he would have known the late viscount well during their many years together in Parliament.

"Thank you," said Richard stepping forward and shaking first the baron's and then his son's outstretched hand.

"Will you be taking up your seat in the House of Lords?" asked Lord Pemberton quite pointedly. "Not every titled man actually shows up as you may be aware."

"Yes, that is the plan," said Richard. "I believe Parliament sits next month."

"Good. I will see you then," said Lord Pemberton. "I hope you will not be as verbose as your father. His speeches had the effect of thinning the numbers if you know what I mean. It takes some fortitude to remain seated for a three-hour speech.

A Forlorn Hope

But your father was ever the strategist. The House of Lords needs only three members for a vote, so his tactics of boring the opposition into leaving often served him well."

"I see," said Richard. "And you, I gather, were his opposition?"

"Yes," said Lord Pemberton with a soft smile. "Perhaps I will be yours as well. But be warned: I am immune to boredom. I like to remain in my seat to the very end of the evening."

"Rest assured, I have no intention of giving any long-winded speeches," said Richard. He was quickly warming to this man and his plain speaking. It was as if he were quite incapable of deception. "I believe my mother is acquainted with your family. If I am not wrong, she has engaged your daughter to paint her portrait."

"Your mother is kind to humour Patience in this way," said Mr. George Pemberton almost apologetically. Apart from the introductions, it was the first time he had spoken.

"Humour?" asked Richard. "Is your sister not a portrait artist?"

"Well . . . yes," said Mr. Pemberton looking a little embarrassed. "I misspoke. What I meant to say was that my sister is glad of the opportunity."

"Ah," said Richard, studying Mr. Pemberton's sombre face. He did not look as glad as he proclaimed his sister to be.

Thomas had been watching the conversation with a bemused expression. Once he and Richard had left the Pemberton men to resume their own discussion, he turned to Richard with a grin.

"She will be coming to your house," he said.

"Excuse me?" said Richard.

"Miss Pemberton. She will be coming to your house to paint

your mother." Thomas shook his head in amusement. "You must tell me all about it."

"It has nothing to do with me, Thomas."

"But it could," said Thomas impishly. "It could."

Patience had found her little sister Grace tucked away in a corner of the yellow drawing room reading. Grace was ten years old and somewhat precocious when it came to literature. She could usually be found with her nose in a novel or writing her own furious and elaborate stories. This time, however, she was reading a periodical and appeared to be doing so surreptitiously. Patience had snuck up on her quietly.

"What is that you are reading?" she asked.

Grace looked up and froze, a bit like a startled deer.

"Nothing much," she said.

"Give it here," said Patience, hand outstretched.

Grace handed over the periodical, and Patience could see it was her mother's subscription to *La Belle Assemblée*.

"I was reading the poetry," said Grace quickly.

"It looked to me like you were reading the fashion component of the magazine," said Patience. "There's nothing wrong with that, so why are you behaving so oddly?"

"I'm not behaving oddly," protested Grace.

Patience opened up the magazine and flipped her way through it. It did not take her long to find the offending passage. A columnist known only as 'Britannicus' gushed effusively over the delicate waists and slender figures he imagined all French ladies displayed. However, he had followed up with a less-than-complimentary commentary on their English counterparts:

An excess of plumpness has been admired in our fair sex ever since a passion for feeding cattle has become the vogue for our lords and gentry. Not satisfied with this redundance of bulk in her figure, she must increase it in certain parts by compressions and bolstering. Her bosom must be pushed up near her chin . . .

Patience lowered the magazine to her side.

"I see," she said. "Where is Mother?"

Grace shrugged. As she did so, George entered the drawing room. He stood tall and handsome, surveying the room with his keen grey eyes.

"No tea?" he asked.

"Ring the bell," said Patience. "It's very easy."

George gave her a look—the look of a brother who felt himself to have endured much when it came to his sister. He rang the bell.

"I just came from the club," he said. "Father and I ran into the new Lord Winter. He is the spitting image of his father—the demon himself but with a younger face."

George shook his head incredulously. It was almost as if he were not talking to Patience at all but to himself.

"We had not expected him to show in London at all this Season. He stayed away last year, so we had hoped he would not be taking up his seat. Thinking about it now, he was probably incapacitated last year due to his wounds. Father is curious to see how he conducts himself in Parliament, whether he will follow in his own father's footsteps. The former Lord Winter took every opportunity afforded him in Parliament to ensure some measure of misery upon those less fortunate. Whether it was widows or tenant farmers or orphans in question, Lord Winter sought to 'teach them a lesson' as it were. And the lesson was always one of enduring hardship and cultivating a mercenary kind of self-sufficiency in the face of the desperate odds Lord Winter himself sought to stack against them."

George shook his head in disbelief at the words he himself was speaking.

"The new Lord Winter looks as grim as his father, but he was polite at least. If the stories are to be believed (and George sounded as if they should not be believed), he is a war hero."

"Is he?" said Patience in the most nonchalant tone she could muster.

"He suffered some terrible wounds at his last battle, so they say. Not that we discussed it. But there is much outlandish talk of his bravery. Have you been reading the papers, Patience? Does the term 'forlorn hope' mean anything to you?"

"I read the papers, George," said Patience irritably.

"And a 'forlorn hope'?" asked George. Patience could tell he was hoping to catch her out.

"A group of volunteers meant to lead the first charge. More often than not, a death sentence," responded Patience. She would not be condescended to by her brother.

George smiled. "You do read the papers! Well, our Lord Winter is said to have volunteered for several such assignments. I do not see it myself—these stories are often overblown in an effort to raise morale and inspire a certain patriotic fervour. Know the father, know the son. And the father would certainly not have sacrificed a hair on his head for anyone."

"Mm," responded Patience. A picture of Lord Winter—a proper portrait—was starting to form in her mind. Bravery was one thing, but this was of another order. It seemed to her

A Forlorn Hope

that the man had a death wish. "Did you speak of anything else besides Parliament?" she asked.

"You mean your painting his mother's portrait?" asked George. "Yes, he did bring it up."

"And?"

"And nothing," said George. "It was just a point of conversation."

"He didn't say anything . . . else?" asked Patience.

"What else would he say?" asked George pointedly. He was starting to look a little suspicious.

"Nothing," said Patience quickly. Then added, "I only thought he might have passed on a message from his mother as to the dates and times of the sittings we were planning."

"I thought those had already been arranged," said George. Patience winced internally. George, like his father, never forgot a detail.

"Oh yes, it slipped my mind," said Patience waving *La Belle Assemblée* up and then dropping it back down at her side. "Your tea, George," she added, nodding towards a footman who had appeared at the door. George turned to make his request, and Patience quickly shuffled past him and out of the drawing room door.

Patience did not know what to make of Lord Winter. It was possible he had spoken with his mother about her behaviour the other night, but if he had, she doubted very much that she would still be engaged to paint his mother's portrait. And he had brought up the subject himself! With her brother and father no less. Could she have misread the situation? She reviewed the events in her mind. *One, having never been introduced to the man, I berated him in front of his friend. Two, I refused to address him as my lord. Three, I then went out of my way to look like a mad woman by curtsying to him from across the room as if he were, in fact, the Prince Regent. Four, he looked displeased by this last display and immediately left the ball.*

Patience was quite accustomed to the feeling of a successful round of self-sabotage, and this wasn't it. It seemed that despite her best efforts she had not, in fact, destroyed her career before it had started. She would be painting the dowager Lady Winter after all!

The unwelcoming face of Lord Winter came into her mind—the lines, the light, the shadows. His face was a puzzle and his behaviour even more so. She stepped into her studio and picked up a piece of charcoal. It didn't take long. She had his likeness before her in black and white, and she held it up at arm's length, screwing up her own face to make sense of his.

She looked down at the table where she had dropped *La Belle Assemblée*, picked it up, and strode from the room in search of her mother. When she found her arranging flowers in a reception room, she waved the periodical back and forth in front of her face.

"Grace was reading this!" she said in an accusatory tone.

"Yes, my dear, can I help you with something?" asked Lady Pemberton with exaggerated patience.

"Have you read the fashion portion of this edition yet?"

"Mmhmm," said Lady Pemberton sliding a long-stemmed yellow rose into the vase in front of her.

"Did you not think Britannicus particularly insulting to English women in particular and women in general?"

"He is always quite pointed, Britannicus," said Lady Pemberton adjusting her rose within the arrangement.

"He compared us to cattle, Mother—cattle!"

"These things happen," said Lady Pemberton, "when columnists attempt to be clever. They like to be noticed."

"Does it not bother you, Mother, that through your subscription, you are paying this man's salary?"

"He would be paid whether I subscribed or not," said Lady Pemberton pertly. "And if not, how would I keep abreast of the latest fashions? Besides, there is much to recommend *La Belle Assemblée* besides fashion news. Essays, poetry, serialised novels. If I do not read what the rest of London is reading, I shall be exiled to the outer limits of every circle of conversation. And so would you, my dear. Unfortunately, paying Britannicus's salary is a necessary evil. Come. Help me with this arrangement."

Patience glanced down at the flowers in the vase. Her mother had a predilection for yellow.

"Add some blue, forget-me-nots perhaps. Lilacs are in bloom early all across London. There's no need for these hot house flowers."

"You are quite right," said Lady Pemberton with a grateful nod. "Thank you."

"Keep this away from Grace," said Patience lifting *La Belle Assemblée* once again. "It is not necessary to subject her to the evils of Britannicus."

"I will be mindful," said Lady Pemberton in a placating tone that Patience knew was intended to disarm her.

Patience returned to her studio. To her sketch of Lord Winter. Lately, she felt herself to be in a constant state of vexation. She felt as if her insides were bubbling up like molten rock. Every time she opened her mouth, ash and soot and fire spewed forth, and it seemed that there was nothing she could do to stop it. If she was not snapping at her brother or scolding her mother, she was berating complete strangers in ballrooms.

I have turned into someone entirely unlikeable, she thought. *Not that I'm usually wrong . . . but do I have to be so unpleasant about it?*

A wave of disappointment and fatigue washed over her. She needed to lie down. Within a few minutes, she found herself in her bed chamber. Sitting down on the bed, she realised that she still had the sketch of Lord Winter in her hand. Looking at it, she could see that something about it wasn't quite right. She placed the paper down on the hard surface of her bedside table and stood to examine it carefully. Then she took a finger and smudged the charcoal beneath both of his hard eyes to create deeper sunken semi-circles of shadow. There. That was better. That was how she remembered his face. Looking at the picture, she realised for the first time that something *could* be seen behind that shield of a face: Lord Winter was a haunted man.

A haunted man with a death wish, thought Patience gazing into his eyes.

Three

Dawn and her Rosy Fingers

One of the best parts about being in London rather than the Pemberton country home was the fact that George, being twenty-nine going on thirty years old, had taken bachelor accommodations in town and no longer lived at the house. Patience loved her brother, but he could be a little overbearing. Since Lord Pemberton did not seem concerned to lace his daughter's life with restrictions and requirements, George felt it his duty to make up for this oversight as if it were his God-given burden. He always seemed somewhat pained by her actions, as if any slight to her reputation as a paragon of obedience and even temperament were some physical injury to himself.

Lord and Lady Pemberton slept late, so it was with great pleasure that Patience looked forward to her solitary early morning ride in Hyde Park. She would sneak out back to the mews in her dark green riding cloak and have the groomsman saddle her black hunter. From there, it was a short ride at a walking pace to the park, the click of the horse's shoes on the cobbles making Patience grimace somewhat. She always breathed a sigh of relief when they arrived at the park, and her horse could tread on softer more pliable ground. Early in the morning, it was as if the park were a watercolour painting— a wash of green and grey-blue with a mist rising off the Serpentine.

This morning was just like any other—a cool, crisp promise of a new day. The park was fairly empty as usual, and Patience trotted her horse along Rotten Row passing the occasional gentleman walking or on horseback, then veered off the path and across an expanse of grass. She squeezed her hunter's sides to pick up the pace—a canter and then a gallop, her hood falling back, the wind washing over her. Eventually, she reined in her horse, coming to rest on a small rise beneath a large oak tree. She looked out across the park with a smile.

This must be what it feels like to survey one's dominion, thought Patience.

Richard had seen Miss Pemberton trotting his way along Rotten Row at some distance. He did not initially recognise her, but a lady riding astride and alone in the early hours of the morning certainly did draw the eye. The hood of her green riding cloak had concealed her face, but as she turned from the path and pressed her horse to a canter, her hood had fallen back, and Richard felt a hard knot tighten in his belly as his mind took in the determined lift of her chin and her sandy blonde hair straining free of a plait thrown over one shoulder.

Dawn and her Rosy Fingers

What was she doing at the park alone?

It was possibly none of Richard's business what the lady was doing or why. He would like to carry on his way. Go home. Eat breakfast. But she was a lady. At the park. Alone. He had met her father and brother only days before, so she could be considered an acquaintance. Richard glanced about him. If he had noticed an unchaperoned lady riding pell-mell across the grass, there were certainly other gentlemen and not-so-gentle men who might have done so as well.

After the events at the Crampton Ball, Richard certainly did not want to engage with Miss Pemberton. Far from it. But he was obliged by duty to do the gentlemanly thing which would be to see to her safety and escort her home. He winced at the thought. For some reason, he doubted very much that she would appreciate an unsolicited escort. Richard heaved a sigh. If he could charge forward into untold ranks of armed French soldiers, he could surely do this. A gentle tug of the right rein led his horse from the path and onto the grass. Squeezing his horse between his thighs, he picked up the pace, watching Miss Pemberton sat atop her little hill. Her gaze scanned the park, then landed firmly upon him and his approach. At first, she lifted her reins looking as if she might flee, but as he came closer, recognition settled over her face, and she settled the reins in one hand and leaned forward to stroke her horse's neck with the other. Her sandy plait swung forward as she leaned. A loosened strand of hair blew across her cheek catching the morning light and shining golden for just a moment before the wind released it once more.

When Richard pulled his horse to a halt before the lady, she said nothing. She lifted herself to an upright seat and stared at him expectantly.

"Excuse me, Miss Pemberton, but I could not help noticing that you are alone at the park." When she said nothing in response, he added, "Without an escort."

She just looked at him and did not respond. In the clear light of morning, her eyes were uncommonly blue—a delphinium blue, shifting to violet depending on the angle of the light.

"I shall escort you home," said Richard. As usual, he spoke without a hint of a question in his tone. He was not asking. Still, she did not respond. "Miss Pemberton, I am speaking to you!"

At that, she seemed to rouse. She squinted her eyes ever so slightly, regarding him with a shrewd look.

"I'm sorry, but have we been introduced?" she asked imperiously.

Richard bristled as he felt his own words—the words he had spoken to her at the ball—thrown back at him. He thought . . . He almost thought she was about to smile. But if she was, she decided against it when he said, "That is beside the point."

"I don't think that it is," countered Miss Pemberton. "A lady must not approach a gentleman, nor a gentleman a lady if they have not yet been introduced. It is a rule, you see, Lord Winter. A rule you seem to hold quite dear."

"There are rules and then there are rules, Miss Pemberton."

"What is that supposed to mean?"

"I have an obligation to see to your safety in this instance—it is another rule, if you wish to speak of it as such. I believe this obligation trumps introductions."

"I am perfectly safe," replied Miss Pemberton. "I am on a very large horse. I will not be accosted."

Richard could feel his ire rising. The naiveté she was displaying would land her in any number of dangerous situations. Dangerous to her reputation, but also dangerous to her person. Richard prompted his horse quickly forward and swiped the reins from her hands.

"Now I have your rather large horse, Miss Pemberton. And if I so chose, I could have *you* as well." He let that comment settle as her big blue eyes grew wider. Then, "It would benefit you in future to be a bit more wary of others and bit less flippant about your own safety."

Richard then twisted his horse in a rather clever equestrian manoeuvre so that they were now both seated side-by-side on their horses and facing in the same direction. He still had her reins. She reached for them and tugged, but he kept his grip tight.

"Lord Winter!"

"Miss Pemberton!"

"You will hand me my reins this instant!"

"I will not. You are coming with me."

"You are being absolutely ridiculous. I have been riding in this park for weeks. I have been perfectly safe. These are gentlemen and gentle ladies." She passed a hand across the distant scattering of park-goers, few though they were.

"You are safe until you are not, Miss Pemberton. A gentleman is often only a gentleman in context—in a crowd at a ball is one thing, alone in a deserted park is quite another. You should not be so trusting. Given the right situation, you may find that the more bestial appetites of any number of gentlemen will come to the fore."

She was looking at him with indignation and not a little bit of annoyance, but he pressed on, wanting to impress upon her the seriousness of her circumstance. He knew it was improper to say what he said next, but he couldn't help himself. She was

A Soldier and his Rules

infuriating.

"Fully one-third of the women in this city are employed to satisfy these appetites of men, my lady. Do you understand me?" He leaned in towards her, angry, but she did not shrink from him. "One third! It is barely comprehensible, is it not? I only tell you this because I do not believe you fully appreciate the situation, or you would not be behaving as you do. I cannot imagine your father or your brother are aware of your current whereabouts."

She stared at him for any number of seconds, and he waited. He felt as if she were examining his face. She looked to his mouth, then up across his cheek to his ear before drawing her gaze back to his eyes. This made him feel odd. That same strange feeling he had encountered when she had dipped into that ludicrous curtsy from across the ballroom. He didn't like it.

Finally, she spoke: "It seems I am in your keeping, Lord Winter. I suppose I am lucky that your appetites are not so base as your countrymen." She paused here. Again, examining his face in that same disturbing manner, exploring it with her blue eyes. "You may escort me home. But I would ask, could you . . . I would very much like to ride down to the Serpentine before we leave."

Richard was at first relieved at Miss Pemberton's capitulation, then taken aback at the casual manner of her request. He had just been scolding her in a rather forceful and angry manner, and despite this, she was asking him to take a jaunt with her down to the Serpentine. As if they were riding companions. She was looking at him in that way again, but this time she was smiling sadly.

"I won't be back, you see. In the early mornings anyway.

Once you tell Father or George about this, I shall be forbidden." She lifted her gaze out across the park. "I like to see the water first thing in the morning. Have you seen it at this time of day?"

Richard nodded his head.

"So you know why I wish to see it," she said.

Patience had seen Lord Winter from atop her little hill approaching at some speed upon his steed. At first, she thought him a stranger, and a quick flash of alarm had her lifting her reins to make off before he arrived. But then, his face came into focus, so familiar to her now. She had made many small adjustments to her sketch over the past few days—wider eyes, a lower cheekbone, square jaw set as if grinding against the upper molars. If she had to title the sketch, she would call it 'Face of Stone'. But she did not have to title the sketch, so the moniker remained in her mind alone.

If she were to believe George, this was a man not to be trusted . . . but if she were to believe her own intuition, this was a man who lacked any malice. Lord Winter had not done the vindictive thing—the expected thing—which would have been to mention her completely outrageous behaviour to his mother. Patience was still grateful for this, and she thought she might perhaps break through his face of stone with a little joke before thanking him.

She should have remembered that ladies are not known for their jests. Her ironic, "I'm sorry, but have we been introduced?" did not go down as expected. The man did not smile or laugh. Nor did he show any sign of amusement

A Soldier and his Rules

upon his face. He just stared at her with a hard expression that she could not read at all and then proceeded to lecture her about her own safety with a contained fury that Patience could not quite understand. She was barely an acquaintance! Patience added 'furious' to her list of descriptors of Lord Winter. *Haunted, furious, death wish.* He was becoming more interesting by the minute.

At first, his unashamed paternalism towards her made Patience want to yell and scream and argue and ignore—all impulses she struggled to hold in check. But the man did now have her horse. *And if he so chose, he could have me*, thought Patience, replaying his words to herself. It had not been a terribly gentlemanly thing to say, but somehow, for some reason, she didn't mind.

The man had quite clearly demonstrated that she was not as safe as she perhaps thought she was. Patience was used to losing this sort of battle with George, so she knew when she had been bested, but she could try for a tiny little win to take the edge off her disappointment, so she said, "I suppose I am lucky that your appetites are not so base as your countrymen." Having said the words, she was careful to watch his face, and sure enough, there appeared a small crack in his shield. His eyelids lowered partially as he looked at her, and his lips parted ever so slightly. It was barely a moment, and then his features set once more against her. That wall of stone. But Patience felt a little thrill travel through her at the feat. She had momentarily breached the wall. When she arrived home, she would make a new sketch of his face with that look upon it.

But first, the Serpentine.

"I will not try to escape," said Patience reaching for her reins.

Dawn and her Rosy Fingers

Lord Winter allowed her to take the reins, and they rode their horses side-by-side down the hill at a walking pace.

"Do you often come to ride in the park this early?" asked Patience.

"Yes, usually earlier than this," replied Lord Winter casting her a quick sideways glance.

"Let us take one last look at the Serpentine before I am locked up in the castle turret," said Patience. "Perhaps I shall grow my hair long. Then you could come to visit me and use my tresses as a rope to climb the tower."

"That is perhaps overly dramatic, Miss Pemberton. I doubt very much that your father or brother have you locked up anywhere."

"Ah, but I cannot leave at will without a maid or a brother or a someone to shadow my every move. How would that make you feel, my lord?"

She noticed that he was quick to turn his head towards her.

"My lord?" he said. "Not so long ago you were adamant that you would not address me as such."

"Yes, but now I have been broken . . . like our horses," she replied, locking eyes with him.

Lord Winter tore his gaze from hers and looked up to the sky as if asking for strength. Patience smiled to herself. She had the same effect on George.

They plodded on for some time in silence. Patience breathed deeply of the cool moist air. George would not be able to let this one go. The viscount himself would bring her home like some naughty child run off to play without leave of her nurse. She found the whole situation quite humiliating. There would certainly be no more early morning rides, for who would bring her at this hour?

A Soldier and his Rules

The Serpentine soon loomed into view. A blue mist rose off the water softening the outline of a stand of trees on the far bank. A perfect reflection of those trees rested beneath them in the water.

"Have you ever dripped a pattern in ink upon one side of a piece of paper and then folded that paper in half?" asked Patience.

Lord Winter looked across at her but made no acknowledgment.

"When you unfold the paper, you have something entirely new, a perfectly symmetrical design that is quite inconceivably different than the dribble of ink you initially made. In the early morning, the Serpentine gives me that same feeling of surprise and wonder. It is always just a little bit different than it was the day before."

Patience was looking out across the water, trying to imprint this memory upon her mind so that she might revisit it when she was trapped at home gazing out across the square from her bedroom window in the early morning. She did not see Lord Winter's face harden into an inscrutable and immovable mask.

"Yes, well, we should be getting on," he said turning his horse in the direction of Mayfair.

Patience turned to him. "You said you came earlier to the park. So you will have seen the Serpentine at its best then, when Dawn shines forth upon it with her rosy fingers."

Lord Winter turned sharply back in her direction.

"What did you say?"

"I was merely being poetic," replied Patience. "I meant to say, when the first pink light of dawn touches the water."

"How did you . . . ? Do you read Homer?" asked Lord

Dawn and her Rosy Fingers

Winter, his face transformed and softened now in a way that Patience had not seen before. There was something there in his features that made her feel as if her heart might break for him right there in the park.

Patience smiled gently. "I do, my lord. Again and again."

"*The Odyssey?*" he asked.

Patience screwed up her face. "I'm afraid not. I mean I *have* read it, but I do not revisit it. *The Iliad* is my favourite."

"The siege of Troy," said Lord Winter in a way that sounded as if he had been there. "It is a bloodbath, that story. I wonder that a lady would find so much interest in it."

"Homer paints with his words," said Patience in answer. "I find even the most repetitive phrases of his quite soothing. Especially that about the Dawn and her rosy fingers. It is always a new day, is it not? Whether you are lying in a ditch choking on your own blood or triumphant as you strip the armour from your enemy's limp body. It is no matter to her—the Dawn. She will shine forth regardless. A new day in which to mourn and fight and die. It is quite beautiful. It is tragic, but it is beautiful. It is life."

"Yes," said Lord Winter slowly, "This very same thought about the Dawn has struck me at various moments in my past."

"When you were . . . abroad?" asked Patience carefully.

Lord Winter locked eyes with her. It was Patience's turn to feel examined now, and it was not an altogether comfortable experience. It was as if the man were trying to peer inside her through the portals of her eyes, and all Patience could think was, *I hope he doesn't find where I've hidden all the ribbons and the gossip.*

Lord Winter finally withdrew his gaze and lifted it up and

A Soldier and his Rules

across the green expanse of park.

"The past is best left where it lies," he said as he raised a shield wall over his features once more. "Come. The hour grows late, and you shall be missed."

They rode their horses at a walking pace in silence across the watercolour park, then out through the enormous wrought-iron gates.

Patience cast a sideways glance at Lord Winter as they made their way along the street only to find he was already looking at her.

"Are you enjoying your time in London?" she asked by way of making conversation.

"No," was his clipped response.

Patience laughed. "I never thought to answer such a question so directly. I shall remember to do so the next time one of my mother's friends is enquiring about whether I am having a good time at a society function. I shall simply say 'no' and be done with it! It would be the truth anyway."

She could feel Lord Winter watching her, but she kept her eyes forward.

"You don't enjoy the Season?" he asked.

"No," said Patience. "I find it difficult and aggravating. It's possible I was overly abrupt with you the other evening on account of my poor mood."

Lord Winter slowed his horse to keep abreast of hers. He was silent so long, she did not think he would respond at all to her little attempt at an apology. When he did speak, his voice was a low rumble beneath the high clip-clop of the horses hooves over the street.

"I should not have spoken as I did," he said. "It was not for your ears, but it was poor form nonetheless." Patience registered his concession with some surprise.

"Our house is this way," she said, turning her horse at a corner.

When they finally arrived outside the Pemberton house on Grosvenor Square, Lord Winter brought his horse to a halt as Patience led hers to the mews at the back. When she realised he wasn't coming with her, she turned back.

"Will you not come in to make a report to my father?" she asked.

"It's another rule of mine, Miss Pemberton," replied Lord Winter. "Don't be a rat." As he said it, he smiled for the first time in her company, and Patience's heart skipped a beat for no reason she could intelligibly discern. "I only hope my warnings for your safety will be taken to heart."

"How could they not, my lord?" said Patience. "It was a most memorable morning."

"It was," agreed Lord Winter, his smile still resting lightly in place. "Good day, Miss Pemberton."

"Good day, Lord Winter."

Four

Rules, Miss Pemberton

Richard rode home in a daze. The morning had taken an emotional toll, and while he had held himself together admirably, now the simple thought of Miss Pemberton returning to the park on her own caused a familiar sensation to rise up from his belly threatening to overwhelm his faculties.

His initial concern for her had been academic. He had simply been doing his duty as a gentleman. But then she had spoken to him—about the Dawn and the Serpentine and drippings of ink that transformed themselves. The image of Charlie Montgomery man-handling that young Spanish woman at the fort arose in his mind, and he could feel the tide waters rising to drown out his sanity. He took long slow breaths and tried to focus on the rhythmic rocking of the horse beneath him. He imagined his childhood horse Bucephalus, the barn-like smell of him, the soft nudge of his muzzle when he was looking for an apple. Richard had only to keep the attack at bay until he arrived home. If it had not dissipated by then, he could lock himself in his bed chamber claiming a splitting headache.

By the time Richard emerged from his room for supper that evening, he was a weakened man. The attack had claimed him with a force he had not experienced in some time. 'Spent' was the word he would use to describe his current state. He would eat supper with his mother, and then he would go back to bed and sleep it off. Tomorrow was, after all, a new day. Dawn would shine forth and stroke him with her rosy fingers, and all might be well.

His mind wandered back to that morning at the park. *Miss Pemberton. What an infuriating woman!* Her defiance made him want to . . . made him want to . . . what? Tame her? No. That wasn't it. But he did very much want to lay hands on her, God help him. Richard flinched at how unpleasant that sounded even in his own mind. That's not what he meant. What he meant . . . what he wanted . . . with Miss Pemberton was. . . Thinking of her aroused that disconcerting feeling once more, and he pressed it aside with distaste. *No point thinking about Miss Pemberton sitting up in her tower growing her golden hair and reading Homer's bloody Iliad.* Richard thought of himself now as only half a man who had no business bringing anyone else into his sphere of shame—a shame that he felt should have killed him long ago.

At supper, his mother sat opposite him at a ridiculously long table. He may be the viscount now, but she was still the dowager viscountess, and matters of the household were under her control. Unfortunately, she liked an imposing dinner table. Richard could let her have that, he thought.

A Soldier and his Rules

If she wants to yell down the length of the table at me every night, so be it. She is in a delicate state as it is.

His father had died just weeks before Richard had returned home battered and bruised from the continent. There had been a horse-riding accident. An awkward fall. A broken neck. Richard's mother had been inconsolable. Neither Richard nor his brother James could understand why. Their father had been a beast of a man who did not appear (at least to them) to love her in the slightest. When he had been alive, she had tiptoed around him as if he were gunpowder and she were holding a candle. Now that he was dead, for some reason, she missed all of that—she missed *him*. Richard wondered what sort of a man he had been with her behind closed doors. There were some things, he decided, that he would never understand, and his mother's grief was one of them. Even over a year-and-a-half later, the dowager viscountess would still pass through waves of melancholy punctuated by bursts of energy and vitality that led one to believe that nothing at all were the matter and that perhaps, finally, her period of mourning was over.

"James will be home by the end of the week," she said (loudly so that he might hear from his end of the table) as she stabbed a single pea with her fork.

And Michael. James and Michael will be home by the end of the week, thought Richard. That was the sentence that would not be spoken aloud.

"Yes," replied Richard. "It will be nice to have him back." *And Michael too.*

"What does Greece have to offer that England does not?" asked Lady Winter as if it were the most rhetorical of questions.

Rules, Miss Pemberton

Richard looked to the darkened dining room windows that were being pounded with rain. The sound was cacophonous. Like distant gunfire.

"I have no idea," he replied.

"You should invite that Captain Walpole of yours around for dinner sometime," offered his mother.

"He has an active social life," said Richard. "I'm not sure he'd be able to fit us in."

"Pish-tosh," said his mother. "He cheers me. So handsome and lively. Make sure you extend the invitation at least."

"I will," said Richard resignedly. "Perhaps he could join us when James is back."

"That would be splendid!" said Lady Winter. "If it is to be a dinner party, I should invite a couple of ladies as well, to even out the numbers."

"No need," said Richard quickly. "Since it's not a dinner party. Simply a family gathering."

Richard certainly did not need his mother playing matchmaker which was exactly what she was conniving to do. James needed her efforts even less.

"We could have music," said his mother.

"Or we could not," said Richard.

His mother gave him a scolding look.

"Richard, I do not ask for much."

No, but your husband did. "As you wish, Mother."

At that she clapped her hands together twice.

"Good boy."

Richard shoved a heaping spoonful of lamb stew into his mouth and chewed without tasting it at all.

A Soldier and his Rules

Dear Patience,

Thank you for your letter. I am so glad to hear you are progressing with your portrait painting. The dowager Lady Winter of all people! How did you manage that? And may I ask, what is she like? John has things to say about her husband that I find myself unable to put to paper.

All is still well with everyone here, so you must not concern yourself. It is enough for me to bear John's unwieldy concern. He has engaged two local midwives as well as a doctor, and now that the time looms closer, he has them visiting daily in a steady rotation! I doubt very much that he will be able to countenance another child. He is beside himself with worry. As you can imagine, I have become quite physically cumbersome, and while I am waddling to and fro like a duck, John insists that I am the picture of elegance! (I only tell you this because I know you will find it funny.)

I have been working flat-out on the first mathematics textbook—my "book of numbers" as John has been calling it. I thought I would be able to continue immediately after the birth, but when I mentioned the idea to one of my midwives, she just laughed at me. It's likely she knows something I do not. Perhaps, I will need more time to recover and adjust to our new life than I had anticipated.

Molly can barely contain her excitement at becoming an aunt. She insists that her presence in the birthing room will be a necessary scientific undertaking, but John says she will attend the birth over his dead body. I think I shall side with John on this one.

I know you said you would travel back from London to be here for the birth, but I do not want you to miss your Season on my account. One never knows when a baby might arrive, and I would not want you stranded here for weeks and weeks. I'd rather think of you enjoying yourself in town—painting portraits and meeting new people. John will send a note with his own driver to inform

you once the baby has arrived.
  Keep well.
  Be yourself.
  I love you.
  Serafina

Patience lowered the letter to her lap where she was seated on her blue-and-white bedspread. She wiped a tear that had somehow emerged of its own volition at the corner of her eye. She wasn't crying. But if she *was* crying, what was she crying about? She placed the letter on her bedside table on top of a sketch of Lord Winter. Not her first sketch—the face of stone. This was perhaps her fifth sketch in as many days. She had drawn his face looking haunted, his face looking furious, and she had even drawn his face in that moment when she had cracked it with her comment about his 'appetites'—lowered eyelids, slightly parted lips. In this last sketch, he was smiling the way he had smiled at her when he had delivered her home. Patience pulled the sketch out from under the letter. Studying it now, she noted that it was not the seductive smile of a rake nor even the disarming smile of a cheerful gentleman engaged in pleasantries. It was something else altogether—a sad wistful kind of smile.

"Patience!" There came a loud rap at the door. Patience pulled out a drawer in her bedside table and placed both letter and sketch inside sliding it firmly shut.

"Yes. Come."

Lady Pemberton swung open the door to her daughter's bed chamber looking resplendent in a pale butter yellow evening dress. Patience did not have any yellow dresses of her own for the simple reason that her mother insisted on decorating their drawing rooms in yellow. Yellow on yellow was a bit too much to bear as far as Patience was concerned.

"Don't look at me like that," said her mother. "You're coming with us to Almack's tonight. Where is Delphi?" Lady Pemberton cast about the room as if the maid might be concealed somewhere nearby. "She should be doing your hair."

"I don't think I'm up to it tonight, Mother," said Patience.

Lady Pemberton cast her an appraising glance.

"Nonsense. There is someone I would like you to meet. You must come."

"Do you not find their refreshments quite stale?" asked Patience pointedly.

"Almack's is not about food, Patience. It is about people." Lady Pemberton stepped over to Patience's closet and threw open the doors. "You cannot wear any of those new dresses of yours, or we shall be turned away at the door. Something classical. A cream silk or . . ." She riffled through Patience's dresses. "Or something pale and girlish. Here we are!"

Lady Pemberton emerged from the closet with an empire-waisted dress cut from an anaemic pink satin and lay it carefully beside Patience on the bed.

"It will be fun. You'll see," she said stepping back.

Patience wanted to argue, to refuse, to remain sullenly in her room as her mother went off for the evening, but she felt worn down. It had been nine long years since she'd first made her debut in society, and doing things her way had not resulted in . . . well . . . results. Did she have to always be so unpleasant towards others? Did she have to keep disappointing her mother? Her family? Patience reached for the dress beside her.

"It is a lovely choice, Mother," she said lifting it up by the shoulders.

Lady Pemberton appeared not to know what to say. She seemed almost thrown by the way Patience had immediately given in to her design for the evening.

"Yes, well, you will look beautiful in pink satin."

Patience gave her mother a smile that did not reach her eyes.

"Pinch your cheeks, Patience. You're looking a bit pallid. I'll see you downstairs."

By the time the Pembertons arrived at Almack's, the evening was in full swing. Lord Pemberton and George had joined Patience and her mother for the outing which Patience thought a bit odd. Lady Pemberton was usually wary of bringing her husband along to large social events. He was terribly frank, and she was never quite sure what he might say or whom he might offend. George, for his part, avoided as many of these events as he could, especially when his mother was present, as she was always angling to match him with some young lady or other.

Candlelight twinkled from the wall sconces and the chandeliers above, and Patience began to tingle with a sensation of ominous foreboding as she watched her mother cast her gaze out like a net across the ballroom.

"Ah, there he is!" said Lady Pemberton. "Come, Patience."

She took Patience by the hand and led her across the room towards a cluster of gentlemen who, from the snatched words that could be heard spoken, might have been discussing horses. Patience, however, suspected from the ribald laughter that

A Soldier and his Rules

they were actually discussing women. As she and her mother approached, one gentleman broke away from the group and came to greet them. He was tall and quite pleasant to look upon—golden hair, a smooth-shaven face, and dark brown eyes that took her in with a single sweep before settling on her mother.

"Lady Pemberton! So nice to see you once more," he said lifting her gloved hand to his lips.

"I would like to introduce you to my daughter Miss Patience Pemberton. Patience, this is Mr. Silas Ruteledge."

Patience's heart felt like lead in her chest. *It was happening. This was it. Her parents had chosen a husband for her.* Mr. Ruteledge took Patience in for a second time. She noticed his eyes dropping from her face to her bosom then bouncing back up again when he caught himself.

"I am charmed," he said taking her hand and bowing over it.

"Pleased to meet you," said Patience. *What else could she say?*

"Your mother tells me you are an artist," said Mr. Ruteledge without letting go of her hand.

Patience gave her hand a little tug to free it and heard her mother's sharp intake of breath. She winced inwardly. Being pleasant wasn't as easy as she thought it would be.

"She has told me nothing of you, Mr. Ruteledge."

"Has she not?" He said it with an amused smile glancing at Lady Pemberton. "Well, we must remedy the situation. Shall we dance?"

Patience looked to her mother who was smiling and nodding at her like a doll whose head was attached to its body with a coiled spring. Patience gave Mr. Ruteledge a polite smile and took the arm he offered her.

Richard had accompanied his mother to Almack's that evening, and she had been delighted to find that Captain Walpole was in attendance as well. That he was wearing his bright red captain's uniform set her off grinning like a girl.

"Captain Walpole! How wonderful to see you," she said striding towards him and reaching out her hand.

"Ah, Lady Winter. The pleasure is all mine," he replied pressing her fingers to his lips. "You are a vision tonight, my lady. Please," he said gallantly placing her hand in the crook of his arm, "you must call me Thomas."

This gesture towards familiarity had Lady Winter tittering at the thought.

Richard threw his eyes up to the ceiling where he spent some time examining the way the crystals of the chandeliers glinted with the occasional rainbow. He could hear Thomas asking his mother to dance. Richard did not have to drag his eyes from the ceiling to know that his mother was completely enchanted with his rascal of a friend. He had told Thomas not to encourage her, but Thomas had never been the discouraging type.

That is fine, thought Richard. *At least she is happy.*

By the time Richard lowered his gaze to the dance floor once more, he was surprised to see Miss Pemberton dancing past him with some gentleman's large hand at the small of her back. She seemed different tonight, her dress an insipid pink that made her look like a drawing someone had tried but failed to erase.

And that man was holding her entirely too close! Her breasts were practically pressed against his chest.

Richard flexed the fingers of his right hand open, then curled them into a fist that he left hanging at his side like a cudgel.

A Soldier and his Rules

When the dance came to an end, he saw the gentleman lead Miss Pemberton over to a refreshment table where she refused his offer of a drink. As she conversed with him politely, a painful smile painted across her face, Richard noticed that she was sending furtive glances about the room as if looking for some sort of escape.

"There she is!" said Thomas sidling up beside Richard. "The storm does not look so stormy tonight for some reason." He grinned at Richard. "Ask her to dance."

"Why don't you?" countered Richard.

"I tried. She doesn't want me," said Thomas. "I'm entirely too congenial for her."

"She doesn't want me either," said Richard without taking his eyes from her.

"But she yelled at you," said Thomas elbowing him in his side. "It's an invitation."

Richard turned on him then with a stormy glare.

"Watch your words, Thomas. What sort of invitation could it possibly be?"

Thomas gave him his usual impish smile. "It's an invitation to yell back, of course."

Richard didn't respond, but Thomas knew him too well. His lack of response gave him away.

"What?" asked Thomas with some excitement. "Are you saying you've already yelled back? You *must* tell me everything."

And then it happened. Richard lifted his gaze towards Miss Pemberton, and she caught his eye. It looked as if she actually sighed with relief at the sight of him. She appeared to speak a few more words to the blonde gentleman she was with, for some reason gesturing in Richard's direction, and then she was walking towards him in her pink satin dress. Richard

Rules, Miss Pemberton

turned towards the exit, but Thomas grabbed his arm and held him fast.

"Let me go," said Richard in a fierce tone.

"Don't be a coward," said Thomas under his breath. "Miss Pemberton! So lovely to see you again."

When Miss Pemberton dropped into a quick curtsy, Thomas turned to Richard wide-eyed and smiling with surprise.

"Captain Walpole," she said. Then gazing up at Richard's great height, "My lord."

"My lord?" said Thomas looking from Miss Pemberton to Richard and back again. "To what do we owe the pleasure?" asked Thomas.

"Please forgive me for being so impertinent, but I needed an excuse to extricate myself from the conversation I was having with the gentleman across the room." She turned to Richard, "I told him I had to speak with you about your mother's portrait."

"I see," said Richard.

"And that is my cue to leave," announced Thomas cheerfully. "Do enjoy yourselves, children!" And then more quietly to himself, "I wonder if Miss Fernside is here tonight."

Richard didn't even cast him a sideways glance as he left. Miss Pemberton's eyes were on him again, but this time they did not roam his face for her usual inspection. This time, they were pleading with him.

"Has that gentleman upset you in some way?" asked Richard.

"No," said Miss Pemberton. "I simply needed an excuse to leave. The evening has become a bit . . . overwhelming."

"In what way?" Richard spoke the words, and as he spoke them, he could not believe what he was hearing. *How could he ask her such a prying question?*

"I do believe my parents have chosen a husband for me."

A Soldier and his Rules

"That man?" asked Richard looking across the room.

"That man," said Miss Pemberton with resignation in her voice.

"And you don't like him?"

"I don't know him," she responded.

"But you would rather not converse with him?"

"Not now. No. It is too much."

"And you would prefer to come over here and pretend to converse with me?"

At this, Miss Pemberton smiled.

"It appears that way, doesn't it? Don't worry—I am under no illusions with you, my lord. I know you are not interviewing me to be your wife."

She laughed then as if it were the most absurd idea, and Richard was struck by the manner in which she resembled her father. So forthright. *What other lady would reveal herself to have escaped her would-be husband under false pretences? What other lady would be so bold as to assuage his fear that she might be expecting something from him?*

As Richard watched her laugh, his chest began to hurt, and he found himself unable to speak. She was so incredibly beautiful. It wasn't her face (although it was certainly fair to look upon), and it wasn't her body (although her full figure certainly appealed to him). What he found beautiful—truly beautiful—was her manner. The way she simply existed as herself . . . even in that terrible dress.

Out of the corner of his eye, Richard could see the blonde gentleman approaching them through the crowd. *He is trying to take possession of her already*, thought Richard. He had the sudden urge to place his arm around Miss Pemberton, to pull her to him in a protective embrace. Of course, he would never

Rules, Miss Pemberton

do so—there were rules to engaging with a lady, although at the moment, he was having a difficult time remembering what exactly those rules were.

Miss Pemberton stopped laughing quite abruptly when she noticed the blonde gentleman's presence.

"Mr. Ruteledge," she said, and Richard could feel her stiffen as if it were a ripple in the air between them. "May I introduce Lord Winter. I am to paint his mother's portrait before the Season is out."

"Nice to meet you," said Mr. Ruteledge extending his hand to Richard. "It seems you have Miss Pemberton here in stitches. Do tell, what is so funny?"

Richard looked to Miss Pemberton. Her face had gone pale, and she was looking at him again with those pleading eyes. He addressed Mr. Ruteledge as casually as he could.

"I told her I was an excellent dancer. As you can see, she does not believe me for a minute. I suppose I must prove myself lest she think me a liar."

He then ever-so-casually reached for her hand and led her out onto the dance floor. The small orchestra had struck up a waltz.

"My lord?" Miss Pemberton looked flushed and flustered as she gazed up into his face.

He placed one hand firmly to her waist, and she hesitantly reached for his shoulder.

"Ready?" he asked. "Hold on. It's a fast one."

She nodded, and then he swung her with some force into the music. They practically flew across the ballroom floor. He was looking down at her face as he guided her flight. The look of sheer surprise in her violet-blue eyes! Clearly, she had not been expecting he could dance. As the music picked up its pace, so did he. He could tell that her feet were barely touching the floor as he swung her around, and my God, she was laughing! A sound of pure delight that sparked its way right down to the base of his spine. She was laughing and gasping for breath with the exertion of keeping up. But she *was* keeping up! He had to look away from her face. It was too bright. He felt blinded, and he worried he might miss a step and cause her an injury. As the tempo finally slowed once more, she looked up at him. He met her eyes.

"Lord Winter?" She said it in a curious way as if she were asking herself a question.

"Miss Pemberton."

"That was . . . (she giggled) that was entirely too much fun, my lord. I could barely breathe. Shall we dance again? I mean, can we? Just for the fun of it."

Richard was so startled by her question, he couldn't at first answer. A lady didn't ask to dance. She was asked. And two dances would certainly not be appropriate. But Miss Pemberton—he looked at her face seriously now—was quite innocent in her question. It had been fun. She wanted to continue. It was as simple as that. Unfortunately, in London nothing was as simple as that.

"Rules, Miss Pemberton," he said as he brought the waltz to an end. "One dance is acceptable. Two will reach the gossip sheets. And I'm sure you wouldn't want that."

Her face fell, and she dropped her gaze from his.

"No, I suppose I wouldn't. I'm sorry. I shouldn't have asked. Thank you for the dance and the distraction. I won't bother you again."

Sweet Heaven, thought Richard. *Bother me. Bother me again and again and again.*

Rules, Miss Pemberton

He said, "I'm always glad to be of service to you, Miss Pemberton."

Patience rode home with her family in silence. She was seated beside her father who was nodding off against the carriage window. Her mother and George sat together on the opposite seat. Both of them looked about to launch into some sort of reprimand, but each time Patience thought they might open their mouths, they seemed to think better of it.

"What?" she finally asked. "What have I done now? You're clearly displeased, so just come out with it."

"My dear," said Lady Pemberton. "We are only concerned. You could have given Mr. Ruteledge a chance to get to know you . . . and you him. Instead of stalking away from him at the first available opportunity."

"I was blindsided, Mother! How do you think I felt when I realised what you were all up to? I mean, I knew it would happen, that you would choose someone for me, but a little warning might have been nice."

Lady Pemberton made a small strangled noise as George leaned forward towards her in his seat.

"Who introduced you to Lord Winter?" he asked, steel in his eyes.

"Lord Winter?" she asked, stalling for time. "The dowager introduced us." The lie came easily. *The dowager introduced us. I have never yelled at him. There are no drawings of him in our house. He has never said he could have me if he so wished in a practically empty park first thing in the morning. And I certainly, most definitely, do not want to feel his hands on my body again.*

"It would be best if you steered clear of that man," said George. "He may be a war hero, and I respect him for that, but he is the spitting image of his father. How far can an apple possibly fall from the tree?"

"I thought you would be happy to see me dancing with an eligible viscount," countered Patience.

"Not him," said George with some finality. "And you weren't dancing. He practically carried you across the dance floor. The whole ballroom could hear your shrieks of laughter. It was indecent."

Here Lady Pemberton made an affirmative sort of sound.

Patience leaned back in the carriage and retreated into her mind. Lord Winter had swung her across the floor as if she weighed nothing (and she knew quite well she weighed a certain something). The man was pure height and muscle and coiled strength. Being held by him, moved by him, had been absolute bliss. The sheer joy of it was impossible to hide. She had laughed up into his stern face, waiting to see it crack, to see him smile. But he had remained impassive. And then he had practically scolded her when she had asked for a second dance. Patience felt the sting of humiliation against her breastbone.

Why would I ask for a second dance? I was begging like a child. What must he think of me?

Five

Strict

Richard lay staring up at the moss green curtains of his four-poster bed. Dancing with Miss Pemberton tonight had been unwise. What had induced him to do it? If he was honest with himself, he would have to say it had been a heady combination of her pleading blue eyes, Mr. Ruteledge's air of possession, and the simple fact that he desperately wanted to lay hands on her. He could feel her now. The laughter shivering through her. The way her soft body yielded to his when they occasionally came into closer contact as they moved through the steps of the dance.

God, I'm a weak excuse for a human being, he thought.

Miss Pemberton was so . . . so . . . unexpected. Her words and her behaviour were quite unpredictable, and this both upset and excited Richard in equal measure. *I mean, who would have laughed like that? Without a care for what anyone thought?* And she would be coming to his house tomorrow. To paint his mother. Richard decided then and there that he would not be at the house when she arrived. He could do that much. He could remove himself.

"George, there is no need for you to come," said Patience wrapping her paintbrushes in a strip of linen and tying them with a cord. "Delphi shall accompany me. And I am painting the dowager all on her own. My reputation is not exactly at stake."

"You are going to that man's house," said George. "You need a chaperone."

"I have Delphi."

George ignored her. "I'm coming, and that is final."

Lady Winter kept them waiting. Delphi stood by the striped blue-and-white couch where George and Patience were seated. Her easel and equipment had already been carried up by footmen to a well-lit room chosen by the viscountess. A grandfather clock marked out the seconds in long slow swings of its brass pendulum. Fifteen minutes became half an hour, and still they waited.

"I told you it would be tedious," said Patience to George.

Presently, a footman entered with a tray of tea and biscuits. George ran an impatient hand through his hair standing it on end. He shifted uncomfortably in his seat.

"Tea means more waiting," he said.

"You're a very clever detective, George," said Patience with

Strict

as much condescension as she could muster. "A real bow street runner."

"Excuse me!" called George to the footman as the man made his way to the door. "Is the viscount in today?"

"No, Sir. Lord Winter left for his club. He said he'd be gone all day."

"Thank you," said George.

The footman left them all alone once more with the tea and the grandfather clock.

"I think," said George standing, "that you are in good hands with the dowager viscountess. I shall leave you to it." He gave Delphi a look as if to say, "Watch her." Delphi nodded once, a quick bob of the head.

Once George had left, and the door had clicked shut, Patience poured and handed a cup of tea to Delphi.

"Oh no, I couldn't, Miss."

"Who knows how long we will be waiting, Delphi? We must stay hydrated."

"I'll be fine, Miss. Thank you."

Patience gave Delphi an affectionate smile. "There's no need for you to suffer this interminable wait as well. I do believe you have a friend in the kitchen. Sarah, is it?"

Delphi nodded with the hint of a smile playing about her face.

"Off you go, then. Have a chat. Help out in the kitchen. And bring me some gossip if you can," said Patience with a mischievous wink. "I'll send for you when I'm done. It might be hours yet."

"Thank you, Miss." Delphi bobbed a slight curtsy and hastened from the room.

Patience ate a chocolate biscuit and then another.

A Soldier and his Rules

I should probably leave at least one biscuit on the plate to be polite, she thought as she hungrily contemplated the last one. And then she ate that one too, washing it down with a cup of milky tea. She looked at the clock. An hour had passed since George had left!

Well, this is absolutely ridiculous, thought Patience. She rose to her feet and went to the door. Opening it, she could hear the front door slam shut on the floor below. She padded silently out of the room to peer down the grand staircase to the foyer. A voice boomed up from beneath her.

"Martin! Martin!" It was Lord Winter. And he was covered head-to-toe in mud!

A footman appeared, rushing forward to take his dirty coat.

"You'd best take these as well," said Lord Winter bending down to remove one filthy boot and then the other, "or I will track mud through the entire house. Bloody phaeton drivers think they own the road. Someone could have been killed."

"My lord," said the footman as he clutched the offending clothing to himself and hurried off.

Lord Winter strode to the stairs in his stockinged feet, placed his hand on the bannister, and then startled Patience by taking the stairs three at a time to the top. He stopped short when he saw her, a look of irritation playing about his stern features.

"I thought you were painting my mother," he said. "Where is she?"

"I've no idea, my lord," said Patience. "I've been waiting for over an hour." She looked him up and down. "Are you hurt? Have you been in an accident?"

"No and yes." He did not elaborate. "Return to the drawing room. I shall fetch her."

Strict

Patience was stung yet again by his demeanour towards her. She returned to the drawing room and waited some more. It was another half hour before Lord Winter returned. He had changed into clean clothing and shoes, but his mother was not with him.

"I'm afraid my mother is unable to attend today's portrait session. She has taken to her bed, and she is not entirely certain the portrait is a good idea after all."

"Oh," said Patience looking down at the cream-coloured carpet so that he would not see the tears pricking at the corners of her eyes. This portrait had been important to her. The disappointment sliced deep. "Is she unwell?" Patience addressed her question to the carpet.

"She is prone to bouts of melancholy ever since my father passed away. They are fairly unpredictable, but they always pass."

Patience remained with her gaze to the carpet.

"Miss Pemberton?"

She couldn't keep her head down forever, so she lifted her wet eyes to meet his.

"Yes, my lord."

Bloody hell. The sight of her pink-rimmed violet-blue eyes wet with unshed tears sent Richard reeling—a feeling of falling, as if someone had pushed him down the stairs. In fact, he would have preferred it if someone had pushed him down the stairs.

What had her brother said to him? She was glad of the opportunity to paint his mother? Clearly an understatement. Richard found himself speaking when he knew he should not.

"You could paint my portrait instead."

She wiped at one eye with the back of her hand.

"My lord?"

"How long will it take?" He tried to sound business-like.

"My lord, it's not necessary."

"Apparently, it is," he said handing her a handkerchief. She accepted his handkerchief but said nothing. "I insist," he added taking her arm and guiding her down the hall and up to the room where her easel had been set up.

Light shone in through south-facing windows illuminating Miss Pemberton's hair—*straw into gold*, he thought. He watched as she took stock of the room. She manhandled her easel to place it at a different angle and repositioned a chair that his mother had chosen for her portrait seat. Watching her move about the room in her sage green dress pained him in a way he could not explain. It hurt him to look at her—she was so lovely.

"Two rules," he said as she gestured for him to take a seat.

She turned and pulled a white linen apron from a case as if she were ignoring him and his rules. Richard watched as she slipped it over her head and tied it tight at her waist. The edges of her green dress stood out against the white of the apron, and Richard marvelled at the way the contrast set off her features to full effect. Finally, she turned back to him, eyes shining now, not with tears, but with something else.

"Rules?" she asked.

"One, I will sit for only one hour at a time. Two, there is to be no talking."

Richard knew he would be lost if she started to converse with him. Or worse, if he said something funny and she laughed (not that he often made humorous comments, but you never know).

"The first rule is yours to keep," she said. "But what happens if I break the second rule?"

"I will no longer sit for you," he answered.

"Strict," she said. And the way she said it, God help him, stirred something deep and animal inside his body. This was exactly why there had to be a no-talking rule.

Miss Pemberton settled into her silence. She adjusted her canvas on the easel and picked up a piece of graphite. She glanced at him once and then set to work. After a few minutes, she stood back to look at her work and screwed up her face. She looked over at him, and then she came around the easel and stepped up to him in the chair. She knelt down in front of him as he tried to remain as still as possible, staring off into the distance. *What the hell was she doing?* She slipped a small soft hand beneath his, adjusting its position on the armrest ever-so-slightly. Then she reached up, took hold of both shoulders, and tilted him slightly more towards the easel.

"Miss Pemberton, I don't think . . ."

His words trailed off as she put one finger to her plump lips to shush him. And then she brought that same finger (along with the hand it belonged to) up to his face and took his hairy jaw firmly in her hand. She turned his face so that he was looking right at her. He could feel her thumb find the scar beneath his beard. Her brow drew together, and she took a closer look, drawing her thumb along the line of the scar from top to bottom. He had to resist the urge to pull her pleasantly soft and pliant body up into his lap. Releasing his jaw, she then stood and leaned over him to smooth down his lapels. The swell of her perfect breasts dipped down towards him as she did so, and Richard had to close his eyes. This was worse than he could have ever imagined.

Patience had a chance to paint the portrait of a viscount! She smiled to herself thinking how soft his heart must be to offer himself up in order to avoid her disappointment. His behaviour in this respect sat in direct opposition to his irritated expression and tone. And while she could not reconcile the two, she would follow his rules, and she would paint his picture, and then the Royal Academy would have to take notice. Since she could not risk speaking to Lord Winter, she decided to adjust his less-than-optimal position herself. Patience did have it in the back of her mind that she would never have done so if Delphi had been in the room. But Delphi was, happily, not in the room, so she could do as she pleased. She could be herself.

Smoothing down his lapels had not been necessary—they were perfectly flat already—but Patience couldn't help herself. The action had been almost involuntary. After dancing with him the evening before, feeling the strength of him around her, she had the desperate urge to place the flats of her hands to his rather wide and (now that she had felt it) muscled chest. Not very ladylike, no, but Patience had never been known for her genteel impulses.

Patience returned to her canvas and sketched out his lordship in broad swift strokes. She marked out the line of his scar even though it would be covered by his beard. It was there. It was a part of him, so she would include it. Then she pulled out her paints and turpentine and linseed oil. She barely had to look at him—she had practised his face so many times before. *Haunted, furious, death wish. Haunted, furious, death wish.* It was like a chant in her head as she poured herself into her work, melting with it, losing herself in place and time until she was nothing but stroke and light and colour. She had disappeared as she always did into the painting.

After what might have been minutes or hours or days as far as Patience was concerned, Lord Winter's voice broke through her trance.

"Are we quite done? It has been nearly an hour," he added checking his pocket watch.

She stepped out from the canvas and smiled. Yes, she was almost done (with this sitting, at least). Just one last thing. She walked right up to him and took his face in her hands tilting it up until she could see his eyes properly. What she saw startled a small involuntary sound from her lips. His eyes were perfect. Hazel didn't quite describe them. They were grassy green pools flecked with gold and held in with an outer ring of orange fire. Gazing into his eyes was like gazing into a star. She felt all tingly and somehow breathless with the wonder of it.

She was still inhabiting that peaceful space she always did while painting. Not thinking of herself at all—her attention focused entirely on how to respond to what was in front of her. Patience's thumb found his scar again and stroked it beneath the crisp hair of his black beard. He stood slowly until she was not gazing down at him anymore but peering up into his eyes. She found she could not bring herself to release his face. He brought his own hands to either side of her waist, and she gave a small gasp. She shifted her thumb down along his scar to his lips which parted ever so slightly. And then, artists being (as her mother liked to say) impulsive creatures, Patience lifted up onto her tiptoes and pressed a kiss to his scar where it was hidden. She heard his sharp intake of breath when she did so, but he did not move. He kept his hands lightly at her waist as if to hold her in place. Feeling emboldened, Patience moved her lips to his and attempted a kiss.

Richard's heart all but melted as she pressed her lips to his scar. That she would find it and then kiss it . . . As she brought her lips to his in a fluttery hesitant gesture, Richard realised that she had never kissed anyone before. She didn't know what to do, and the thought drove him out of his mind with desire. He pulled his face away slightly, adjusted hers with his hands.

"Like this," he said, pressing a kiss to the corner of her mouth, teasing her lips apart with his tongue.

She opened to him, and he delved further into the sweet recesses of her mouth. She surprised him by responding with her own exploration, taking his bottom lip in her mouth, biting him gently. He rubbed his cheek against hers, and she responded by pressing her breasts and hips to him, throwing her head back so that he might kiss her neck. *How could he not when she offered it up to him like that?* He ran his tongue up her neck to her ear, and the gasping sounds she let loose as he did so made him feel as if he might blackout with the sheer pleasure of it all.

Sweet Lord, what was he doing? While his brain was not entirely functional at that particular moment, Richard suspected somewhere at the back of his mind that some very serious rules were being broken. For the first time in his life, he didn't

Strict

care.

Miss Pemberton pulled her face from him and reached her hands up through his hair as she gazed into his eyes. He slid one hand down her back to squeeze and lift the soft rounded flesh of her ample bottom which provoked an involuntary sound from her that had him struggling to regain control of himself, to muster some restraint.

"May I speak?" asked Miss Pemberton, his hand still on her bottom, her fingers still woven through his hair.

Good Lord, she was asking for permission!

He nodded.

"I hope you wouldn't think . . ." she said, ". . . that I do this often."

"Miss Pemberton," he said, releasing her bottom and sliding his hand back up to the small of her back, "I would never think that."

"I have never felt the urge to kiss someone before."

He pressed his forehead to hers. "I know it was your first kiss."

"Was it that obvious?" she asked quietly.

He didn't answer.

"Why did you do it?" he whispered, his forehead still pressed against hers. "You don't know me at all."

She shrugged.

"How did you come by that scar on your face?"

"Bayonet," he said.

"Did it cut deep?"

"Yes."

"How long did it take to heal?" she asked.

"The wound is still festering," he replied cryptically. And that was as close as he'd ever come to telling anybody about his past.

She looked at him then in a way that made him feel as if she could see right into the very depths of his broken soul. He didn't like the feeling before, and he didn't like it now.

"You say I don't know you, but I do know you," she said. "You are haunted by your past, furious about the present, and . . . and . . .

"And what?" he asked quietly as his entire body tensed.

He could feel the hesitation in her.

"And you have a death wish."

Richard felt as if she had stunned him with a blow. *How could she know? And how could she speak it?* He felt so incredibly exposed, and the shame of it—of her seeing him as he was—was too much to bear. He started to pull away from her, but she closed her fists around his hair and held him tight.

"Miss Pemberton, release me!" he said prying her fingers from his hair and stepping back. "This was a mistake. I should not have taken advantage of you as I did. It will not happen again. Please take your painting and leave. There shall be no more sittings."

The look on her face squeezed at his heart, but he ignored the pain. It was better this way. He could not give her what she wanted. He could not be a whole person for her. He was, after all, on his darkest days, flirting with some kind of madness. A husband should be someone you can count on, not an invalid trembling on the floor.

Miss Pemberton was frozen in place, the white of her apron smeared with colour, her face flushed, her eyes wet once more. He had engaged in this enterprise to prevent her from crying, and now here she was welling up again. Richard cursed himself to the very depths of Hell.

Strict

Miss Pemberton removed her apron quietly and set about packing up her things as if he weren't even there.

"Miss Pemberton," he said. "I am sorry."

She tossed him a frosty glare as she wrapped up her paintbrushes.

"My name is Patience," she said.

Patience was silent on the carriage ride home with Delphi. She had managed to pack up the painting using some pins and a piece of board to prevent the wet paint from smudging and, more importantly, to prevent the portrait of Lord Winter from being seen, especially by George. He would be livid if he found out how she had spent the afternoon.

What was I thinking? thought Patience. *The problem was that I wasn't thinking. That's what happens when I paint. There is only feeling and responsiveness and smoothing the way for something beautiful to appear. Well, the kiss was certainly beautiful. Until I had to go and ruin it.*

Patience knew she would remember that kiss for the rest of her life. The way he had teased her mouth open with his tongue. The soft velvet heat of his breath inside her. She could feel herself flushing just thinking about it.

Serafina said it would be like that. That I would know beyond a shadow of a doubt. That I would want it with every fibre of my body.

When Patience arrived home, she went straight to her room. Normally, when she was in a state such as this, she would throw herself down on the bed and wallow for a couple of hours, but looking at the bed, it seemed too exposed.

She wanted to hide, to curl up and die somewhere with the humiliation of it all. So she stepped into her dressing room, found a dark corner, and slid her back down the wall until she was sitting on the floor in-between two blue gowns that were hanging from a rail.

Why can't I do anything right? Why do I have to displease everyone at every turn? I always have to be clever, to open my big mouth.

She dropped her forehead to her knees, and a sob escaped her lips. Before long, she was wracked with them. Deep, body-shuddering convulsions that went on for what seemed like an eternity until her eyes were raw and her face was puffy. She blew her nose on the green skirt of her dress. Being herself was too hard. It seemed easier to give up. To give in to what everyone seemed to be asking of her.

I will go to bed tonight, and tomorrow I will be better. I will do better.

Six

Crossing the Alps

After Miss Pemberton's departure, Richard went on a frustrated rampage across the room, smashing every breakable thing in sight. Two vases (one with an elegant arrangement of white flowers still in it), an ornate Turkish plate, a lamp, and two side tables—he plunged his fist through the top of one table and threw the other one at the wall. When he was done, he brushed off his jacket and strode from the room. He spent the rest of the afternoon and much of the evening at his gentlemen's boxing club, taking on one opponent after another. He won the first few matches but soon tired, allowing himself to be punched and pummelled until the manager himself had to have him dragged off.

"Lord Winter, while I appreciate your patronage of this establishment, I think you can understand why I am insisting you return home."

"What's he done now?" said a familiar cheerful voice.

A Soldier and his Rules

"Captain Walpole. Could you please escort his lordship home. He may need tending to."

When Thomas stepped up beside Richard who had been propped up on a stool in a corner, he whistled. Richard's face was starting to bruise and swell, his bandaged knuckles were bloody, and he had a vacant look in his eyes as he stared blankly into the middle distance.

"Jesus, Richard! You look like hell. What's going on?"

Richard did not look up or respond.

"Let's get you dressed and home then," said Thomas hoisting his friend up by the arm.

In the carriage on the way home, Thomas sat across from his friend willing him to say something. He knew Richard well enough to know that something had upset him—something of more than a little consequence. After some time staring out the window, Richard finally spoke.

"Having done what we've done, and having seen what we've seen, do you think it at all possible that we could lead normal lives?"

Richard knew he was prying open the lid of the box with this question. Not lifting the lid properly, mind you. Just testing it out. He could sense Thomas recoil slightly at the question.

"Anything is possible," said Thomas in a noncommittal tone.

"That's the thing, though, Thomas. People say that, but 'anything' is *not* possible. There are some things reality will not allow. The laws of nature are set. There are rules that the world must by necessity follow."

"What has happened?" asked Thomas.

Richard went silent then for a very long time. The carriage bumped its way over the cobbles, and he watched out the window as the lamp-lighters lit the gaslights along the street.

"She told me her name was Patience," he said, his eyes fixed out the carriage window.

Thomas leaned forward towards his friend, hands clasped, elbows resting on his knees, and Richard continued, still staring out the window.

"After I had taken advantage of her and then humiliated her with my rejection, she just gave me this cold look, and said, 'My name is Patience'. Why would she say that?"

"And by 'taken advantage' you mean . . . ?" asked Thomas trailing off.

"A kiss Thomas. She kissed me. And, God forgive me, I kissed her back."

"Just to be clear, we're talking about Miss Pemberton here."

Richard gave a grunt of ascent.

"Good Lord, Richard. I saw you dancing with her last night, and now you say you've already kissed her and had your first fight."

"It's not a joke, Thomas."

"I know, I know," said Thomas raising his open palms in surrender. "But I don't understand. Why did you reject her? What's the problem?"

Richard fixed him with a look.

"I'm the problem," he said.

Thomas knew immediately what he meant. Not exactly what he meant but close enough to it. Thomas had his own demons. He had been trying to ignore them, but they were there nonetheless, clutching greedily at his ankles, plaguing his every move.

Once Thomas had returned with Richard to the Winter residence, he realised that he could not leave his friend there

A Soldier and his Rules

with only the servants to see to him. Lady Winter was in bed with what Richard referred to as a bout of melancholy, so he would have no support there. She had been so happy the evening before. Thomas wondered that she could come crashing down so easily within the space of one night's sleep. But of course, he had been known to do the same on occasion, so why not Lady Winter as well? *We all have our demons to contend with.*

Thomas had Richard cleaned up, his cuts bandaged, and a poultice placed to one eye that was swelling shut. He saw Richard to bed and then took himself downstairs for a drink or four before settling into one of the guest rooms for the night. In the morning, he found Richard at breakfast but his mother nowhere in sight.

"Is your mother not up yet?"

"She will not come down," said Richard. "It's like this sometimes."

"May I go to see her?"

"By all means," said Richard shoving a piece of bacon into his mouth.

Thomas got up, went to the sideboard, and put a plate of food together, then made for the door.

"Thomas," said Richard.

"Yes?" said Thomas turning.

"Thank you."

"Don't say that," said Thomas with a smile. "You don't know what I'm going to do next."

A few days later, Mr. Silas Ruteledge came to call on

Crossing the Alps

Patience at the Pemberton London house. When the footman announced his arrival in the yellow drawing room, Patience felt her heart sink into her belly.

Here we go, she thought. *Be better. Do better.*

Lady Pemberton looked to her daughter, and Patience gave her a smile.

"I'm ready," she said.

"Ready for what?" asked Grace who had only just lifted her nose from a book in the corner of the room. Nobody appeared to hear her.

"Show him in," said Lady Pemberton.

Mr. Ruteledge was everything that Patience had remembered him to be—suave and confident, polite and reassuring. He was dressed in a dark green jacket which was the perfect counterbalance to his thick blonde hair and dark eyes. There was no denying that he was an attractive man. He was holding an enormous bouquet of salmon-pink roses sprinkled with white baby's breath.

"For you, Miss Pemberton," he said, offering her the flowers.

Patience smiled. They were actually quite lovely (and not yellow which was another point in their favour).

"Thank you," she said burying her nose in the satiny petals and inhaling deeply.

She noticed Mr. Ruteledge looking to her mother as if for support.

"Mr. Ruteledge, do sit down, and I shall call for tea," offered Lady Pemberton.

"No one has introduced me yet," said Grace coming forward from her chair in the corner.

"Mr. Ruteledge, my youngest, Miss Grace Pemberton," said Lady Pemberton. To Grace she said, "I think you have a lesson

A Soldier and his Rules

beginning any minute now. Off you go."

Grace remained where she was. "No," she said. "It's not for an hour still." Turning back to Mr. Ruteledge, "And what brings you to our fine home today? Are you courting my sister?"

"Ah . . ." He looked to Patience. ". . . Yes, that is, I would like to be courting your sister . . . if she is amenable."

"And what do you have to recommend yourself?" asked Grace with an imperious air. "Besides being handsome."

"Grace!" scolded Lady Pemberton.

"No, no. It's alright. A perfectly legitimate question," said Mr. Ruteledge. He took a seat on the yellow sofa where Grace joined him. Patience sat opposite them on the edge of a chair, and Lady Pemberton went to ring the bell for tea.

"So?" asked Grace.

Patience bit her lip. *Poor Mr. Ruteledge*, she thought.

"Well, let's see. I have several large estates and a reasonable income. I have never been the subject of a scandal." He passed his eyes over Patience's face, and she gave a soft smile to encourage him on. "And I have all my own teeth." He opened his mouth to show Grace, and Patience couldn't help it—she laughed.

Grace did not look amused.

"That is all well and good," said Grace, "but I asked what there is to *recommend* you."

"Are those not good things?" asked Mr. Ruteledge with some humour in his tone. He was, after all, speaking to a child.

"They're mediocre things," said Grace with gravity. "Have you ever fought a duel? Do you read Homer? Do you think true love exists?"

Crossing the Alps

"Grace. That is enough!" interrupted Lady Pemberton as she rejoined the group.

She took Grace by the elbow and led her from the room. Mr. Rutledge and Patience could hear her furious whispers as she dismissed Grace at the door.

"So, Mr. Rutledge," said Patience, "have you ever fought a duel?"

Mr Rutledge lifted his eyebrows. "No, Miss Pemberton, I have not. I hope that does not come as too much of a disappointment."

She shrugged.

"And do you read Homer?"

"I know the stories, but I have not read Homer's work in its entirety myself. Quite long-winded and repetitive if you ask me, especially *The Iliad*."

"And do you believe in—"

Lady Pemberton took a seat.

"—true love?" asked Mr. Rutledge.

"Come now," said Lady Pemberton laughing nervously and fiddling with her skirts.

"No," said Mr. Rutledge, "I don't."

"Good," said Patience, and Lady Pemberton turned her head so sharply in her daughter's direction that she nearly gave herself whiplash.

"What was that about?" Lady Pemberton asked Patience once Mr. Rutledge had left.

"What was what about?"

"You know very well of what I speak, Patience."

A Soldier and his Rules

"If Mr. Ruteledge is to be my husband," said Patience, "should I not ask him questions? Find out what he is like? What he believes? What he expects?" Patience took a sip of tepid tea that was left in the bottom of her gold-rimmed cup.

"Yes, but you mustn't go speaking of love with a gentleman so early on in the courtship. It frightens them."

"It didn't frighten Mr. Ruteledge," replied Patience. "He was quite forthright."

"His answer did not seem to frighten you either," said Lady Pemberton in a measured tone while looking at her daughter carefully.

"Why should it? This is an arranged marriage after all. You're the one arranging it, Mother. Mr. Ruteledge appears willing to court me for no other reason than the sight of my face and the knowledge of my sizeable dowry. Why should love play a part? Could we not have a happy, possibly an affectionate, marriage without it?"

"Yes, but love must be given a chance to grow, my dear. Do not salt the earth before any seeds have been planted."

Patience placed her cup back on its saucer and lowered them both to the table in front of her.

"If we are done here, I have some painting to do."

In her studio, Patience looked to the board-covered portrait of Lord Winter, then turned and locked the door. She uncovered the canvas and placed it on her easel.

"What are you so furious about?" she asked him as she prepared her palette and brushes.

He may not want her, and he would never have her, but *she* had *him* right here in her studio, and she would certainly make use of him. He owed her that much. Patience didn't need him to sit for her again. His form was burned into her mind like a

Crossing the Alps

brand. She took out her tiniest brushes to recreate his eyes—those grassy, fiery stars. She then turned to his scar, painting it down the length of his cheek before covering it with his beard. For a moment, she closed her eyes, remembering the feel of his beard against her face and the smell of him—oranges and spice and the scent of laundry that has been dried in the sun. Patience opened her eyes and swore quietly to herself.

For Heaven's sake, it was just a kiss.

Over the next couple of weeks, Patience spent a great deal of time with Mr. Ruteledge. He would call on her at her home, or they would go for long ambling walks in the park trailed closely, of course, by Delphi or Lady Pemberton or both. In the evenings, Patience would always make sure to save a dance for Mr. Ruteledge, and she noticed that he took great pleasure in pulling her to him and sliding his hand into hers—more pleasure than perhaps she herself felt, but that was no matter. Being courted by Mr. Ruteledge was easy and simple. He did not give her any brooding looks or scold her or humiliate her. He acted the perfect gentleman, unaffected by any fits of anger or passion on her account. She became accustomed to the sight of his handsome face and started to wonder what it might be like to kiss him. If he were to be her husband, she would definitely have to kiss him—that would be the least of her marital obligations.

Patience was painfully aware over the course of this time that she had not seen Lord Winter about. Not at Almack's or the Blackmore Ball and not at the park (although she was never there in the early mornings anymore, so that might be why).

A Soldier and his Rules

She tried not to think of him, but it was almost impossible when she spent every moment she could shut up in her studio working on his portrait. When it was finally finished and dry, she bundled it up, carefully attaching an informative note to the front of the package with her name (P. Pemberton—no need to advertise the fact that she was a lady), the title of the painting (Portrait of Lord Richard Winter), the materials used (oils) and the date (1814). She included her address as well so that she may be informed of whether or not it had been accepted for the Royal Academy's exhibition. Then she took it along with Delphi and a footman to Somerset House.

"Please see that this painting is delivered to the office," she told the footman.

To Delphi, "Go with him, and make sure he hands it over properly. It is a submission for the exhibition. Tell them we know that it is late to submit, but they might be interested to take a look nonetheless."

Patience would not be accompanying them. There was no need for anyone to see the artist. The portrait should be judged on its own merits.

"I'm going up to the Great Room to look at some of the paintings," she told Delphi. "I'll meet you back at the carriage."

Patience took her time climbing the steep spiral staircase all the way up to the domed room at the top of the house. There was one painting in particular she wanted to look at, and she wondered if it was still there. When she finally arrived, the room was just as she remembered it—high walls soaring up to meet the domed roof, every inch of space covered in ornate-framed oil paintings. Light filtered down through the high windows just beneath the roof. It took her breath away every time. It must have been the early hour of the day, but there

Crossing the Alps

was no staff about and only one other person in the gallery—a tall gentleman in black with his back to her. He was gazing at the painting she had come to see—J. M. W. Turner's *Hannibal Crossing the Alps*.

As Patience gazed at the wide back of the gentleman on the other side of the room, she realised with a jolt that she recognised his muscular frame, his short curly black hair. An electric charge shot through her as the man turned. It was Lord Winter!

When he saw her, he froze in place and stared. Patience stared back. One of his eyes was slightly puffy and surrounded by a greenish bruise that appeared to be fading. He had a wound across one cheek that had closed and healed but was still quite red.

"Lord Winter."

"Miss Pemberton."

"You look as if you've just come across the Alps," she said glancing behind him to the stormy painting he had just been viewing.

A slow smile crept over his face.

"I was just leaving," he said.

She advanced towards him. "Isn't that odd? I came to see that same painting," she said curiously.

He turned to look at Turner's masterpiece with her.

"I am not overly fond of Mr. Turner himself," said Patience. "He is a crotchety sort of man, condescending at times. But his paintings—my God, they're something, aren't they?"

Lord Winter turned his face to hers as she swore. She was still looking at the painting.

"With Turner, it's all about the light. Just look at that. Everything shrouded in darkness so that he can show us the light to full effect. Could you ever expect to see so much hope in such a dark and ominous landscape?"

Richard drank her in as she spoke, completely ignoring the painting.

She turned to him. "What happened to your face?"

Her hand lifted itself towards the wound on his cheek, but before she could touch his face, he caught her quite firmly by the wrist.

"Don't touch me, Miss Pemberton!"

Patience stared at him, her breath coming hard. She knew she shouldn't, but there was some part of her that wanted to provoke him, so she lifted her free hand to the opposite side of his face. He caught that wrist as well which, for some reason, pleased her in a perverse sort of way.

"Can you not follow instructions?" he asked furiously. Patience thought he looked like Mr. Turner's storm, as if he were about to crash down over her—a turbulent wave of wind and ice.

"I'm not yours to command," she said defiantly.

That statement appeared to set him off which gave Patience a sense of enormous satisfaction. His jaw clenched, and he carefully lifted both her arms by the wrists until they were above her head. Then he turned her around and with control backed her slowly against one of the paintings on the wall. He lowered her arms slightly out to the sides, pinning her against the painting like a bug. Patience noticed his eyelids had lowered and his lips were parted. She couldn't look away from his mouth.

"My lord?"

"Don't speak!" he barked.

"*You* may touch *me*," she said quietly as his pupils dilated to swallow up the green of his eyes leaving only a wide expanse of black surrounded by a ring of orange fire.

They stood like that for some time, their hot breath mingling in the small space between them.

Mercy! This woman! thought Richard. *What is she doing to me?* His breathing was laboured, and he could practically hear the blood pumping through him.

Of all the minutes in all the days, why was she here now to look upon this one particular painting? And why was he so enraged? He knew why. He was angry because the mere sight of her took the breath from his body like a punch to the gut. He was angry because when she spoke of light and hope shining through the darkness, he wanted to believe her. And he was angry because his impulses were so selfish. He wanted her for himself when he knew he had nothing to offer her.

Richard had not quite realised what he was doing as he was doing it. He had simply wanted to prevent Miss Pemberton from touching him, but now he had her pinned against a painting as if he were some sort of fiend. *And she didn't appear to mind! She was inviting him to go further!* He took a long slow breath, released her wrists, and stepped back.

"Don't tempt me, Miss Pemberton. It's not a game you can win."

"What happened to your face, my lord?" she asked again, changing the subject.

He gave her a long hard stare before answering.

"Somebody kissed me," he said. Then he backed slowly away from her until he felt sure she wouldn't follow before turning and leaving the room.

Patience was left standing in the Great Room feeling extremely hot and terribly bothered and not a little bit wet between her thighs.

Sweet heavens—that man! she thought. She gave her own cheek a little slap. *Don't be a fool, Patience. You must stop putting yourself in these compromising positions. What were you even thinking? You may touch me? Good Lord, how did that sentence leave your lips?*

Patience knew her behaviour had been coloured by the fact that Richard had been here to see that particular painting. It meant something to him, and somehow she had already known that. How? It was as if they were connected somehow by an invisible thread. She thought of his portrait that was sitting in a room somewhere downstairs. She had pretended to herself that it was just another portrait, but it wasn't—it was so much more than that.

When Richard arrived home and stepped into the foyer on the ground floor, he could hear his mother and Thomas chatting animatedly from the drawing room at the top of the stairs. Richard handed his coat to Martin and proceeded up the stairs. He tried to walk quietly by the drawing room, but his footsteps were noticed.

"Richard? Is that you?" called Lady Winter.

"Yes," he said peering in through the doorway.

Crossing the Alps

"You should know that Thomas and I have been planning something."

Richard threw an accusing look Thomas's way. He knew they had been up to something, but he hadn't asked what it was because he didn't want to know. Thomas had spent the last two weeks reading Gothic romances to his mother, taking her cups of tea, and finally, coaxing her from the bedroom and out into the world again. It was what Richard should have been doing if he were any son at all, but he doubted that he would have been as successful as Thomas. It hadn't helped matters that his brother James had not arrived home when expected. He had sent no note to explain, and the dowager viscountess was worried that something was amiss. Richard had his suspicions that James was simply avoiding London and the prying eyes of the ton. He certainly would be if he were in James's position.

"We are to host a musicale!" said his mother brightly. "And I don't want to hear any excuses. The invitations have already been sent out."

Richard stepped into the room.

To Thomas he said, "This was your idea?"

"Not exactly," said Thomas with a grin. "But I *have* encouraged it."

Richard bit back the words that were collecting on his tongue. Thomas had taken care of both him and his mother for the past couple of weeks without a thought for himself. Now his mother was up and out of bed and looking forward to something with a spark in her eye. The least Richard could do was acquiesce to their little musicale. He would hate it, obviously. But he would not ruin their fun.

"It sounds like an excellent idea," he said, surprising them both.

"The Fernside girls have agreed to provide some of the music. Lady Blackmore says that her daughters are quite adept at harp and pianoforte, so they shall be playing as well—all four of them! I did ask Lady Pemberton if her daughter would agree to play something, but apparently she has no talent for music. I daresay I owe her a rather large apology for standing her up the other day. I never did ask, Richard, was she terribly upset?"

"She was only concerned for your well-being, Mother," said Richard. In his mind, Miss Pemberton was kissing him all over again, biting his lower lip, and driving him insane as she pressed her soft warm body against his.

"I shall apologise properly at the musicale," said Lady Winter. "She is, of course, invited along with the rest of her family and that lovely Mr. Ruteledge who is rumoured to be courting her."

Thomas searched Richard's face, but he had erected a shield wall over his features, and nothing could penetrate it.

Seven

Winsome and Amiable

Mr. Ruteledge was looking exceptionally dashing in his russet-coloured coat with his blonde locks shining golden in the afternoon sunshine. Patience examined his open face. Nothing to hide there it seemed. He was smiling at her pleasantly as she held his arm. Their faces were mere inches apart.

"You are the most winsome company, Miss Pemberton. I do not believe I have met so amiable a young lady in quite some time." He looked down to her lips then back up at her eyes.

'Amiable' was not exactly a word Patience was used to hearing attached to her personality. But she had been trying. To be better. To do better. Clearly, it was working. She smiled back at him.

"You flatter me, Mr. Ruteledge."

"You deserve to be flattered," he said, stopping mid-stride to take both her hands.

A Soldier and his Rules

His hands were warm and large and took full possession of hers. Patience glanced along the path to where her mother was pretending to brush some lint from her pelisse.

"I would like to give you something," continued Mr. Ruteledge. He reached into a coat pocket and brought out a dark blue velvet box, opening it to reveal the most beautiful bracelet Patience had ever seen—delicate gold filigree with a blue flower at its centre composed of sapphire petals arranged around a central diamond.

"Mr. Ruteledge, I couldn't," said Patience.

"If you agree to be my wife," said Mr. Ruteledge clasping the bracelet to her wrist, "you shall not want for pretty things . . . and *you* shall be *my* pretty thing." He stroked her body with his eyes and reached out a hand to lift her chin.

"You are too kind," said Patience.

They walked on for some time, nodding at people as they passed.

"Do you like to ride?" asked Patience. "I am fond of riding in the mornings."

"Would you like me to accompany you sometime?"

"That would be lovely."

Patience had decided that Mr. Ruteledge would do nicely. Her experiences with him were not overly complicated. He appeared to have some genuine affection for her, if not passion . . . or love. And being twenty-seven with not a proposal to her name, Patience feared that he may be her last chance at a family. *He is kind and attentive and generous*, she thought. *All wonderful qualities.* She did have it in the back of her mind that she had not been as honest with him as he had been with her, and this did prick at her. Would she be able to be 'winsome' and 'amiable' for an entire lifetime? As it was, she had only

Winsome and Amiable

succeeded in cultivating these qualities over the last few weeks, specifically with Mr. Ruteledge in mind.

I'm never winsome or amiable around Lord Winter, she thought. *I don't even think to try.*

Richard had spent every night since that day at Somerset House tossing and turning in his bed. He could not rid himself of the spectre of Miss Pemberton hovering before him, repeating the same thing over and over again: *"You* may touch *me."*

Was that what she was like with this Mr. Ruteledge? Somehow, Richard thought not. She had been a complete novice at kissing him. And the way she had confided in him afterwards. *What had she said?* "I hope you don't think I do this often. I've never had the urge to kiss someone before." He could feel the truth of it, and it shook him to his core. He wanted to pull her to him and never let her go.

He awoke late that morning as he always did—covered in sweat and clutching a pillow to his hairy chest. He could hear his mother's voice floating along the hallway outside his door giving instructions to the staff.

Bloody hell—the musicale was tonight.

Thomas poked his head in through the bed chamber door.

"What?" asked Richard gruffly.

"Sleeping Beauty is awake!" called Thomas down the hall to Lady Winter. Then to Richard, "She has a few things for you to do before this evening."

"Haven't you done enough, Thomas? Why are you still here?"

A Soldier and his Rules

"Oh, that's simple," said Thomas stepping into the room. "I'm here because I love you."

"Thomas!" said Richard in a scolding tone as he sat up in bed.

"What?"

"Don't let the servants hear you talking like that."

"Why not?"

"It's undignified," said Richard. *And it might add to the gossip*, he thought. *Where the hell was James, anyway?* After the musicale was over, he would make a point of finding his brother.

"I don't see why we all have to go," said Patience adjusting the skirt on her new violet dress.

The bodice was cut somewhat lower than she had expected, and while she was feeling a little exposed, Lady Pemberton had insisted she looked every inch the lady and that Mr. Ruteledge would approve.

"Mother, why would you respond to the invitation without asking the rest of us?"

"For once, I agree with Patience," said George. "Nothing good can come of this."

Lady Pemberton turned on Patience. "The dowager asked specifically for you to come."

"Oh?" said Patience, surprised.

"And I decided it was a good idea," interrupted Lord Pemberton as he strode into the room, gloves in hand.

"Thank you, my dear," said Lady Pemberton to her husband.

"But Father—" said George.

Winsome and Amiable

"Allies, George," replied Lord Pemberton in his usual authoritative tone. "We have a chance here with Lord Winter."

"The man cannot be any different from his father," said George. "Nothing could survive that poison."

"Imagine the surprise in Parliament if we could convince him to vote with us. He is a war hero. Respected. He may have influence we cannot foresee," said Lord Pemberton.

As usual, his father was right. But George still didn't like the idea of bringing Patience anywhere near that man. The thought of him swinging her around the dance floor set George's teeth on edge. He eyed Patience from across the room.

Just then, a footman arrived to announce Mr. Ruteledge.

"Show him in, show him in," said Lady Pemberton brightly. "Patience, stand up straight."

Lady Winter and Thomas had arranged for the music to be heard in the ballroom. A number of chairs had been set up in front of a slightly raised stage that hosted a pianoforte and two enormous golden harps. The lighting had been kept low so as not to distract from the music. Richard watched from across the ballroom as his mother's guests trickled in and took their seats. Judging from the number of chairs, she appeared to be expecting up to eighty people or so!

When Miss Pemberton arrived on the arm of a handsome blonde gentleman in a black tailcoat, Richard's heart started to beat a little louder. He had only met the man once, but Mr. Ruteledge's face had imprinted itself on Richard's mind like a brand.

A Soldier and his Rules

Richard watched unobserved from his position across the room. Miss Pemberton's perfect bosom was on display in that devastating violet dress, and Richard noticed several gentlemen gazing appreciatively her way including Mr. Ruteledge. He didn't like it, but he remained where he was. He saw his mother approach Miss Pemberton to pull her away from Mr. Ruteledge and take her on a turn of the room as she pointed out this and that. She stopped with Miss Pemberton at one end of the room, took both her hands, and Richard could only assume she was making her apology. Miss Pemberton was shaking her head and smiling her acceptance.

"Now's your chance," said Thomas coming up behind Richard. "While she's on her own."

"I don't know what you're talking about," said Richard.

"Talk to Miss Pemberton."

"I don't think so."

"Well then at least talk to her father."

"Why would I do that?" asked Richard.

"Because he's coming this way," said Thomas glancing over Richard's shoulder. "Look sharp!"

When she entered the ballroom, Patience could feel Richard's gaze upon her, sensing his presence even when she refused to look his way. She felt him like she could feel a storm collecting over the horizon or thunder waiting in a darkened cloud. So she was glad of the distraction when Lady Winter came to peel her away.

Once Lady Winter had left Patience in order to see to her other guests, Patience noticed Lord Winter deep in

Winsome and Amiable

conversation with her father at the other side of the room. She smiled to herself thinking of the way her father took every opportunity to advance his various causes in Parliament. The world was a better place for having him in it.

Patience quickly and stealthily departed the ballroom using a side door. If only she could track down a maid. Perhaps she could borrow a shawl to cover herself. (She berated herself for not asking Lady Winter when she had the chance.) *Every inch the lady, indeed.* It hadn't escaped her attention that every male gaze in the room (and not a few of the ladies') had fallen directly upon her decolletage. Her mother had simply wanted to give Mr. Ruteledge a peek at the pie so to speak.

She is such a conniving woman, thought Patience. *A conniving woman with my best interests at heart. But still.*

Patience made her way up a set of stairs and down a blue-carpeted hallway until she finally found a maid stepping out of a room as she wiped her sooty hands on her apron.

"Excuse me," said Patience. "I can see you aren't Lady Winter's lady's maid, but could I ask you for a favour? I'm Miss Pemberton, one of the guests. My maid Delphi knows Sarah from the kitchen."

The maid gave her a wide smile and a curtsy.

"Yes, Miss. We all know Delphi."

Patience followed the girl down two sets of stairs. It didn't take long for one maid to find another. And Sarah was only too happy to help. No one would dare provide Patience with anything from Lady Winter's wardrobe, but Sarah lent Patience her best shawl. It was a rather lovely burnt orange silk, and Patience could not believe the girl's generosity. It must have been special to her, the way she had it folded and wrapped in paper as if it had never been worn before.

A Soldier and his Rules

"I will take great care not to damage it," said Patience. "And I will return it to you at the end of the evening. Thank you so much, Sarah. I'm in your debt."

"Not at all, Miss. Happy to help," she said adjusting the shawl across Patience's shoulders.

Patience liked the way the orange contrasted with the deep violet of her dress. It was a shocking combination of jewelled tones that she thought much more deserving of attention than her bosom. *This will give them something to look at*, she thought as she mounted the staircase to the main floor. As she returned along the blue-carpeted hallway, she could see Mr. Ruteledge approaching her with some concern.

"Where did you disappear to?" he asked. "And what is that hideous thing you are wearing?" He said it with a laugh as if he had just realised how he had spoken, and he wished to lighten the moment.

"Hideous?" asked Patience looking down at the shawl. "I think it quite fetching. Do you not like the bold colours?"

Mr. Ruteledge gave her a smile that did not reach his eyes.

"You are always beautiful, my dear. But pretty things are meant to be seen," he said as he stepped up to her and pulled the shawl from her shoulders. "There. That's much better." His eyes lingered at her breasts. "When we are wed, I should like you to wear more dresses like that one."

"Mr. Ruteledge, I should like my shawl back."

"Don't be silly, Miss Pemberton."

"I'm never silly," said Patience biting back her irritation. *Try to be pleasant.*

"Give her the shawl," said a murderous voice from down the hall. Patience looked up to see Lord Winter looking more furious than ever. The viscount strode towards them in quick long steps.

"I'll have you know," said Mr. Ruteledge to Lord Winter, "that this is my fiancée."

Patience looked at him with some alarm.

"You haven't even proposed yet," she said.

"And I'll have you know that you are in my home," said the viscount taking the shawl from Mr. Ruteledge and handing it to Patience. "In this house, the ladies can dress as they wish."

Mr. Ruteledge was red in the face, but he did not argue. Richard was large and oozing a kind of violent menace that would brook no argument. Patience gave him a nervous smile. It was a bit like smiling at a mountain since she received nothing back in the way of acknowledgment. Richard remained stone-faced as he accompanied them back into the ballroom.

"Take your seats," he said. "It's about to begin."

Lady Pemberton gave Patience a wide-eyed look as she took her seat with Mr. Ruteledge. Her mother was clearly not pleased with the shawl either. Patience shifted in her chair to put as much space between herself and her 'fiancé' as she could.

The nerve of him! This is exactly the sort of thing her friend Serafina had warned her about all those years ago. Gentlemen hide themselves behind their manners like masqueraders behind their masks. It's entirely possible you could unknowingly marry a complete stranger only to find out the truth of him once you were well and truly under his control. Well, to hell with that, thought Patience. *I've been sleep-walking into a nightmare.*

A Soldier and his Rules

Richard had had a very interesting conversation with Lord Pemberton. It was clear the baron was feeling him out, trying to decide if he could trust him. Richard did not blame him for being unsure. His father had set a parliamentary precedent for the Winter name that was as hard as it was cold. He knew how his father had behaved in Parliament because he knew how he had behaved at home. He would stack the odds against those less powerful than him and then sit back and watch the misery. If he could inflict the misery directly himself, so much the better. Richard remembered the gleam in his father's eye when he was about to assert his authority.

"You know the punishment for defiance, Richard. Come here!"

It would be a beating with a cane. Richard was always being beaten as a child. To the point where it became a matter-of-fact part of his life. He would take one beating for himself. And then because he knew James was too sensitive to endure it, he would take the blame for whatever accusation his father levelled against James, and he would receive his beating as well. His father knew full well he was covering for James, but he never called him out on it. The evil man merely increased the intensity of the beating in an attempt to break Richard and have him turn over his brother instead. Even as a child, Richard sensed the twisted game they were playing, and he committed himself to winning at all costs. He withstood the pain on James's behalf, and he did so silently without a tear being shed which infuriated his father all the more.

There is something about being thrashed by your father—not smacked or spanked, but actually thrashed, sometimes to within an inch of your life. It flays the spirit from you. It makes you feel as if you have no value. That there is no part of you worthy of love. Richard had at least saved James from that fate. James knew he was worthy of love, and he had found it with Michael. Not an altogether conventional way of finding it, but Richard had accepted that this was who his brother was. Which was not to say he had not struggled to understand. He had. But the way Richard saw it, he also struggled to understand many other couplings. Why had his mother agreed to his father's suit, for example? She'd thought it a love match! When you placed James and Michael's relationship against that of his parents, it seemed much more comprehensible, Michael being without a doubt a wonderful, kind, and trustworthy person.

Richard stood in a doorway at the back of the ballroom, his eyes fixed on the back of Miss Pemberton's head as the music began. He had seen the way she shifted herself away from Mr. Ruteledge as they sat down. He had heard the irritation in her voice when she had spoken to him. These two small things pleased him more than they rightfully should have. She looked like a sunset, he thought to himself, all wrapped up in orange and violet. A sunset like one he had seen before. A picture came to him in his mind, orange light striking the crenellations at the top of the fort of Badajoz just before the darkness descended and the slaughter began. And then, as Miss Fernside graced the audience with a soulful melody upon one of the harps, Richard found himself kneeling in the dust of that street, a bayonet pulled from his belly, a gunshot breaking the air beside him, and a small Spanish boy falling down dead, killed by a British soldier in a dirty red uniform. Back in the ballroom, his heart began to race, and a cold sweat broke out across his forehead. His hands had gone numb. The sound of the harp came to him as if from a great distance. It was all

A Soldier and his Rules

Richard could do to remain standing. He felt for the doorjamb near him, but his hand would not obey him, and it slipped. He stumbled backwards, catching himself against the wall.

Strong hands took hold of him from behind, pulling him out of the ballroom and into the hall. He could hear a man's voice, but it seemed so distant, he couldn't make out what he was saying. He felt himself stumbling as a large arm came around him. When Richard finally returned to the world, he found himself seated on a couch with Lord Pemberton crouched in front of him holding his shoulders firmly. He was still struggling for breath, but some sensation had returned to his hands, and his hearing had returned.

"Breathe," said Lord Pemberton. "Slowly. That's right. Inhale. Exhale. Let's count it out, shall we? Inhale for one. Exhale. Inhale for two. Exhale. Slowly, man! Slowly. Are you with me now? I lost you there for a little while."

"Yes," said Richard. "Thank you." He couldn't look at the man in front of him. Richard felt as if he might drown in the shame of it all.

Lord Pemberton rose from his crouched position, took a step back, and sat in a chair opposite Richard.

"Keep breathing," he said.

After Richard had recovered himself, and his heart rate had slowed a little, he looked up at the baron. The older gentleman was seated in a cream-coloured wingback, leaning forward, his elbows resting on his knees and his hands clasped. This was exactly how Thomas had sat in the carriage when Richard had spoken to him about Miss Pemberton.

"I've heard of this sort of thing," said Lord Pemberton.

"I'm destined for the mad house," said Richard. "It's only a matter of time."

Winsome and Amiable

"I think not," said Lord Pemberton leaning back in his chair as if to give Richard more space to breathe. "As a member of Parliament, I have made it my business to meet and speak with many of the men who served our King and country against Bonaparte. Often, it is their wives or sisters who tell me about their condition rather than the soldiers themselves. Nightmares, cold sweats, loss of breath, rapid heart rate." Lord Pemberton counted off the symptoms on his fingers like a laundry list. "Sometimes, a soldier might feel he is in the midst of battle once more and all that that entails. It is different for everyone."

"How could they shame their husbands, their brothers by telling you this?" asked Richard.

"There is no shame in being human," said Lord Pemberton. "But I see your meaning. Not everyone will understand, and the ton does so like to whisper. That is why I dragged you away from the musicale. Too many tongues wagging and all that."

"You will not speak of this to anyone?" asked Richard slowly.

"Not a word if that is your preference," said the baron.

"And what would you ask of me in return?" Richard knew this man had a parliamentary agenda, and now he had him exactly where he wanted him, pinned at the point of his sword.

Lord Pemberton looked quite openly surprised at the question.

"Nothing, Lord Winter."

"Nothing?" Richard didn't believe him. His own father would have owned the man gasping for breath in front of him. The humiliation his father would have piled on someone who was as demonstrably weak as he was could barely be contemplated. He would have had him dancing like a puppet.

A Soldier and his Rules

The blackmail would have been strung out from week to week, month to month, year to year, ending only with the sweet release of death.

"How about you have a brandy with me, save me from listening to the rest of that musicale your mother has forced us all to attend, and we'll call it even?"

Richard lifted one trembling hand. Looking at it, he said, "I'm afraid you'll have to fetch the brandy yourself if you don't mind." He gestured to the drinks cabinet.

Patience was glad when the music finally ended. Her friend Abigail had played the harp like a dream, but the evening had been poisoned by Mr. Ruteledge and his behaviour. As the applause faded, a murmur rose from the audience as they began to rise from their seats. Lady Winter had arranged for refreshments to be served in an adjacent room.

"Go and mingle," said Patience to her mother. "I will be right back. I need to visit the ladies' retirement room."

Mr. Ruteledge had clearly heard her as well, so she gave him a curt nod before heading off. Patience did not need to visit the ladies' room, but she could not spend another minute beside Mr. Ruteledge. His presence now sickened her, and she was afraid he might reach out and touch her. If he did so, she would flinch, and her mother would suck in her breath, and the evening would become even more unbearable.

On her way out, Patience passed her father who, for some reason, was only now joining the company in the ballroom.

"Did I miss much?" he asked with a mischievous smile.

"Only the entire musicale," said Patience. "Mother will be

looking for you."

"I'd best hurry up then," said Lord Pemberton glancing past her to the crowd of people who had all risen from their seats. He did not ask her where she was going, and she loved her father for that. He treated her just as he did George.

Patience thought to hide herself away, at least for a little while. She made her way to the drawing room where Lady Winter had left her and George and Delphi waiting so many weeks ago. No one would be there. She could sit in the dark and wait out the evening with the grandfather clock as company.

Pressing down the handle of the door, she entered the room and turned around quickly to close it behind her lest anyone notice she had come in. She took a deep breath and stepped into the large drawing room, only then noticing that Lord Winter was seated in a chair at the far end of the room staring into the fire.

"My lord?" she said quietly.

He looked her way.

"You shouldn't be here," he said, but he didn't get up.

It struck Patience that something was wrong. He didn't look well.

"My lord, you look pale. Is anything the matter?" She walked up to him, but he still did not rise from the chair.

"You don't listen, do you?" he said irritably. "You shouldn't be here."

"Well I can't be out there," said Patience sitting down opposite him. "Mr. Ruteledge might reach for my hand, or he might try to undress me again."

"Will you marry him?" asked Lord Winter.

It was an inappropriate question. Patience noticed the

A Soldier and his Rules

empty brandy snifter on the table beside him.

"What business is that of yours?" asked Patience softly, willing him to make it his business.

Lord Winter gave her a resigned look.

"None," he said. "It is none of my business."

Patience examined his face.

"You are too pale, my lord," she said rising from her seat and stepping up beside his. "Perhaps you are ill. I should call for a footman to help you to bed."

She placed her hand to his forehead, but he had no fever. If anything, he was too cold, too clammy.

"Miss Pemberton, I think you should leave." He spoke more forcefully this time as he took hold of her hand and removed it from his forehead.

"My name is Patience," she said. "And I told you, I can't leave."

"If someone finds you here, you will be compromised," he said, but he hadn't let go of her hand. Patience shrugged.

"It's a risk I'm willing to take," she said. She could see some colour rising in his cheeks at that statement.

"You look like a sunset in those colours," he offered, looking up at her from his seat. His eyes were earnest. The shield wall was down.

Patience smiled. She couldn't help it. This brute of a man knew what was beautiful—the Dawn, the Serpentine in the early morning, Turner's light shining through the darkness, a burnt orange shawl against a violet dress. There was so much more to him than his gruff exterior.

"I imagine that is a line you use with all the ladies," said Patience rubbing her thumb slowly along his palm.

He pulled her to him gently, and she fell into his lap more

than willingly.

"Just sit with me," he said wrapping his arms around her and pulling her to him.

Patience melted silently into his embrace, resting her face against his neck, feeling the tickle of his beard against her skin. She could feel his chest rise and fall with his breath beneath her, and as the minutes passed, her heart began to beat in time with his. She closed her eyes and surrendered to the warm feeling of connection. It was such a comfort to sit with him like that, to be held by him. She could have done so for an eternity.

When Patience finally roused herself, Lord Winter was fast asleep. She stood and smoothed down her skirts, adjusted her shawl, and with a lingering glance his way, slipped quietly out the door.

Eight

The Darkness and the Light

It was an awkward and silent ride home in the carriage with the Pemberton family and Mr. Ruteledge. Lady Pemberton tried her best to make conversation, but each of her comments and questions died a quick death—their corpses littered the floor of the carriage leaving everyone (except perhaps Lord Pemberton) feeling extraordinarily uncomfortable.

Once they had dropped off Mr. Ruteledge and arrived home themselves, Lady Pemberton pulled Patience into a reception room off the main entrance.

"What has happened?"

Patience looked at her mother. She said nothing.

"With Mr. Ruteledge?" added Lady Pemberton.

Patience could feel her ire rising. "He thinks I am a pretty thing, Mother."

"Well I don't see what's wrong with that," replied Lady

The Darkness and the Light

Pemberton pertly.

"And I shall be *his* pretty thing," added Patience. "When we are wed, he would like me to wear more dresses like this one." Patience gestured to her breasts. "In fact, when I covered myself with that orange shawl I had borrowed, he told me it was hideous and pulled it off my shoulders. When I protested, he called me silly. Silly!"

"Oh dear," said Lady Pemberton sincerely. "My poor girl."

"Are you not going to berate me, Mother?" asked Patience with annoyance. "Or you, George? I know you're listening at the door!"

"But Mr. Ruteledge gave the shawl back to you, did he not?" asked Lady Pemberton.

"No. It was taken from him by Lord Winter," said Patience. She never blushed, but she could feel herself redden as she spoke the words, and she cursed herself for being so transparent.

"I see," said her mother looking at her carefully in that way mothers do. "I do believe I owe you an apology, my angel."

"Yes. You do! What were you thinking when you insisted on me wearing that dress?"

"I wasn't thinking," said Lady Pemberton.

"I do *not* want to marry that man," said Patience as if it still needed saying.

"Of course not," said her mother. "No one is forcing you, my dear."

I suppose I was sort of forcing myself, thought Patience. *What a fool I have been.*

Her mother pulled her into an embrace.

"Don't despise me," she said. "I only want what's best for you."

A Soldier and his Rules

"I know," said Patience. "But maybe I can't have what's best."

"Nonsense," said Lady Pemberton. "All my children shall have what is best. I do believe I have been going about this all wrong." She pulled back, kissed Patience on the forehead, and then made her way from the room.

When Patience went to follow her out a few seconds later, George was waiting outside the door.

"Where did this happen?"

"What, George?" asked Patience. She wasn't in the mood.

"Where were you when Lord Winter took the shawl from Mr. Ruteledge?"

"I don't know, George. In the back hall somewhere."

"Alone?"

"Well, I wasn't alone. There were three of us."

"Patience!"

"George!"

"Clearly, I can't take my eyes off you for a second," said George. "Perhaps I should move back into the house."

"Please do," said Patience.

"Patience," said George. "It's important that you are not compromised. Even the appearance of being compromised could ruin your chances of finding a husband."

"No one wants to marry me anyway," said Patience. "Or have you not noticed?"

The tears began to tumble down her cheeks, and she brushed them away with an angry hand before fleeing up the stairs to her bed chamber.

If she was being honest with herself, she didn't particularly care that no one wanted to marry her. She only cared that Lord Winter did not want to marry her. If he did, he would be behaving differently.

The Darkness and the Light

And how was he behaving?

She thought of the way he had kissed her when she had been painting his portrait, how she had ruined the moment, and how he had then asked her to leave. The angry look on his face when she had provoked him at Somerset House. And then his words tonight: he had agreed with her that whether or not she married Mr. Ruteledge was indeed none of his business.

But then he had told her she looked like a sunset. He had held her hand and pulled her to his lap. "Just sit with me," he had said. He hadn't pawed at her or pulled her shawl down (not that she would have protested either). He hadn't even tried to kiss her. He had simply wrapped his arms around her, and it had been the sweetest, most decadent moment of her life.

He was probably under the influence of the brandy he had been drinking, thought Patience. Nothing else quite made sense. It was all so confusing. *Surely, love isn't confusing. Perhaps this is something else. Perhaps it's simply a physical attraction—lust and nothing more.* She certainly could not deny the way Lord Winter's body seemed to call to her from across a room.

Whatever it is, thought Patience, *Heaven help me.*

Richard awoke to a dying fire and an empty lap. At first, he thought it must have all been a dream, but no, he could still smell her on him. She smelled all fresh and new, like a garden in springtime—lavender and mint and something else . . . possibly just herself. He rubbed his face with both his hands. *What was he doing? Why couldn't he stop himself?* He knew it wasn't a good idea to lead her on, but he had been in a

A Soldier and his Rules

weakened state. He had been drinking, and he hadn't been thinking straight. Despite what her father had said to him earlier, Richard suspected that no man in his right mind would hand over his daughter to someone so debilitated, so broken.

She deserves so much better, thought Richard as he stood and removed his jacket.

Thomas poked his head around the doorjamb.

"Heading up to bed?" he asked.

Richard grunted.

"All done cuddling with Miss Pemberton?"

Richard felt the shock of that statement course through him. Thomas had seen them. Patience had been thoroughly compromised in his arms. *I am the most selfish man in the entire world.*

"I didn't want to disturb the two of you," said Thomas with a twinkle in his eye.

Richard glared at him. "Not a word, Thomas. Do you hear me? Not a word! She would be ruined."

"You insult me." Thomas placed his hand over his heart. "I am nothing if not discreet. If I may," said Thomas stepping into the room.

"No you may not!" said Richard.

"It seems to me," continued Thomas, "that this is something more than a passing fancy. You were holding each other as if nothing else in this world existed. Neither of you even noticed that I'd opened the door."

"I may have been drunk," said Richard.

"On love," said Thomas playfully.

His suspicions were confirmed when Richard ploughed roughly past him, shoving him with some force against the wall as he strode from the room.

The Darkness and the Light

A few days later, a letter arrived for Patience.

"What is that?" asked her mother looking up from her needlework as the footman presented the missive to Patience on a silver tray.

"Nothing important," said Patience tossing it to the table beside her as if she did not care to read it. She returned to her book.

But it *was* something important. It was a letter from the Royal Academy, and it was all Patience could do not to rip it open on the spot. *Best not to make a fuss of it. There will be enough fuss as it is if they find out I painted Lord Winter's portrait, that he sat with me alone in his house.* And by 'they', Patience meant George and her mother, but especially George.

Patience turned a page of her book. She was rereading *The Iliad*. Lady Pemberton thought it pretentious to read *The Iliad* in Greek, but then why had she agreed to those language lessons for so many years? As far as Patience was concerned, the lilt of the poetry, the meaning of the story came across entirely differently in Greek. Just as it was meant to do. Patience reread the same page four times as she waited for her mother to give up on her needlework and leave the room. She knew from experience that if she left first—with the letter—her mother would be suspicious.

Finally, Lady Pemberton rose from her chair and stretched gracefully. She stepped across the room to Patience and casually picked up the letter from the table.

Turning it over, she said, "I think it *is* important, Patience dear. It's from the Royal Academy."

Having called Patience out on her little deception, she smiled brightly and left the room.

Patience grabbed the letter and ripped it open.

A Soldier and his Rules

They had accepted the portrait! It would be a valuable contribution to the exhibit. Such an important man painted in such an impressive manner. It was hoped that the viscount would be able to attend the exhibit on opening day as well.

They had sent him a letter.

Oh dear, thought Patience.

Richard stood in front of himself under the domed roof of Somerset House. He had been shown in early by special request. Soon the ton would descend upon the building for the opening day of the Royal Academy's exhibit. Not everyone who came was actually interested in art, but it was one of the highlights of the Season and certainly the place to see and be seen. There would be a lot of people, and Richard planned to be well clear of the building before the well-dressed mob descended upon it.

When Richard had received a letter from the Royal Academy, he did not know what to think. *How could Miss Pemberton have finished the portrait after only one sitting?* Reading the letter, he realised that the Academy was under the impression that his portrait painter was a man, and this made him smile.

The sly little fox. She knew exactly how to give herself, if not the advantage, then at least an even playing field. There were other paintings at the gallery done by ladies, but they were few, and often the lady artists in question were wives of Academy members.

Richard could not comprehend how she had done it, but Miss Pemberton had painted his portrait as if it were Turner's *Hannibal Crossing the Alps*. That particular painting was

The Darkness and the Light

no longer hanging in the Great Room, so it was unlikely anyone else would notice what Miss Pemberton had done. But Richard could see it as clear as day. His figure was there, but shrouded in darkness. The brush strokes were stormy, violent, and quick. You had to peer carefully to make out the details as you might in a darkened room. A soft golden light shone down on him from the top left corner. Not enough to illuminate him in his entirety, but enough to give his face a subtle glow. His stern features were highlighted in the palest gold, and the light struck him in such a way as to emphasise the dark hollows of his eye sockets. In contrast, the irises of his eyes were aflame, bright and green and lit orange at the edges.

It's not often that a person feels seen. Not just noticed but seen for who they are, blemishes and all. Richard felt that way now, and it was an overpowering sensation that made him surprisingly weak in the knees. He should leave, but he found it impossible to tear himself away from the portrait. He wasn't simply looking at himself. He was looking at himself through Miss Pemberton's eyes, and he didn't want to let go of the connection he felt with her there in that moment. He had held her the other night in that chair by the fire. But here in the gallery, he could see that she was the one holding him. One minute tumbled into another, and Richard forgot himself entirely as he stood there. It was only when he heard the murmured voices ascending the spiral staircase that he realised he had tarried too long. He descended the staircase quickly with his head down, passing by those first few enthusiastic attendees heading in the opposite direction.

"Lord Winter!"

Richard lifted his gaze to see Mr. Henry Howard, secretary

of the Academy, advancing up the steps towards him. He was a man with a friendly open face, a large nose, and dark bushy eyebrows that arched into a permanent expression of surprise.

"Mr. Howard," said Richard.

"You're not leaving so soon, are you, my lord?"

"I am," said Richard.

Mr. Howard turned around to join Richard in descending the stairs.

"Your portrait artist is a marvel, Lord Winter. Mr. Pemberton has somehow managed to transform a simple portrait into an epic struggle between the darkness and the light. I have not seen the like, and I cannot wait to speak with him about it when he arrives."

"*She*," said Richard. "*She* is a marvel."

"My lord?" said Mr. Howard in confusion.

"My portrait artist is Miss Patience Pemberton. The baron's daughter."

Mr. Howard stopped on the stairs.

"Miss Patience Pemberton," he repeated. He looked at Richard curiously. "You engaged her to paint your portrait?"

"You could say that," said Richard.

Mr. Howard broke into a smile. "How very forward-thinking of you, my lord. I will seek her out when she arrives."

Richard knew Mr. Howard would have much to say to Miss Pemberton. Ten years ago, he had exhibited a painting at the Academy titled *The Sixth Trumpet Soundeth.* He had used the darkness and the light to dramatic effect, creating a painting that was as grand as it was awful (in the original sense of that word).

By the time they arrived on the ground floor, there was a crush of gentlemen and ladies rustling and chattering as

The Darkness and the Light

they made their way through the front doors. Among them, Richard saw the entire Pemberton family. Lady Pemberton was clinging to the baron's arm. George Pemberton followed behind. And there was Patience—Miss Pemberton—wearing a moss green pelisse and holding the hand of a little blonde girl beside her.

That must be her sister, thought Richard.

Miss Pemberton immediately spotted him through the crowd. And for a brief second, as their eyes met, it was as if the crowd fell away, and it was just the two of them with a stretch of open marble floor between them. Miss Pemberton gave him an apologetic look, and Richard wished he could tell her that there was no need for an apology. Richard knew that he should keep his distance from her and her family, especially today. Once they saw that portrait, her parents and brother would suspect that there was something between him and Miss Pemberton. His presence would only add to their discomfort and probably hers as well.

"There is the baron and his family now!" said Mr. Howard stepping forward to greet them.

Richard took the opportunity to slip into a side room.

Here we go, thought Patience as Mr. Howard approached them.

She hadn't exactly told her family that she was exhibiting a painting this year, although she suspected that her mother knew something was up. The Pembertons always attended the opening day of the exhibit at the insistence of Lady Pemberton who would not have her social standing among the gentle ladies of London falter by being absent or late to such an

A Soldier and his Rules

important social event in the Season.

Mr. Howard introduced himself first to the baron and Lady Pemberton. With the charm of someone who has been caught off her guard, Lady Pemberton then introduced the rest of the family.

"I am so pleased to finally meet you Miss Pemberton," said Mr. Howard stepping forward. "It is an honour. I was just speaking with Lord Winter . . ." He looked behind him, but Patience could see that Lord Winter had taken the opportunity to sneak away.

"Lord Winter?" said George reaching out and taking hold of Patience's arm in a protective grasp. Patience felt her heart begin to knock against her chest. *George is not going to like this.*

"The viscount was here just a moment ago," said Mr. Howard smiling. "Come, come! You must see where we've hung the portrait. Pride of place, Miss Pemberton."

He led the Pemberton family up the spiral staircase following the clicking footsteps of the crowd, the sound of silk skirts rustling, and the laboured breathing of those less athletic attendees who were perhaps regretting their decision to attempt the climb up to the top floor. George had not released his grip on Patience's arm. She turned to him and smiled nervously, but of course, he did not smile back. He never smiled.

Just as they reached the last few steps, Patience leaned into George and whispered, "Please, brother, do not make a scene. This is an important day for me."

George looked down at her and loosened his grip, but he made no promises.

When they finally emerged beneath the domed roof of the Great Room, they could see a crowd of people clustered

The Darkness and the Light

around one painting at the far end.

"Make way! Make way!" said Mr. Howard as he led the Pembertons through to the front. "I have the artist with me here. Perhaps you would like to ask her some questions."

As the crowd parted, Lord Winter's portrait came into full view of the Pembertons. Lady Pemberton stopped short with her husband. Patience could hear her mother gasp. Looking up at George beside her, Patience could see a vein begin to throb at his temple. Lady Pemberton stepped forward and took Patience by the hand.

"You painted this, my dear?" she whispered.

Patience nodded.

"Your daughter is quite talented," said Mr. Howard to the baron.

"Of course she is," said Lord Pemberton smiling. "Of course she is."

Mr. Howard gestured for Patience to step forward.

He raised his voice to address the crowd. "We're lucky to have the artist Miss Patience Pemberton with us here today. Miss Pemberton, do you have anything you would like to say?"

Patience felt the tears pricking at her eyes. It was all a bit more than she had bargained for when she had submitted the painting to be considered. Swallowing back the wealth of emotion that threatened to engulf her, she gathered herself together and stood up a little straighter. She could hear the sound of two small hands clapping and looked down to see her sister Grace smiling brightly and encouraging her on.

In the carriage ride on the way home, Patience sat quietly with

A Soldier and his Rules

her family.

"I thought," said the baron, "that you were to paint the dowager viscountess."

"Yes," said George, throwing her an accusing look.

"Lady Winter changed her mind, and the viscount was kind enough to sit for me in her stead," said Patience as casually as she could.

"Kind enough," repeated George with some sarcasm.

"Yes, kind enough," said Patience. "He is a busy man, and he made time for me."

"I'm sure he did," said George.

"Now, now," interrupted Lady Pemberton. "I'm sure it was all done properly." She looked at her daughter. "You had Delphi with you?"

"Of course," said Patience, willing herself not to blush. She did not say that Delphi had been in the kitchen with Sarah, but she could feel George's eyes burrowing into her as if he somehow knew or at least suspected.

"Lord Winter is a gentleman," said Lord Pemberton, and everyone turned to him in surprise. The baron so rarely inserted himself into any of these little family bickerings.

"He is a man. I would not say he is gentle," said George.

"A war hero," said Lord Pemberton.

"His father's son," countered George.

"There are sons, and then there are sons," said the baron cryptically, leaning back in his seat.

"Lord Winter only sat for me the once," said Patience in an attempt to put an end to the conversation. "He did not want to sit again."

Everyone turned to her.

"How could you have possibly completed that portrait with

The Darkness and the Light

only one sitting?" asked Lady Pemberton.

"I finished it at home," said Patience quietly. "From memory."

"Hah!" laughed the baron. "Do you see your daughter, Agnes? What a talent!" To Patience, "I am so proud of you today, my love."

"Thank you, Father," said Patience. She could feel herself welling up again.

Grace had been uncharacteristically silent as she listened to the adults in the carriage. She reached for Patience's hand and gave it a little squeeze.

When they arrived home, Patience went directly to her bed chamber. She needed a rest, but she had only just laid down when there was a soft knock at her door. It was Grace. She came into the room and lay down beside Patience on her bed, both of them staring up at the white bed curtains draped over the four posts of the bed.

"Even if he has never been in a duel, I suppose 'war hero' is a point in his favour," said Grace quite out of the blue.

"Excuse me?" said Patience turning to her sister.

"Lord Winter. War hero. That's one point. So here's a question for you: has he read Homer?"

Patience stared at her little sister. She couldn't believe what she was hearing.

"I'll take your silence for a yes," said Grace. "That's another point for the viscount. And there's only one more question to answer for the full three points. Does he believe in true love?"

"You've been reading too many romance novels," said Patience trying to deflect her sister.

"And you haven't been reading enough. I'd say you've read none."

"That's a point in *my* favour," said Patience. "Those books

A Soldier and his Rules

are full of nonsense." She gave her sister a shove that sent her off the side of the bed.

"Ouch!" said Grace as she slid awkwardly to the floor. "That wasn't very ladylike!" As she stood up, she said, "But I suppose that's what the viscount likes about you. You're different."

Patience threw a pillow at her sister who shrieked and then fled the room laughing.

On the floor below, George was sitting at a heavy oak desk in his father's study pouring himself a rather large glass of whiskey. He downed it in a few gulps, then placed the flats of his hands to the surface of the table and stood with some resolve. He called for a footman and told him to have the driver ready the carriage once more. There was somewhere he needed to be.

Nine

You Burn so Bright

~~~~~~

Richard had been home from the Royal Academy exhibit for only a couple of hours before George Pemberton came calling.

"Show him in," said Richard to the footman. He rose to greet his guest.

Miss Pemberton's brother stepped through the doorway. He was tall and lean, and he did not have the soft look of a man who sat around all day. In fact, at that particular moment, he appeared to be a bundle of rigid muscle and barely controlled anger.

Mr. Pemberton watched the footman leave, and when the door clicked shut, he pierced Richard with his grey gaze.

"What can I do for you, Mr. Pemberton?" asked Richard.

"Have you touched her?" asked Mr. Pemberton, a vein throbbing at his temple.

"Excuse me?"

A Soldier and his Rules

"Have you touched my sister?" He said it, and as he did so, he stepped forward two paces.

Richard did not answer. *Have I touched his sister?* he thought. A picture of Miss Pemberton's face in his hands flashed before him, her lips parted and wet. Then he had her by the wrists, pinned to a painting. Richard could feel her soft body moulding to his lap as he held her in front of the fire and buried his face in her hair.

Richard knew he should answer, that he should say 'no', but he found he could not bring himself to lie so baldly to Miss Pemberton's brother.

It was likely the too-long pause that did it, but before Richard could understand what was happening, Mr. Pemberton had launched himself forwards, toppling Richard with an enormous crash to the floor.

"I will kill you!" yelled Mr. Pemberton, knocking Richard's face sideways with a punch.

Good, thought Richard.

"You're a bloody predator just like your father," said Mr. Pemberton landing another punch.

Richard's body instinctively wanted to fight back, to protect itself, but Richard willed himself to remain passive. If he was good at anything, he was good at this: he could take a beating willingly.

And why should Mr. Pemberton not be angry? I have thoroughly compromised his sister. Without even a promise of marriage. Not that that is at all possible.

It was a few minutes before Richard found himself freed of Mr. Pemberton's body-weight. Thomas must have heard the crash to the floor and come to see what was the matter. He had pulled Mr. Pemberton from Richard, and he was struggling to

You Burn so Bright

keep the man's arms pinned behind his back. Richard stood and wiped some blood from his mouth with the heel of his hand.

"Now, Mr. Pemberton," said Thomas. "I'm sure whatever the matter is, it can be discussed civilly, like gentlemen."

"I'm not dealing with a gentleman," spit out Mr. Pemberton. His sandy hair had been thrown wildly on end, and he looked more than ready to attack again. Thomas held him firmly while tossing Richard a questioning look.

"What is this about then?" asked Thomas.

"Your friend," said George trying to pull his arms from Thomas's grip, "is in the business of compromising young ladies."

Richard said nothing.

"I see," said Thomas. "This is about your sister."

George whipped his head around to try to see Thomas who was still holding him fast from behind.

"You know?"

"Well, it's an easy guess since you're here, and you're clearly upset. I for one don't know anything about anyone being compromised," continued Thomas smoothly. "But what would you say if I told you they were in love?"

"Thomas!" yelled Richard.

"I'm just asking," replied Thomas.

Mr. Pemberton appeared to go completely mad, growling and twisting away from Thomas. He hurled himself at Richard once more, and then they were on the floor again, this time taking a lamp crashing down with them.

"Good heavens," said Thomas as if he were a nurse and they were two children squabbling on the carpet. "What am I to do with the two of you?"

A Soldier and his Rules

By the time Thomas had wrestled Mr. Pemberton away from Richard once again, everyone was sweating and breathing heavily.

"Alright, Mr. Pemberton," said Thomas. "That is quite enough now. I'm going to have to ask you to leave."

Mr. Pemberton kept his eyes fixed on Richard as he tugged his arms free of Thomas's grip.

"I will see you at dawn, Winter."

"Good Lord," said Thomas. "Not a duel! This is too much, Mr. Pemberton. Just ask the viscount to marry your sister, and be done with it."

"The hell I will," said Mr. Pemberton. "He'll marry her over my dead body."

"Well, after tomorrow morning," replied Thomas astutely, "that just might be the case."

Ignoring Thomas, Mr. Pemberton fixed Richard with a steely glare. "I will kill you," he said quietly.

George had not joined the rest of the family for dinner that evening which was not unusual. He no longer lived in the London house, and he had his own engagements, so no one thought anything of it.

Afterwards, Grace announced quietly to Patience that she was going up to her room to write "an epic romance about a war hero and a painter and their at first unrequited—then later *very* requited— love."

"Don't say such things in front of Mother . . . or George," Patience whispered angrily.

Grace looked hurt. "I would never," she said. "I'm just

teasing."

"It's enough, Grace. It's not funny."

Grace huffed. "Fine, but I *am* going to write it," she said before leaving Patience on her own in the drawing room.

It had been an emotional day, and Patience took the opportunity to simply sit and contemplate all that had happened. She had already received several commissions to paint various well-to-do ladies about town, and that was certainly something to smile about. Although Lord Winter had come to the exhibit, he had not made the situation any more awkward than it already was. She quietly thanked him in her mind for sneaking out when he had the chance.

When Lady Pemberton finally joined Patience in the drawing room that evening, she looked hesitant and concerned.

"My dear," she said. Patience waited, but her Mother appeared to be having trouble with the rest of her sentence. After a long pause, she continued, "I do not want to cast a pall over this day. Your father and I are very proud of you. I hope you truly know that." Another pause. "But it has come to my attention over the course of this afternoon that there are some rumours circulating."

"Rumours?" asked Patience.

"There was that waltz you danced with the viscount," said Lady Pemberton. "At Almack's. It was rather a spectacle, and people remember it, especially now."

"Why now?" asked Patience.

"Because of the portrait, my dear. Quite a fuss is being made over it. It is . . . rather an intimate likeness."

"It's a portrait," said Patience. "Nothing more."

"Everyone can see that it is something more," said her mother giving her a curious look. "And coupled with the memory of that waltz . . . There is talk that you and the viscount are having an affair."

"But that is preposterous, Mother!"

Lady Pemberton made a sound that Patience could not decipher.

"Is there anything you would like to tell me, my dear?"

"No Mother. There is not," said Patience. "These rumours are just that—rumours."

"Well, then, I think it may be time to take that trip out to see Serafina and John. If you arrive before the baby is born, you could be a source of strength for your friend when the time comes."

Patience heaved a sigh. Despite coming from her mother, it wasn't a terrible idea.

"Alright," she said. "I'll pack tomorrow. Not because there is any truth to the rumours, but because I do so want to see Serafina again. I should not have left her to come to London in the first place."

"Good," said Lady Pemberton. "Distance and time always work to weaken the rumour mill. It will come to nothing," she said.

It must have been past one o'clock in the morning when Delphi snuck up to Patience's room to wake her.

"Miss," she said shaking Patience's shoulder gently. "Miss."

"What is it?" asked Patience still half asleep.

"Forgive, me," said Delphi. "I didn't know what he was asking."

Patience didn't understand. "What who was asking?"

You Burn so Bright

"Mr. Pemberton, Miss."

At the sound of her brother's name, Patience sat up in bed. Delphi was holding a candle, and the look on her face was one of sheer terror. All the colour had been drained from her face.

"Earlier today, Mr. Pemberton asked me about that day when we went to Lord Winter's house to paint the dowager viscountess. I didn't realise . . . I mean, I didn't know that you had been painting the viscount himself." The maid took a deep shuddering breath. "Your brother knows that I was not with you."

"Don't worry yourself, Delphi. I'm leaving London tomorrow anyway. George's suspicions will fade with time."

"You don't understand, Miss," said Delphi, tears welling up. "There's going to be a duel in the morning."

"What?!"

"Mr. Pemberton and Lord Winter. I heard it from the driver."

"Of all the nerve!" said Patience swinging her feet from the bed. To Delphi, "Don't worry yourself, Delphi. It's not your fault."

"I believe it is, Miss."

"Nonsense. My brother is a pig-headed fool, and that will never be your fault. Go to bed now. I'll take care of it. Don't worry yourself." She took Delphi's head in her hands and kissed her forehead. "Go to bed," she said again.

When Delphi had disappeared back into the darkened hallway, Patience began pulling on her boots in a panic.

Bloody George and his bloody protective nonsense! At first she thought to go after her brother, but conjuring his stubborn face in her mind, she could foresee that she would make no headway with him. What he didn't understand was that Lord

A Soldier and his Rules

Winter would not hesitate to allow himself to be killed. He wouldn't mind. Then not only would Lord Winter be dead, but George would be a murderer, and all because she had danced a waltz and painted a portrait. *The situation was too ludicrous for words!*

Patience pulled a riding cloak over her nightdress, stepped quietly down the stairs, and made her way to the mews at the back of the house.

Richard could not quite understand what was happening when he was woken in his bed to be told that Miss Pemberton was waiting downstairs in the drawing room in the middle of the night. He did, however, have the presence of mind to warn the footman that discretion was advised.

"Martin, not a word of this. To anyone. Not the other servants, not your sweetheart, not your mother. No one."

"Of course not, my lord," said the footman.

Richard pulled on a pair of trousers and grabbed a shirt as he left the room. He paused outside the drawing room door. Then taking a deep breath, he entered the room.

Miss Pemberton was facing away from him and staring into the fire. She was wearing her dark green riding cloak, and as she turned to him, his breath caught in his chest. She had that softened look of someone recently roused from sleep. Her eyelids were heavy, and her hair fell down over her shoulders, a cascade that glinted golden in the firelight.

"It seems that boys will be boys," she said. "I apologise for my brother."

"He's not wrong," said Richard. "And you shouldn't be here.

You Burn so Bright

Did you come alone?"

Miss Pemberton ignored his question.

"Promise me you will not go through with this duel in the morning," she said.

"Your brother has a right," said Richard. "Gentlemen have rules."

"Rules!" said Miss Pemberton, her voice increasing in volume. "If you followed the rules, you would have asked me to marry you by now!"

"You wouldn't like that!" Richard snapped back. "You don't know me."

"Don't tell me what I would like!" said Miss Pemberton advancing on him as her cloak fell open at the front to reveal a white muslin nightdress clinging to her soft round curves. Richard stepped back until he was up against the door. Miss Pemberton walked right up to him and took his hand.

"Please," she said. "Please don't do this. I know you do not care for yourself, but think of George. You will make a murderer of him."

Richard looked down to where she clasped his hand. *This woman! This fiery, impossible woman!* Miss Pemberton looked up into his eyes as she tightened her grip on his hand.

"Patience," he whispered. It was the first time he had used her Christian name. She waited. "How did you . . . I saw the portrait today," he said. "How did you do it?"

She slid her hand up to his wrist. "When I close my eyes, I can see you," she said quietly as she moved her hand up a little further along his arm beneath the open cuff of his linen shirt.

Richard felt himself coming undone like a worn piece of clothing unravelling at the edges. He was struggling to hold himself together as he felt her small cool hand slide up his forearm.

Patience could feel her pulse quicken when Lord Winter spoke her Christian name. Coming from his mouth, it was somehow even more intimate than a kiss. He was quite dishevelled, his shirt untucked and open at the neck to reveal a slab of hairy chest. She desperately wanted to touch him. To stroke every inch of his body with her fingertips. Patience slid her hand up his forearm, revelling in the sensation of sinew and muscle beneath her fingers. *Sweet merciful heavens, she wanted this man in a way she could not quite comprehend.*

"You are a marvel," he said with wonder in his voice.

"So are you," she said.

"Don't say things like that."

"Why not?" asked Patience. "Is it a rule?"

"Yes," said Richard.

Patience slid the sleeve of his shirt up to his bicep and inspected his large hairy arm. The veins and tendons, the muscles beneath the skin. She would memorise that arm so that she would be able to draw it later.

"You shouldn't do that," said Richard, but he didn't pull his arm away.

"Another rule?"

"Yes."

"Fine," said Patience.

She dropped his arm and turned to the fireplace. Unfastening her cloak, she threw it across a chair and sank herself into one of the sofas.

"What are you doing?" asked Richard. He hadn't moved

from the door.

"I can't leave until you promise me you will not duel with my brother in the morning."

"I can't promise you that," said Richard firmly, stepping up to her and handing her her cloak.

"Then I can't leave," said Patience, taking the cloak from him and tossing it to the floor.

"Miss Pemberton, you must leave! You cannot be found here in my house in your nightdress."

Richard reached for her upper arm and hoisted her to her feet. He had the look of a man who would brook no opposition. Patience began to panic. She could not allow the duel to take place. If Lord Winter died . . . she couldn't even bear to think it. She struggled against him.

"I'm not leaving!" she cried.

He tried marching her to the door by the arm, but she allowed her legs to give way, sinking to the floor. He couldn't exactly drag her by the arm. He might dislocate her shoulder.

"For Christ's sake," muttered Lord Winter under his breath. He reached down, and scooped her entire struggling body up into his arms.

"Put me down!"

"I will put you down in front of your house," said Lord Winter firmly. "You're going home!"

Patience could feel the strength of him surround her to hold her in place. Her mind worked frantically to find a way to stay, to stop the duel. She kicked and thrashed her body against him, but he drew her tightly to his chest, refusing to release her. She pounded at him with her little fists, and when that did nothing, she actually bit him on the shoulder. Richard, for his part, did not appear to register any of her pathetic attempts at violence. It was like throwing pebbles at a mountain.

Finally, just as he was approaching the door with her, she reached her hands up to his head and took his hair in two fists. Pulling his head down to hers with as much strength as she could manage, she kissed him—hard.

Patience could feel Lord Winter's entire body go slack as her lips touched his. He was still carrying her, but his muscles had somehow relaxed. She softened her mouth against his, probed tentatively with her tongue. She could feel his momentary hesitation. And then his arms tightened around her once more as he opened his mouth to take her in. Patience luxuriated in the heat of him, the way he knew exactly how to kiss her, to stroke her lips, her mouth with his silken tongue. An involuntary moan escaped her, and she heard him growl—deep and low in his throat. She released her grip on his hair, slid her hands to his broad shoulders. He pulled his mouth from hers to look into her eyes, and she tilted her head to kiss his bare neck, his exposed chest where his shirt had fallen open. She could feel him tremble beneath her touch.

"You need to leave," he said in a hoarse voice as she slid a hand inside his shirt to skim her fingers over his chest.

"No. I need you," she said quite honestly.

The words she spoke seemed to do something to him. His eyes darkened, and she could feel his heart start to beat a little harder against her body.

"Richard," she whispered as she offered her mouth up for another kiss.

He was growling again as his mouth took possession of hers with an animal intent that set her toes curling. The white hot heat of the moment sank down through her body, and she could feel herself begin to swell and throb between her legs as he kissed her senseless. She didn't realise he had moved with her across the room until he lay her down upon the couch. He straddled her body with one knee on the couch and one foot to the floor. Leaning over her, he propped himself up with one arm planted on the couch beside her. The anticipation of what he might do next set Patience's heart racing. Her breath was coming quite fast. He paused over her, and for one painful, disappointing moment, she thought he might stop. But then he took the back of his free hand and lightly stroked it over the front of her nightdress. As he grazed the tip of each nipple, Patience let out a small gasp, arching herself towards him, searching for more. The feathery nature of his touch was agonising in its restraint. He brought his fingers to her throat, the same delicate touch, stroking up to her jaw, then her lips. Patience was trying not to whimper with the overwhelming need that engulfed her.

"Richard," she whispered once more. It was a plea.

He took his hand from her and leaned his face down beside hers. His beard grazed the side of her face as he brought his lips to her ear.

"I'm going to need you to say it," he said.

His hot breath on her ear sent her momentarily to a place where words didn't exist, and she had to struggle to put a sentence together.

"Richard, I need you," she said in a husky voice.

"You're going to have to be more specific," he said as he ran a finger from the divot at the base of her neck down between her breasts.

Oh Lord, thought Patience. *I can't even remember my own name. How can I possibly be specific?*

"Touch me wherever you want," she said breathlessly. "Take

whatever you want."

Richard leaned down to her ear once more, breathing heavily this time.

"You shouldn't say that," he whispered.

And then he was unbuttoning the front of her nightdress. Patience noticed that his fingers had a slight tremor to them. She sat up and placed her hand over his on her chest.

"Let me," she said, unbuttoning herself with practised fingers as she gazed up into his darkened eyes.

She slipped the nightdress from one shoulder and then the other to expose her breasts to his hungry eyes. She had never felt so vulnerable, so completely at someone else's mercy. Richard lifted his shirt over his head to reveal a hulking torso composed of overlapping slabs of taut muscle. His skin bore the scars of many battles, the slice of swords and bayonets. Patience reached up to stroke the black hair of his chest. When she ran a thumb over one of his nipples, she heard him take in a sharp breath.

"Dear God, Patience," said Richard leaning over her as she lay herself back down beneath him. "You are so incredibly beautiful. You burn so bright, it hurts me to look at you."

Patience couldn't speak. She had never felt so wanted in her entire life.

I'm going to burn in Hell for this, thought Richard as he lowered his face to hers to explore her soft mouth once more.

He was drunk on the permission she had granted him. She had said he could take what he wanted, but what he wanted most of all was to please her, to make her ache for him, to make her scream and beg for more.

As he kissed her gently, she pulled him to her, responding with her own kisses which were neither tender nor gentle. It was as if she were struggling to take in more—more of him! He responded by biting her lip and sliding down her body, leaving a trail of kisses along her neck. He took her nipple between his teeth, and she gave a small cry of pleasure, arching into him. He licked and sucked at her until she was writhing beneath him, her hands in his hair, holding him against her body. Richard slowly reached a hand down between her soft thighs, hiking her night dress up to her waist. He lifted his head to look her in the eyes as he placed his fingers to the petals of her flower. She was gripping his shoulders tightly now, and he could see she was holding her breath, waiting. He moved his fingers in slow, lazy circles around her perimeter, teasing her with his touch.

"Richard," she whispered. "Please," she said more loudly.

"You want more?" he asked.

"Yes," she said pleadingly.

He slipped one finger partially inside her as he watched her face, careful to monitor her reaction. She threw her head back and pulled him down to her. As he bit her ear, he gently slid a second finger inside her. Her breath was ragged as he began to pump his fingers slowly and very tenderly in and out.

"Oh God," she whispered, barely able to form the words. "What are you—?"

He had pressed his thumb to her bud of pleasure, his fingers still inside her. It was taking all his energy to keep a rein on his own bestial impulses as he worked her little bud into a swollen frenzy. Patience tossed her head from side to side, her nails digging into his shoulders. He could feel her tense and still before she let out several breathy cries in swift succession as she arched her generous breasts up against his hard torso. The sight and sensation of her losing control beneath him caused Richard to lose the precarious grip he had on himself, and with a groan, he spilled himself into his drawers.

Ten

Grey Clouds

As Richard held Patience across his lap, she nuzzled her face into his neck. They were both still bare from the waist up, and the feel of her soft ripe body against his was the worst kind of pleasure—the kind that hurt him to contemplate. Richard realised in that moment that he would do whatever she asked of him. If she didn't want him to fight the duel in the morning, he wouldn't.

Morning! Bloody hell—it was almost morning!

"Patience," he said stroking her hair, "We have to get you home."

He could feel her burrow closer into him.

"I told you I'm not leaving," she said into his neck.

"I promise not to fight your brother," said Richard.

Patience pulled her face from his neck to look into his eyes. In the firelight, she looked all golden and flushed, lips plump with his kisses. *Sweet mercy, he had to return her home before his desire overcame his good sense.*

"I have to leave London anyway to search out my brother James—he should have arrived home by now. I'll send your brother a note, although I don't think he's going to like it."

"Duels are illegal," said Patience. "George doesn't have to like it." A pause. "Thank you."

She placed one hand to his hairy jaw and tipped her face to kiss him once more. It was soft and slow, and Richard drank it up, savouring every hot wet second of it.

He knew he should ask her to marry him, that it was the only honourable course of action at this point, but there was the matter of her brother hating him, and there was also the fact that he was not the man she thought he was. He felt physically ill when he contemplated telling her about the broken state of his mind. He imagined how she might look at him, as if he were less than a man, certainly less than any husband should be, and he couldn't bear the thought. It certainly wouldn't be the way she was looking at him now—as if he were some sort of Homeric hero, strong and powerful, if not invincible.

Patience arrived home on horseback escorted by Richard in the opalescent light that preceded the rising of the sun. Dawn and her rosy fingers were only just beginning to stir. Patience did not kiss Richard in the street or touch his hand as she desperately wanted to, but she did steal a backwards glance at his large frame silhouetted against the early morning light before she stole quietly towards the mews with her horse. She crept up to her room to find Delphi half asleep in an armchair beside her dressing table. When she entered the room, Delphi

Grey Clouds

stood.

"I came back, and you weren't here, Miss," said the maid. "I didn't know how long you would be, and I thought I'd best stay in case Lady Pemberton eventually came knocking. I shouldn't like to lie to her ladyship, but . . ."

"Not to worry, Delphi," said Patience. "It's nice to know I can count on you, but it's all been sorted."

"Really?!" said Delphi with surprise.

"George will not be shooting anyone today."

"That's certainly a relief, Miss. I don't think I could have forgiven myself if anything had happened. But how . . . ?"

"Never you mind how," said Patience.

With a great deal of heavy petting and open-mouthed kissing—that's how, she thought. *Oh Delphi, I'm sure you would not approve.*

When Delphi left the room, Patience crawled beneath the covers of her bed. She was tired, but the events of the night had been enough to keep her heart pounding and her mind alert . . . until now. She could feel her eyelids grow heavy as she reached up to stroke her breasts the way Richard had stroked them, imagining his hands on her again. Her friend Serafina had given her a primer in what to expect physically if she ever became intimate with a man, but no amount of explanation or diagrams (they had drawn diagrams, and they had laughed, for it was all just a little embarrassing) could have prepared her for what had happened that night. She had offered herself up to him, but he had taken nothing from her. Every stroke, every touch had been a gift. Just thinking about the way he had touched and teased her until she was breathless and needy sent her eyes rolling up in her head.

Heaven help me, thought Patience.

A Soldier and his Rules

As she slipped quietly towards sleep, her angry words came back to her from earlier that night: "If you followed the rules, you would have asked me to marry you by now!"

What had Richard said?

"You wouldn't like that! You don't know me."

There was something he was hiding, thought Patience, like that scar he had concealed beneath his beard.

The next few days were spent packing clothes and daydreaming about Richard. Patience had sent off a letter to Serafina, but it was entirely possible that it would not arrive before she did. Serafina wouldn't mind a surprise visit. It was not as if the whole family were coming—it would just be her and Delphi with a footman and driver along for the journey.

George, for his part, appeared at the Pemberton house for dinner a day after the date of the unspoken duel.

"It seems Lord Winter has quit London," said George lifting a spoonful of soup to his mouth.

"What a shame," said Lord Pemberton. "Parliament sits in a few weeks. I thought he would take up his seat."

"It's probably better if he doesn't," said George as he glared at Patience. "His father has wreaked enough misery as it is. Hell is too nice a place for that man."

"George!" said Lady Pemberton.

"It's the truth, Mother. He was evil."

"Nevertheless," said Lady Pemberton. "You can conduct yourself as a gentleman, even if it is only a family dinner."

George said nothing, but Grace who had been listening as she ate, said quietly, almost to herself, "Every story needs a villain."

"His father never went to war," said Lord Pemberton with some force in his voice. All eyes looked down the table to him. "It changes a man."

"In what way?" asked George in a clipped tone.

"It forces you to grow up," said Lord Pemberton with an accusing look at his son. "To take stock."

"Of what?" asked Patience affecting a casual manner as she sipped broth from her spoon.

"Of who you are. Of your life. Of what is important. Death has a way of bringing these things to the fore. I have seen it time and again in my interviews with veterans and their families. The horror of war also has a way of breaking you down, highlighting your own weaknesses and fears. We walk around pretending that we can control the world, make it bend to our will. A soldier knows this is an illusion. The world happens, and all he can do is react."

"Father," said Patience curiously, "have you been reading Homer?"

Lord Pemberton laughed. "No, my dear. I simply listen when people talk."

"Enough talk about war and death and fear," said Lady Pemberton. "Patience, I should like you to come with me to the party the Hastings are hosting before you leave.

"Where are you going, sister?" asked George quickly.

"To stay with Serafina and John until their baby arrives," said Patience. "I should never have left her to come to London this Season."

This news appeared to mollify George. Patience could actually see his shoulders relax. By the time dessert had been served—a very fine rhubarb pie with custard—George dug into it with apparent gusto. He even took the time to offer Grace some advice about training Potato, her small pug of a dog.

"I don't know," said Grace. "Potato likes to do what Potato likes to do. She's a free spirit."

"Free spirits need manners too," said George in between bites of pie.

"But I was so looking forward to the duel," complained Thomas quite disingenuously. "I had Martin wake me early and everything. Look, I polished my own boots for the occasion."

He stuck out one shiny black-booted foot and then another to show Richard his handiwork.

"Don't be annoying, Thomas," said Richard.

"What made you call it off?" asked his friend.

Richard didn't answer.

"It was the storm in a dress, wasn't it? Did she come round? Tell me she didn't visit you last night, Richard. Mr. Pemberton will have all the more reason to shoot you. If I were a proper upstanding citizen, I would turn you in."

"Nothing happened," said Richard.

"Oh. My. God," said Thomas peering up into Richard's thunderous face. "Something actually *did* happen last night. I was joking about turning you in, but seriously, Richard, what are you doing? She's the baron's daughter, an innocent young lady—not some lonely widow from down the street. You have to propose."

"I'm leaving town," said Richard. "I need you to watch Mother while I'm away."

Grey Clouds

"Where are you going?"

"I'll be back. I just need to find James and Michael, make sure they're both in one piece."

"And avoid this duel," added Thomas.

"And avoid this duel," repeated Richard.

"For Miss Pemberton's sake," said Thomas.

Richard glowered at him. Thomas was the best of men and a loyal friend, but he could be incredibly irritating sometimes.

"Tell me why I have to attend this party again?" asked Patience.

"So that it doesn't look like you are fleeing London due to the rumours about you and Lord Winter," replied Lady Pemberton in a somewhat exasperated whisper. "The appearance is the thing as always, my dear."

"Appearances. Yes," said Patience distractedly as they handed their coats to a footman and took in the scene in the Hastings's ballroom.

It seemed as if all of Mayfair had been packed into the room—jewels glinting, silk shimmering, and the occasional flash of a brightly-coloured waistcoat partially hidden beneath a dark jacket. Patience saw her friend Abigail dancing with Captain Walpole and wondered that Richard had not taken his friend with him. But then the dance ended, and she watched as Captain Walpole handed Abigail over to her next dance partner before making a line for Lady Winter. She could see his charm melt the dowager viscountess into a girlish smile. He fetched a drink for her and stayed to chat.

Richard has left Captain Walpole to watch over his mother, thought Patience.

A Soldier and his Rules

The small orchestra struck up a waltz, and Patience was taken back to the night she had danced with Richard, holding onto him for dear life as he swung her about the room in time to the quick pace of the music. It had been possibly the most fun she had ever had in her life. Richard had put his foot down when she had asked for a second dance that evening. What would it be like to live in a world where she could dance with him again and again without fear of gossip or rumour or ruined reputation? *Would she tire of it? Would he?*

"I thought we would see both the artist *and* her muse tonight," said Lady Hastings as she stepped up to Patience and her mother. "But it seems Lord Winter has been called away on business." Looking directly at Patience, "It was quite something, the portrait you painted of him."

"Thank you," said Patience, steeling herself for what she assumed would follow.

"You must have spent a great deal of time with the viscount to render his likeness so . . . so . . . intensely."

"Not really," said Patience. "There was just the one sitting. He's not a man with a lot of time on his hands."

"One sitting?" said Lady Hastings incredulously. "That can't possibly be true."

"But it is," said Patience. "He only sat for an hour. Then he became cranky, and I had to leave." Patience could see her mother give her a look. 'Cranky' may not have been the best word to use—a bit too familiar perhaps.

"Well. Yes. I suppose Lord Winter is not known for his affable disposition. You certainly captured that aspect of him in your painting."

When Lady Hastings had left, Lady Pemberton leaned her head towards her daughter.

Grey Clouds

"Well done, my dear. I'll make a society lady of you yet."

"I hope not," said Patience.

"One sitting *does* sound a little unbelievable though."

"But it's the truth!" said Patience.

"Pfft! You can't go relying on the truth when you're trying to dispel rumours, my dear."

Patience couldn't believe what she was hearing.

"Why not?"

"Because it's often more ludicrous than a lie," said her mother knowingly. "You did well, but next time, think it through."

"The next time I am the subject of gossip?"

"Yes, my dear," said Lady Pemberton lifting her eyebrows and smiling. "Don't look at me like that, Patience. Chin up, eyes bright—you have a gentleman approaching."

It was Captain Walpole in his crisp red jacket.

"Lady Pemberton. It is lovely to see you," he said. "I was just wondering if Miss Pemberton would grace me with the next dance."

"She would love to," said Lady Pemberton smiling.

Captain Walpole looked to Patience questioningly, reaching out his hand.

"It would be a pleasure," said Patience in a measured tone as she slipped her gloved hand in his.

As they took to the dance floor, Captain Walpole said, "I have already danced with Miss Fernside, so there is no need for your clever machinations this evening."

Patience laughed.

"If you are referring to the evening we first met, I believe the machinations were yours. I didn't even know you, and you were approaching me for a dance. It was a ballroom ambush

A Soldier and his Rules

if ever I saw one."

Now it was Captain Walpole's turn to laugh.

"You have me, Miss Pemberton. May I apologise for my behaviour that evening. It was my little attempt to taunt Richard into participating more fully in his life. The past two years have been difficult for him."

"His recovery?" asked Patience. Quiet now. Listening carefully.

"Soldiers are scarred by more than the physical wounds of war," said Captain Walpole.

His cheerful, playful manner had disappeared quite suddenly, and Patience could see now that it was simply an affectation. Beneath the surface, Captain Walpole was like a bank of grey cloud looming low on the horizon.

He continued, "It's not as if Richard ever came across as a barrel of laughs—that much is true. His childhood was less than idyllic. But something happened to him on his last campaign that sank him into a dark place, and he has only recently been able to pull himself out into the open." Thomas looked at Patience with concern in his eyes. "You must never tell him I spoke to you like this, but I am asking you now: do not give up on him, Miss Pemberton. Give him time."

"Captain Walpole," protested Patience. "I don't know what you think, but there is nothing—"

"Save your polite objections and pretence for the society ladies," said Thomas. Then registering the concern on Patience's face, he added, "You mustn't fear, Miss Pemberton. I am the soul of discretion. Now. What are we to do about your brother?"

"Excuse me?" said Patience. "George?"

"When Richard returns to London, your brother will want

Grey Clouds

to kill him all over again. Please don't pretend as if you did not know of the duel, Miss Pemberton. I assume it was you who managed to dissuade Richard from engaging with your brother."

Patience affected a look of affront.

"Your acting skills are lacking, my lady," said Captain Walpole.

Fine, thought Patience. *There is no use pretending with this man. It's a wonder Richard does not find him quite irritating.*

"Richard finds me irritating as well," said Captain Walpole as if reading her mind. He gave her a mischievous wink, and just like that the low grey clouds parted, and it was all blue skies and sunshine once more as he guided Patience across the floor.

"Leave my brother to me," said Patience as the dance came to an end.

As Captain Walpole and Patience parted ways, she spied Abigail approaching her with some hesitation.

"Your dancing is coming along," said Patience brightly. "A bit of a disappointment, that. I was hoping for some mayhem on the dance floor." Patience gave Abigail a friendly nudge with her shoulder.

"Captain Walpole has been helping me along. He's quite a good teacher."

"Is he?" said Patience as she searched out his red jacket in the crowd.

Abigail followed her gaze.

"How old do you think he is?" asked Abigail.

Patience gave her friend a quizzical look. "As old as—" She realised she was about to say "Lord Winter," but she caught herself just in time. "I'd say he's in his early thirties. Why,

A Soldier and his Rules

Abigail? Do you fancy the captain?"

Abigail's porcelain complexion flushed bright pink.

"That would be a yes," said Patience reaching for her hand. "Don't worry. I won't tease."

"It's no matter anyway," said Abigail. "I do believe he thinks me a child at only twenty. He seeks me out for a dance at every social function, possibly out of pity. We have a lovely chat, he makes me laugh, and then he excuses himself for the rest of the evening."

"Gentlemen are sometimes difficult to fathom," said Patience. She looked to her friend with concern. "You must never allow someone else to determine your self-worth, Abigail. You are clever and kind and talented, not to mention beautiful. Any gentleman would be lucky to have you."

"Hm." Abigail pressed her lips together as she stared out across the floor to Captain Walpole who was engaging yet another beautiful young lady in conversation and laughter. "But I doubt very much that *I* would be lucky to have just *any* gentleman," she said.

Patience smiled. It was a very clever thing to say.

"You are absolutely right—never forget that," said Patience.

Patience had her trunk packed and was planning on leaving later that morning. George had come by to breakfast with the family before she left. Her brother did love her, thought Patience. It was just that he was unbearably stubborn as well. She hoped he would be more amenable to her request now that the situation had been somewhat diffused.

After breakfast, Patience managed to corner George alone

Grey Clouds

in her father's study.

"I know about the duel that didn't happen," she said.

"He told you?!" said George, face flushing a pale pink as he stood.

"Of course not. Delphi did. Don't think you can do anything around here without more than a few servants noticing." Patience took a breath. "Lord Winter sat for me only the once, George. For exactly one hour. Then he asked me to leave."

"Delphi wasn't with you," said George accusingly.

"My fault," said Patience. "I was expecting Lady Winter, so I sent Delphi off to help in the kitchen with her friend Sarah. It all happened so fast. I didn't even think of a chaperone."

"I blame myself for leaving," said George. "I should never have left you in that man's house."

"He isn't his father despite looking quite like him," said Patience. "I know it is a difficult distinction for you to make, but you should look to his actions rather than his appearance. I was devastated when Lady Winter decided against having her portrait painted. It was kind of him to sit for me. I could tell he would rather not have done so."

All true statements, thought Patience. *But there is such a thing as lying by omission.* She hoped her acting skills were good enough to fool George if not Captain Walpole.

George didn't look entirely convinced.

"George, I'm leaving soon, and I need to know that you will not insist on duelling with Lord Winter if or when he returns. If either of you were hurt or, God forbid, killed, I could never forgive myself. It would be silly and tragic. And all because I sent Delphi to the kitchen one afternoon."

George sat down once more at his father's desk.

A Soldier and his Rules

"I hope you have a nice trip," he said. "Give my best to Serafina and John. And Molly."

"George!" Patience couldn't believe he was ignoring her request.

"And while you are gone, I shall not engage in any duels," he said avoiding her eyes and shifting some papers around the desk.

"Is that a promise?"

He looked up at her abruptly. Angry grey eyes. "What do you want from me, Patience?"

"I want you to promise."

"It's my job to protect your honour," he said. "You're my sister."

"I appreciate that," said Patience in a more placating tone. "But sometimes you go too far."

"Fine," said George, standing and showing her to the door. "I promise."

He did not sound pleased.

"George," said Patience turning at the door. "I love you."

She pressed a quick kiss to his cheek and pretended not to notice the look of vulnerable surprise on his face as he registered her words. It's possible she had never said it before. She was always butting heads with him and finding clever ways to cut him down.

I have not been the easiest sister, she thought. *Everyone wants to feel appreciated. Even my pig-headed brother.*

Later that morning, Grace and Lady Pemberton waved Patience off in the carriage.

"It's going to be a long ride," said Patience to Delphi as she looked out the window. It was a crisp and cool April morning. The sky was blue, but each time a cloud obscured the sun, the

Grey Clouds

temperature seemed to drop considerably. Patience snuggled into her coat and rested her head against the deep purple curtains beside the window.

They trundled along for a couple of hours before Patience noticed a significant chill in the air. She peered out the window to see dark clouds gathering in the east, and while she hoped the storm would hold off until they arrived, she knew it was unlikely since they were driving right into it.

The thunderstorm came upon them quickly. Blue sky one minute, near complete darkness the next, and a torrent of heavy water falling down upon the roof of the carriage like bricks being dropped from above.

"Do you think Charlie will pull over soon?" asked Patience of the driver. She knew the driver and footman would have their waxed coats with them, but the downpour was torrential.

"I don't see where," said Delphi, squinting out the window. There wasn't a village or farm house or shelter of any kind in sight.

It was not long before the dirt road was awash and the horses too tired to pull the carriage through the torrent of water and mud. When the carriage came to a complete halt, Patience impulsively opened the carriage door to see what was going on. A cold wash of rain water drenched her within seconds. A flash of sheet lightening across the sky was followed almost immediately by a crack of thunder so loud she heard Delphi squeal with surprise. As the rain battered her head and shoulders, she could see that Charlie and the footman were standing knee deep in mud, squelching their way around the carriage. Eventually, Charlie mounted once more while the footman remained at the back. Patience pulled herself into the shelter of the carriage and closed the door.

A Soldier and his Rules

"I think we're stuck. They may be trying to push us out."

"Miss!" said Delphi looking at Patience's dripping form, "You'll catch your death."

"I'm sure they'll have us clear in no time," said Patience ignoring her concern.

Time passed, and while Patience and Delphi could hear the driver and the footman yelling to each other above the sound of the storm, the carriage did not budge an inch. The sun remained completely obscured, and Patience began to shiver in the dark space of the carriage. Delphi found a blanket beneath the seat and wrapped her up tight, but it was of little use. The cold had sunk into her bones, and Patience was feeling increasingly lethargic. Delphi wrapped herself around Patience and her blanket and murmured encouraging words.

I just want to sleep for a little bit, thought Patience. At the fringes of her mind, she could hear shouting outside the carriage, and just as she was drifting off into a sweet dream, the door of the carriage opened with a bang, and a cold spray of water on her face roused her ever-so-slightly.

"Bloody hell!" boomed a voice she quite thought she recognised.

Richard had found James and Michael without any fuss. They had been at Avery House—the viscount's country seat. He had suspected as much, but he was still glad to see that they were alive and well.

"Mother is worried sick about you," he told his brother. "You could have at least sent a letter."

"We wanted to prolong the holiday," said James looking at

Grey Clouds

Michael who had just seated himself at the pianoforte and was plunking out a tune with one hand. "If Mother knew I was home, it would have been the beginning of the end. You know how she is—I would be forced to London to attend soirées and musicales, and in the mornings, she would make me read her those dreadful Gothic romances."

"You'll be happy to know that Thomas has been doing all that in your stead," said Richard. "I think you owe him a debt of gratitude."

James laughed. "But Thomas actually *likes* it. Have you heard him reading those novels to her? He does the voices and everything!"

"Who's to say what Thomas likes," said Richard. "He's been a good friend."

"The best," said Michael quietly from the pianoforte.

Richard had spent the next few days with James and Michael. They went riding in the mornings and played billiards and cards in the evenings. In between, Richard saw to the estate. He thought he may as well get a few things done while he was there. Each day, he rode out to visit various tenants in order to listen to any grievances they may have and to make a note of any buildings that needed mending. The tenants were reticent at first, holding their tongues out of a mistaken fear that he was a viscount like his father. Complaints were not something his father took lightly—punishment would be swift, and it would be severe. So Richard had his work cut out for him.

If he wanted to know what was actually going on, what needed doing, he was going to have to soften his image with the farmers. He tried to make a point of smiling even though it did not come naturally to him most of the time. Upon

A Soldier and his Rules

dismounting his horse, he would remove his riding gloves so that he might shake hands properly with his tenants. And while Richard was used to barking commands in the military, he tried his very best to pay each tenant a compliment—whether it be the care he had taken with the sheep or a new fence he had built—before getting down to business. It became easier with each passing day, and Richard was beginning to feel quite accomplished and satisfied in his role.

As he rode home from the tenant he had been visiting that afternoon, he knew he would not be able to outride the storm that was threatening at his heels. It would be a slog if the roads became muddy, but he was dressed for the weather in a waxed riding cloak, so at least that was something. Then the darkness had descended, and the rain had begun. The force of the downpour was so strong, it was like standing under a waterfall, but somehow Richard didn't mind. He revelled in the sensation, squeezing the sides of his horse with his thighs to spur the gelding on through the torrent. Richard was nearly home when he rounded a copse of trees to see a carriage stuck in a dip in the road. Through the curtain of rain, he thought he could make out the fancy green trim that graced the Pemberton carriages, but this one couldn't be theirs. The baron's country home didn't lie in this direction.

Either way, whoever it was needed help, so he approached. He could see two men had placed several branches in front of the back wheels to give them some purchase in the mud. One of the men looked up from his task as Richard rode up and dismounted.

"We'll have it out soon enough!" the man yelled to Richard. "If you could give us a push, it would be most helpful."

Richard walked around to the back of the carriage and

Grey Clouds

inspected the wheels.

"Something's wrong with the axle!" yelled Richard above the sound of the downpour. "These wheels are not going to turn!"

The man whom Richard assumed was the driver came around to take a look, and when he saw what Richard was pointing at, he swore himself blue in the face.

"My house is just over that rise," yelled Richard. "I'll send a groom with some fresh horses for you to ride. How many in the carriage?"

"Just two," said the driver. "The lady and her maid."

Richard felt he should introduce himself, put the lady's mind to rest over the situation. When he opened the carriage door to find the ashen-faced maid clutching Patience's limp body to hers, he felt himself to have been plunged into the middle of a nightmare. Patience's hair was wet, and her face was as pale as death.

"Bloody hell!" said Richard as he took in the scene, his mind working to understand the situation and determine next steps. "Don't let her fall asleep! Give her a smack."

"My lord," said the maid, "I couldn't."

Richard entered the carriage, filling the small space with his hulking body.

"Give her here," he said grabbing Patience roughly from the maid. Her breathing was so quiet. His heart was pounding. He slapped her across the cheek. "Wake up, Patience!"

Her eyes fluttered open, and Richard took a breath and clutched her to him.

"Don't make me smack you again," he said gently.

He could see her try to smile, but she was too weak to do even that.

"Her coat and dress need to come off."

"My lord?" said Delphi.

"Now! Where is her luggage?"

"Under the driver's seat," said Delphi. Richard swore again as he left the confines of the carriage to fetch her trunk. When he brought it inside, they found most of her dresses were wet with the rain that had made its way in through the cracks. Digging down, he finally found a peacock blue velvet dress, somehow miraculously dry.

Patience could feel herself being handled by many hands. Layers peeled away from her skin.

"Dry her off with the blanket," said Richard. "Really rub her down. It will warm her up, at least a little. The chemise is wet and needs to come off. Put this on her once you're done."

Patience felt a cool wet gust of air as the carriage door opened and closed once more. She was still cold and weak, but she was not feeling quite so sleepy as Delphi rubbed her methodically from head to toe. Before she knew it, she had been changed, and Richard returned. He covered her in his waxed riding cloak, pulling the hood up over her head, and she was carried outside to a horse in the pouring rain. She felt his strong arm around her as he mounted the horse and held her between his thighs. Her head dropped weakly back and to the side to rest against his chest as he spurred the horse into a canter.

Eleven

Broody and Unsociable

Patience was so weak and drowsy, she couldn't quite register what was happening. She could feel and hear Richard's presence, but it all felt so dreamlike that she wasn't sure if any of it was real. Eventually, she heard the crackle of a fire close by and felt its delicious warmth permeate her numb body. As her faculties slowly returned to her, she sat up on the couch where she had been bundled beneath several blankets.

"Who is she?" asked a man's voice at the other end of the room.

"Lord Pemberton's daughter." That was Richard's voice.

"The artist?" asked the first man.

"You know her?" asked Richard.

"No. I know *of* her," said the other voice. "You seem awfully concerned for her."

Patience could feel the weight of Richard's silence.

"Hello," said Patience craning her neck to see over the back of the couch.

"Patience!" Richard was at her side in a heartbeat. He placed a warm mug in her hands. "Drink this."

"Patience, is it?" said the other man's amused voice from behind the couch.

When the person attached to the voice stepped around the front of the couch, Patience's breath caught in her chest. He was the most golden, most beautiful, most dazzling man she had ever seen in her life.

"My brother James," said Richard. The shield wall had descended once more over his features.

"Miss Pemberton, it is a pleasure," said James dropping to one knee in front of the couch and taking her hand. "Your maid will be with you shortly. Richard sent horses to fetch the rest of your party. Until then, I suppose I had better act as chaperone."

"Would you like another blanket?" asked Richard, ignoring his brother.

"I'm fine, thank you," said Patience looking down at the many wool blankets that were already covering her. She took a sip of the hot broth he had given her. "This is perfect," she said.

"What were you doing in that storm?" asked Richard, standing over her now, his tone severe.

Was he angry?

"Travelling to visit friends," said Patience calmly. She took another sip of broth.

"Why were you wet?" he asked accusingly.

"When the carriage became stuck, I opened the door to see what was going on."

Broody and Unsociable

"It was a very foolish thing to do," said Richard. He was glaring at her furiously. "I've seen men die of the wet and the cold. You could have died!"

"You're one to talk!" countered Patience, a flush creeping into her cheeks.

"Oh my," said James looking from Patience to his brother. "Is this . . . ? Richard, are you and Miss Pemberton . . . ?"

"Shut up, James!" snapped Richard.

He sat down beside Patience with a look of contained rage and took her hands in his as if to gauge their warmth. He pressed a hand to her forehead, felt the skin at the back of her neck. Patience gazed into his stormy face, but he refused to make eye contact. She looked to his lips longingly.

"As chaperone," said James, "I'm not sure I should condone this sort of thing."

Richard glared at him, and Patience stifled a giggle.

"I like your brother," she said. "Do you think I could paint him?"

"No!" said Richard at exactly the same time that James said "Of course!"

The rain did not let up for the next two days, and Patience was forced to remain where she was. In Richard's house. He didn't know how to be pleased about it. Her surprise appearance made him feel nauseous for some reason. Sitting with him at the table, passing the salt, making small talk with James and Michael—it was too much. She fit right in, and this made things so much worse. Even the servants seemed pleased to have her around. She spent the rainy afternoon making

A Soldier and his Rules

sketches of anyone passing through the drawing room, and the maids were only too delighted to be given their likenesses in charcoal.

"My very own portrait," said one with wonder in her voice. "I feel like royalty, Miss."

"Everyone should feel like royalty some of the time," said Patience.

She was always saying things like that. Things that made other people feel good. James and Michael were no help. They fawned over her as if she were a new puppy brought into the household. Richard could barely tolerate the situation, and he ended up sequestering himself in his study for much of the first day. It was not lost on Richard that the last time he had seen her, she was pressing her naked breasts up against his bare chest. He tried not to think about that because when he did he became painfully aware of the void that lived inside him, the one she might have filled if only he were worthy of her. If only he were a complete person.

That evening, Patience came to knock at his study door. She looked like an angel in her blue velvet dress, and it was all Richard could do to keep his voice steady.

"James and Michael are going to teach me how to play billiards." She spoke as if she were trying to quiet a nervous horse, all soft and calm. "Will you not join us?"

"I don't think so," said Richard.

Patience stepped further into the room, and Richard stood from his desk.

"Don't be like this," said Patience.

"Like what?" asked Richard.

"All broody and unsociable."

"I'm always broody and unsociable," said Richard keeping

Broody and Unsociable

the desk between them.

"Mm," said Patience walking around the desk and taking his hand. "You're right. Perhaps that's what I like about you. Why don't you come and be broody and unsociable in the billiards room. James and Michael and I will play, and you can stand in the corner and glower at us. Just like you're doing now," she said smiling and tugging him by the hand.

What could he do when she put it like that? It's not as if he could actually refuse any request she made of him. Richard allowed himself to be led towards the door, but just before they left the room, he spun her towards him and wrapped his arms around her, holding her close and tight. He felt her little hands slide to his back.

"Thank you for saving me," she said into his waistcoat.

"I'm still angry with you," he said tilting his lips down to the top of her head, inhaling the scent of her hair.

"Come and be angry with me in the billiards room," she said pulling him through the door and into the hall.

"Richard does spend a lot of time in that study," said Patience to Michael.

The three of them had been drinking whiskey and chatting in the drawing room after dinner. Delphi, of course, had been shadowing Patience all day as if she might be accosted at any time by any of the three gentlemen present. The maid was now sitting quietly in a corner pretending not to listen.

"Not usually," said Michael with a look towards James. "I think you've scared him away."

Patience gave a self-conscious laugh. She had warmed to

A Soldier and his Rules

Michael immediately. He had dark eyes and a kind face. Where James was startlingly handsome, like some sort of Achilles in trousers and jacket, Michael was quite plain. There are some people, however, who become more attractive the more time you spend with them, and Michael was one of those people. His self-deprecation, humour, intelligence, and warmth turned him into a kind of social magnet that drew you in. It was difficult to leave the room if he was in it.

"Well, I won't be responsible for forcing him out of your company," she said standing up. "I shall invite him to join us for billiards. I can't believe you're so kind as to teach me to play!"

Patience strode to the door, and Delphi rose to follow. Turning at the door, Patience said, "Just so you both know, I am having a wonderful time. Whiskey and billiards after dinner—hah!—I'm living the life of a proper gentleman. Next thing, we'll all be smoking cheroots!"

"To make things even, tomorrow, you can teach us how to embroider a handkerchief," offered Michael. "Even better— regale us with all the gossip from London."

"That's a promise," said Patience laughing. "Just let me fetch the viscount."

In the hallway, she turned to Delphi.

"I think you can relax, Delphi. I am perfectly safe in Lord Winter's house."

"It isn't right, Miss," said Delphi, concern lacing her features. "You should have a proper chaperone."

"Well, there simply isn't one," said Patience. "And I'm not exactly a blushing young girl making her debut, am I? I would like you to take a break. See to your own needs for a change. I am going to speak to Lord Winter, *alone* if you don't mind."

Broody and Unsociable

Delphi made a small disapproving sound.

"Off you go," said Patience making a shooing motion with her hands. "I'll be in the billiards room if you need to find me later."

Once Patience had Richard out the door of his study, she started leading him down the hall by the hand. He walked slowly, a pace behind her as if he were reconsidering following her.

"I don't actually know the way to the billiards room," said Patience, "so you'll have to take me there even if you've decided against coming after all."

Richard squeezed her hand. "I'm coming," he said. "This way."

When they entered the billiards room hand-in-hand, James and Michael looked up from their game with raised eyebrows.

"He's going to glower in the corner," said Patience, which provoked a laugh from James. Michael was a bit more circumspect with Richard actually in the room.

"I'll play," said Richard.

"Really?!" said Patience turning to him with surprise.

It may have been the whiskey she had just imbibed, or it may have been the feeling of freedom that enveloped her in this house, but she impulsively pressed herself up on her toes and kissed Richard on the cheek.

James and Michael had stopped playing entirely. They were standing holding their cues and staring quietly. Richard flushed beet red. James cleared his throat and looked away as did Michael.

"Pass me a cue," said Richard in a stiff voice. "One for Miss Pemberton as well."

"Two against two?" asked James. "I'll take Miss Pemberton."

A Soldier and his Rules

"Miss Pemberton stays with me," said Richard keeping his eyes on the balls as he reset the table. Patience could see James send a wink towards Michael. They both smiled.

Richard proceeded to explain the rules of the game. He watched Patience attentively, adjusting the way she held the cue, explaining the angles of the various shots. Patience, for her part, noticed Richard's manner of play. While James and Michael were good shots, Richard took the time to strategise, to play defensively when necessary. It was all quite good fun, and Patience found herself laughing and cheering as the most unlikely shots were made by her companions.

At one point in the game, James lifted his head from aiming his cue: "Brother, did you ever think these walls would hear such laughter?"

Patience looked to Richard, but his face was stone-still. He had retreated inside himself, and he would not answer the question.

The next morning, Patience found herself early at breakfast with James. Michael and Richard had not come down yet. Patience went to the sideboard and piled her plate with ham and eggs and toast. She was contemplating where on the plate she might fit some fruit, when James offered her a small bowl.

"I find my eyes are quite big at breakfast as well," he said, looking down at his own plate which was piled even higher than hers.

As they sat down at the table and unfolded their napkins, Patience wondered if she could ask James her question. Was it too intrusive?

"I was wondering . . ." she said, "You and your brother . . ."

"—are so different?" offered James.

"Yes," said Patience. "It's quite striking. Not how you look," she said quickly. "Although that's striking too, but how you are," she clarified.

"We had different childhoods," said James quietly contemplating his toast.

"You don't have to answer if you don't feel comfortable," said Patience quickly. "I shouldn't pry."

"Richard says the past is best left in the past, so we never talk about it between ourselves, but I think you should probably know," said James fixing her with a warm gaze. "You seem important to him." James rearranged the food on his plate as he thought about how to begin. "We both lived here in this house with the same parents, but we had different experiences."

Patience waited for him to continue as James hesitated and looked down to fiddle with his napkin.

"Our father was an extraordinarily cruel man. He was quite brutal with anyone who displeased him. As you can imagine, two young boys managed to displease him quite a lot. We were always getting into trouble, but somehow, I rarely received my due punishment. When I became old enough to understand what was going on, I realised it was because Richard would always take the blame for my transgressions." Here, James looked up from his plate to fix Patience with his piercing hazel eyes. "My father would beat him quite senseless."

"Good Lord!" said Patience bringing her hand to her mouth.

"I tried to take my own punishment once, but Richard was absolutely furious. He could not have been more than ten years old at the time. He cornered me and told me that I didn't know what I was in for, that Father might actually kill me.

He said, 'Let me do this for you. It's the only thing I can do. Father won't kill me.'

'Why not?' I asked.

A Soldier and his Rules

'Because he likes beating me too much,' said Richard.

And he was right. That man lived for it. It was as if it were his God-given mission to break Richard, and Richard specifically. He must have known that Richard was taking the blame for me, and he didn't care—he just beat him harder."

Patience took a breath expecting James's reminiscence to be over, but he continued.

"As a child, Richard had a horse. He was a beautiful white gelding. Bucephalus. Bucie for short. Richard loved that horse so much. The stables and fields were his place of refuge. Just him and Bucephalus. They would ride out in the morning, and we might not see them again until sun-down."

James let out a heavy breath and shifted some ham around on his plate with a fork.

"One day, our father met Richard out at the stables on his return home. He said that Bucephalus was too poorly and needed to be put out of his misery. He handed Richard a pistol. Richard must have been around twelve-years-old." James looked out the window away from Patience. "There was nothing wrong with that horse. He was fighting fit. Young and healthy. But Richard loved him with all his heart, and our father knew it."

Patience could feel her heart pounding in her chest. She was feeling quite sick to her stomach.

James continued. "Richard refused to shoot his own horse which infuriated Father. He took the pistol from Richard and shot Bucephalus in the head as Richard watched. Then he proceeded to beat Richard for his disobedience."

Patience pressed a hand to her belly. She was no longer hungry.

"It was the first and last time I ever saw Richard cry. After

Broody and Unsociable

that, he was never quite the same. He erected a kind of wall around himself so that no one could approach close enough to peer in. So you see, we are different because Richard loved and protected me, but there was no one to love and protect him."

"What about your mother?" asked Patience.

"It was as if our father had cast some sort of spell over her," said James. "He would apologise to her, and she always imagined things would get better. Who knows what went on between them behind closed doors? I don't think that he ever physically harmed her—there were no obvious signs of that— but occasionally, he would lock her in her room so that she could not interfere. Her own family were not particularly kind, so perhaps she thought it was in some way normal. And what could she have done anyway? She was his property as much as we were."

"James," said Patience placing a hand over his across the table. "Thank you for telling me." She took the napkin from her lap and placed it back on the table. "I don't think I'll be having breakfast," she said standing.

Richard found Patience later that morning curled up in a chair in the corner of the sunroom with a book in her hand. Her gauzy white dress stood out against the bright blue pots, the flowering plants and greenery that surrounded her. Rain pelted the enormous windows, and the sound was a low roar. She looked sad.

"I couldn't find you anywhere," he said.

"I'm hiding from Delphi," she answered.

A Soldier and his Rules

"What are you reading?" he asked.

She gave a sad smile. "It's my copy of *The Iliad*," she said lifting it. "A bit damp, but still readable." She looked down and stroked a hand across one of the pages. "Sometimes I feel that if I read it carefully enough, I will receive some great wisdom. That all of a sudden I will Understand—with a capital U, if you know what I mean."

"Understand what?" asked Richard crouching down in front of her chair and gently taking the book from her.

"Everything. Life. Death. Love. Loss. It's all right here in these pages. The story floats on top, and the wisdom of the ages flows beneath. Like the sea holding up a ship."

Good God, this woman is something special, thought Richard. He looked at the book in his hands.

"You read Greek?" he asked with some surprise.

"Mother says it's pretentious."

"I don't think you have a pretentious bone in your body," he said, handing the book back to her. "What can I do?" he asked.

"About what?" she said looking confused.

"You're sad. How can I fix it?"

"Ask me to marry you," she said without missing a beat.

Richard felt her candid response like a dagger to the chest. She wasn't begging him. It was not that kind of request. He knew she wasn't trying to wheedle a proposal out of him. It was simpler than that. She was just being honest. *How?* thought Richard. *How in the world does she think I could make her happy?*

"I can't do that," said Richard hoarsely.

"Why not?"

"It will make you even sadder."

"I don't like riddles," said Patience. "You'll have to tell me what you mean."

Richard shook his head and offered her his hand.

Taking her to a back door, he bundled her up in her own coat and then slipped a waxed cloak over her. She locked eyes with him as he reached back to pull the hood up over her head, and he felt the shock of her violet-blue gaze course through him. He donned his own cloak and then pulled her by the hand out into the rain. They ran across the yard to the stables, boots squelching in the wet grass and mud, Patience laughing as the torrent pounded down upon her head and shoulders.

When they arrived inside the warm stable which smelled of hay and leather and horse, Patience turned to Richard with a grin.

"If I'd decided to do that myself, you would have been quite upset with me," she said.

He tipped her hood back from her face.

"Yes, I would have."

"It's one rule for you and another for me then, is it?"

"Always," said Richard narrowing his eyes at her.

"I don't see how that's fair," said Patience shrugging off her cloak. He could feel her good-natured prod like a warm embrace.

"Do you know who treats me quite well? Your brother. He offered me whiskey and the chance to learn billiards. He also promised to pose for me—and not just for an hour," she said bumping Richard with her shoulder. "I should think he would make a good Achilles. I could paint him outside the walls of Troy."

"Would this be Achilles in all his glory or Achilles gone mad with grief as he drags Hector's mangled corpse behind his chariot day after day?"

Richard had snapped out the question with some irritation. He knew she was teasing him by comparing him to his brother, but it cut to the quick in a way he didn't quite understand.

"I don't see the difference," said Patience ignoring his tone and reaching up to wipe a drop of rain from his brow. "Achilles is glorious *because* he loses his mind. And who wouldn't have under the circumstances?"

What was she saying? Did she know? Had her father told her about his mental affliction?

Richard gave a grunt and turned away. She was too warm and too soft and altogether too understanding. For some reason, he didn't like it.

He strode along the stalls with Patience in tow and introduced her to each horse in turn. Patience cooed over each one, scratching behind ears, stroking necks, and rubbing her sweet face against the muzzle of a friendly brown bay. There was a barrel of apples in one corner, and Patience dipped her hand in. He thought she might feed it to one of the horses, but she bit into it herself.

When he looked at her questioningly, she said, "I didn't eat breakfast."

Richard led out one of the horses. He had chosen a black hunter named Midnight that resembled Patience's own. When she had finished her apple and fed the core to Midnight, Richard handed her a brush.

"Are we grooms today?" asked Patience taking the brush and sliding it along the flank of the black hunter.

"I thought it might lift your spirits," said Richard. "This is where I come when I need to feel better." Patience paused her brushing of the horse, and he could feel her take him in with her wide blue eyes. *Were they welling up? That's not what he'd intended at all!*

Patience sniffed and turned back to grooming the horse. "Thank you," she said quietly. "I quite like it here."

They brushed the horse in silence then—doing so quite thoroughly from head to tail. Richard was surprised when Patience bent down to check each of the horse's hooves for stones. Clearly, she'd done this before. Not exactly the activity of a baron's daughter—most ladies would leave this to the grooms. Finally, Patience came around to Midnight's neck and with deft fingers, began plaiting his mane.

Richard chuckled. "I don't think he's ever looked so fetching," he said.

"The thing about horses," said Patience as she continued her work on the mane, "is that they can sense how you're feeling. When you're riding, there isn't only the physical connection of body against body, there's an emotional connection as well. I suppose that's why I enjoy riding so much. It's a comfort to me when I cannot find that connection elsewhere."

Richard was staring at her as she worked, his entire body warmed by her words.

"Do you think it is luncheon yet?" asked Patience finishing up her work on the mane and turning to him. "What is it, Richard?"

"Nothing," he said stepping up to her.

He wanted to hold her again. *Merciful heavens, he wanted to do more than that—so much more than that.* His urge was not simply physical: he wanted to be able to give her everything. A home and a family and a husband who was a whole unbroken person. Someone strong who could protect her from anything. He shouldn't touch her. He had no right to touch her, but . . . Richard reached his hands out to cup her face, and the contact

A Soldier and his Rules

felt so completely right. He could feel her hands slide around his waist. He closed his eyes.

"If you're going to kiss me," said Patience, "you'd better do it quickly. I'm becoming very impatient for luncheon."

Richard opened his eyes, smiling. *Dear Lord, he actually loved this woman.*

"You're hungry, are you?"

"Very," whispered Patience, tilting her face up to his, stretching herself up on her toes.

Instead of bending down to kiss her, Richard removed his hands from her face, and slid them to her waist. He lifted her up, so that her face was on a level with his. Then he took three steps forward to press her up against the stable wall with his body. Richard was a little more than surprised when her legs came around his waist, her thighs gripping him close and tight.

"Why do I feel like you've done this before?" he said with some amusement.

"Would that bother you?" asked Patience. He could feel her searching his heart, his mind.

"No," he said. Then thinking better of lying, "Actually, yes. But I'm sure I'd get over it."

"Well I haven't done anything like this before," said Patience stroking his hair. *Sweet heavens, it felt good to be touched by her.* "It's just that I've had some instruction."

"Have you?!" said Richard with a wolfish smile.

"Lessons from my friend Serafina. The one I'm travelling to visit. Serafina is very methodical, very thorough. We drew diagrams and everything," said Patience. "I'm a quick study."

Richard shook his head with amazement.

"You are something else. Do you know that?"

Before she could answer, he brushed his lips against hers, a feathery touch that made her shiver. She opened her mouth to him, and he tasted her—gently at first, savouring the flavour of apple on her tongue. And then there was no more gentle. Patience was kissing him back with a feverish passion he could barely comprehend, as if she wanted to consume him in his entirety. With her legs wrapped around him, and her breasts pressed against him, it was all Richard could do to hold himself in check. He could feel himself swelling beneath his trousers, and he groaned into her mouth.

His conscience reared its unwelcome head. *What right did he have to take from her when he could give her nothing in return? And yet, somehow, this didn't feel like taking. She was giving so freely. It was exhilarating to feel so wanted, and Richard's desire pressed his conscience back into the shadows.* Unfortunately, his conscience was not going down without a fight. *Here she was, stranded in his house, without a chaperone, completely at his mercy. No. He had to stop.*

"Patience," he said reluctantly pulling his face from hers.

She ignored him, tilting her head to bite his neck, to take his ear in her mouth.

"Patience," he said again unwrapping one of her legs and then the other with his hands. Releasing her back down to the floor.

"Changed your mind?" she asked quietly looking up at him from under her lashes.

"It would be taking advantage of you," he said.

"You didn't mind doing so before." She looked hurt and disappointed.

"I was wrong before," he said.

The look on her face nearly broke his heart. He certainly

didn't want her to feel rejected or unwanted.

"Just so you know," he said stroking a strand of golden hair behind her ear, "you are perfect. In every possible way."

Patience heaved a sigh.

"What's for lunch?" she asked changing the subject.

"Whatever you want," said Richard placing the cloak over her shoulders once more. "Whatever you want."

Twelve

Touché

Patience was still feeling wounded by the way Richard had pushed her away in the stables. Captain Walpole had asked her to give him time, but Captain Walpole didn't know just how impatient she could be. She tried to put her feelings aside as she sat down for lunch with everyone. It was a spread of roast chicken and buttered smashed potatoes with spring salad and freshly baked bread. She spied some jam tarts along the sideboard as well. *Thank goodness for men and their appetites!* She had once been served a lunch of cucumber sandwiches and lemonade while visiting a friend of her mother's, and her mother had scolded her afterwards for accepting seconds.

"But it was only cucumbers!" she had protested. "She may as well have served us water. I thought my stomach was going to eat itself."

"Ladies do not stuff their faces," said her mother. "People

will talk."

Hah! thought Patience with her mouth full of chicken as Richard passed her the bread basket and a silver pot of butter. *If Mother could see me now, she would probably die of embarrassment.*

Patience looked up from her plate to see both Richard and James gazing at her approvingly. Michael, for his part, was looking at James in a way that gave Patience a familiar sensation. She tucked it away in the back of her mind to contemplate later.

"I'm glad your appetite has returned," said James.

"Richard put me to work in the stables," said Patience as she buttered her bread.

"Did he?" asked James, giving Richard a look.

Richard shrugged but said nothing as he kept his eyes on Patience.

"The rain looks as if it's letting up," said Michael, pulling the bread basket towards him and helping himself. "You may be able to travel tomorrow with any luck. Not that we want you to leave," he added quickly. "It's been jolly good having you here."

"Oh . . . Yes," said Patience slowly.

She didn't want to leave at all. Ever. She wanted to stay in this house drinking whiskey and drawing portraits and playing billiards and eating enormous lunches. She thought she could do that forever. At the same time, although she was trying her best not to think about the awkward situation with Richard in the stables, she was still feeling stung by the way he had behaved with her. Perhaps she was foolish to hope he would eventually want something more.

"It's Bosworth Manor, correct?" asked Richard. "Your

Touché

friends' home?"

"Yes, John Thornton and his wife Serafina," said Patience. "They're due to have their first child delivered soon."

"I've heard of Mr. Thornton," said Michael. "Have you known the family long?"

"I've known Serafina since I was a child," said Patience. "She married John—Mr. Thornton— last year. She had been governess to his little sister Molly."

Michael raised his eyebrows at that. "Really?" he asked.

"It's a fair ride from here," said Richard interrupting. "I'll escort your carriage tomorrow if the weather lets up."

His assumption that he would accompany Patience after pushing her away not fifteen minutes ago made the heat in her body rise.

"No need," said Patience pointedly, giving him a cold look. "I've taken up enough of your valuable time as it is, and you are certainly not responsible for my welfare."

As she watched Richard's face, she could see the shield wall fall to reveal the hurt she had caused him with her words just spoken. *Well what did he expect when he sent such mixed messages? How was she supposed to react?* As she continued to stare him down, willing him to challenge her, his expression turned dark and stormy. The air practically fizzed with electricity, and Patience half expected lightening to strike right there in the middle of the dining room.

James cleared his throat and pressed his chair back from the table. Michael looked to James, then longingly back at his half-finished plate.

"If you will excuse us," said Michael placing his napkin on the table. "There is a matter needs attending."

The two of them left the room but not before James tipped

A Soldier and his Rules

his chin to the two footmen standing by. Soon, only Patience and Richard remained in the room, their eyes locked in an unspoken stand off. Delphi happened to step into the room at just the wrong moment.

"OUT!" boomed Richard.

She skittered from the doorway like a terrified mouse, closing the door behind her.

"Do NOT speak to my maid that way!" said Patience putting down her fork.

"My house. My rules," said Richard.

"Perhaps I should leave then," said Patience standing.

"You will leave when I deem it safe to travel and not a moment before," said Richard standing and blocking her exit from the room.

"Who do you think you are?" asked Patience incredulously.

"I'm the viscount," he said, "and you will do as you're told."

"Viscount or not, you have no claim on me, Lord Winter. And for the record, I *never* do as I'm told."

Patience stalked angrily past him, heading for the door, but he grabbed her by the arm.

"You will leave when it is safe," he said sternly.

"I'm leaving *now*!" said Patience pulling her arm free of his grip.

Patience could hear her heart thumping in her ears. *She was not going to cry. She was not going to cry.* She walked on shaky legs towards the door, and just as she reached for the handle, Richard spoke once more. His words were so quiet, she thought she must have misheard.

"What if I did have a claim on you?" he asked.

Patience remained as still as a stone with her hand on the door handle, her back to Richard.

Touché

"Excuse me?" she said to the door.

When he didn't answer, she started to turn the handle.

"What if I did have a claim on you?" he asked again, this time much louder.

Patience turned to answer him and was shocked to find him standing before her with a look of absolute terror painted across his face. This man, who had charged into the jaws of death itself an untold number of times, was afraid. His bottom lip quivered, and she found her heart stretching itself, as if it might be able to reach out to him across the dining room.

"Patience," he said softly, apologetically.

Patience walked up to him, took his hand in hers, and looked up into his face.

"If you had a claim on me, then you would be responsible for my welfare," she said kissing his hand. "But I have to warn you, I rarely do as I'm told."

"I thought you *never* do as you're told," he said pulling her into an embrace, his body trembling slightly as he held her.

"I have a tendency to exaggerate when I'm emotional," said Patience. She felt his chest shake with a silent laugh that may have been a sob.

Richard could not understand what had caused him to speak those words to Patience. One half of his heart knew full well he couldn't make her happy, that once she found out about his affliction, she would not be able to see him in the same way, and the emotional connection between them would fray. But the other half wanted desperately to be by her side, to be able to look after her and keep her safe. If he didn't, it would be someone else, and this thought pierced him through with what he at first thought was jealously, but later realised was actually fear. *What if she ended up with a Mr. Ruteledge? Would someone like him keep her safe? He certainly wouldn't have made her happy—that much was more than apparent.*

Richard took some deep slow breaths to calm himself as he held Patience to him.

It had been her words: "Viscount or not, you have no claim on me, Lord Winter." Those words had made him feel helpless. They struck to the core of him like an electric shock jolting him from slumber. She hadn't been wrong. He was not a brother or a father or a husband or a husband-to-be. He had absolutely no right over her. No right to care for her. For some reason, he could not let that stand.

Patience looked up at him, her arms still around his waist. Her face had the look of a flower turning itself towards the sun, and Richard marvelled that she could look upon him that way, that she wanted him with such open ardour. He blinked back his own trepidation at the circumstance he had created.

"Just to be clear," she said softly, "is this a proposal, Lord Winter?"

Richard nodded. He couldn't speak.

What about her brother? This was not going to go down well with George Pemberton. A proposal was one thing. Reality was another. Her family needed to be in agreement. Her father knew about Richard's affliction, and Richard could only assume he would not hand his daughter over without some assurances, if indeed, he handed her over at all.

Richard took another long slow breath as he stroked the back of Patience's head, holding her against his chest. *She was with him now. He would see her safely to the Thorntons', and then .*

Touché

. . and then . . . he would need to devise a strategy.

"So I suppose this means you're coming with me tomorrow?" said Patience.

"Yes," said Richard. "I have a claim on you now."

Her eyebrows lifted. "Not yet," said Patience. "If this is a proposal, I haven't given you an answer." Richard could feel her searching his face. "I have a stipulation," she said.

"Which is . . . ?" asked Richard.

"You will not yell at the servants. Delphi deserves an apology," said Patience.

"I can do that," said Richard. "No yelling."

"I didn't say 'no yelling'. I said no yelling *at the servants*. You can yell at me whenever you like," she said huskily, her eyes darkening. "And I shall yell back," she added.

He could feel her words dripping down his neck like hot wax. *This woman will undo me*, thought Richard.

"What would we be yelling about?" asked Richard in a low gravely voice, his hands sliding up from her waist to her ribs, thumbs resting just beneath her breasts.

"Oh, I'm sure I shall displease you in many ways," said Patience with a mischievous smile as she reached up to grab two fistfuls of his black curly hair.

"You could never displease me," said Richard allowing his face to be pulled to hers.

When their lips were nearly touching, she said, her breath hot on his face, "I'll have to try my best then, won't I?"

Richard growled—a harsh throaty noise that sounded more animal than anything else. He kissed her then, hard and rough. She stumbled backwards, and he caught her in a fierce embrace, lifting her up to seat her at the edge of the dining room table. She was staring at him wide-eyed now, with the

A Soldier and his Rules

look of a deer who has stumbled upon someone unexpected in the woods, and he wondered if he should have reined himself in a little.

His hesitation must have shown on his face because she said, as if reading his thoughts, "Don't hold back, Richard. I like it."

He shifted her further up onto the table and stepped between her thighs. She was looking at him expectantly.

"You mustn't say things like that," he said.

"Why not?" she asked less-than-innocently.

"Because you will have me on my knees," he said pulling her dress down to expose one soft rounded shoulder, biting it gently, then dragging his tongue up her neck to her jaw before taking her plump mouth in his once more.

As he kissed her beautiful mouth, Richard was lost—lost in the scent and the taste and the heat of her, lost in his own desire. He was quite heedless of where they were or what they were doing. It was only when he felt her small hand slide down between his legs to stroke the swell of him through his trousers that he was able to centre himself once more.

Reluctantly, he pulled himself from her, held her by the shoulders. Her hand was still between his legs.

"We shouldn't," he said. "I have a claim on you now, and you are also a guest in my home."

"What do you mean by that?" asked Patience maintaining eye contact as she stroked him slowly over his trousers.

He groaned. He couldn't believe he was about to say this.

"I need to do this properly," he said. "You are too precious to be taken like this. We need your father's blessing. And your brother . . ."

"We could elope," she said with a smile, her lips full and wet, her face flushed. Her hand was still manoeuvring itself over

Touché

him in a gentle rhythm.

"Patience," he said, warning her, eyes flashing fire.

"What?" she asked.

"You're going to have to stop." He looked down at her hand.

Patience bit her bottom lip as she dropped her gaze to the bulge beneath his trousers.

"You're so full of self-restraint and respect today," she said with a playful smile. "I'm not sure I like it."

"Patience." His voice was stern now. He had to be, or she would have him take her right there on the table in the middle of all the dishes. And that was certainly no way to treat your bride-to-be.

"Alright. Alright," she said taking her hand from between his legs. "You're in charge, *my lord*."

James cornered Richard in his study later that afternoon.

"I hope you told Miss Pemberton that you will do anything to have her in your life. I know you don't like being told what to do, but Richard, you must ask for her hand in marriage," said James. "You simply must. And if you don't, I will!"

"Don't be ridiculous," said Richard.

"She is far and above the only woman who could possibly manage your nonsense. That, and she is absolutely gorgeous and clever—did you know she speaks Greek? The magic she conjures with a piece of charcoal and a sheet of paper resists all logic. She is kind and funny and not afraid to defy convention . . . or you. Richard, are you listening to me?"

Richard slowly slid the jumble of papers on his desk into a pile and looked up at his brother.

A Soldier and his Rules

"Does Michael know you feel this way?"

James stared at him incomprehensibly.

"About Miss Pemberton," said Richard with a soft smile. "I don't think he'd like it."

"Are you joking with me, Richard?! You never joke. What in the hell is going on? Have you proposed already? Did she say yes?!" James was now round the side of the desk and shaking Richard by the shoulders.

"It's not as simple as that," said Richard fending off his brother. "I have to bring her family on board. Their experience of the last Lord Winter has left them with a bad taste in their mouth."

"I see," said James. "Can't fault them there."

"No," agreed Richard.

"You look a lot like him," said James breaking protocol. They never spoke of their father if they could help it.

"But *you* don't look like him in the slightest," said Richard. "I need you to come with me to London."

Richard knew he was asking a lot, so he was surprised when James agreed without any further convincing.

"I don't think Michael will come with me," he said. "There's Mother to deal with, and then there are the gossips."

"Mother can grow up," said Richard, "and the gossips can go hang."

"Still," said James thoughtfully, "he won't come." He offered Richard a brilliant white smile that lit up his handsome face. "Probably best considering our mission. Muddying the waters with extraneous gossip won't be helpful."

Richard heaved a sigh. His brother was right, but he didn't have to like it. As James left the study, Richard slid his gaze to his left hand which was trembling slightly as he lifted it from

Touché

the desk. He knew this wasn't one of his usual attacks. Rather, it was the very reasonable fear that Patience's family would rightfully find him wanting, that Patience herself would find him wanting if she saw him as he really was. He stilled his left hand with his right, placing both on the desk, and for the first time since he was a very small child, Richard bowed his head and said a prayer.

Patience felt quite giddy as she rode out in the carriage with Delphi the following morning. Richard had proposed. His mixed messages had dissolved into one unambiguous missive—*I want you*. Clearly, there was something that had made him hesitate. She knew he wasn't being entirely up front with her, but now that she had him within her sights, she was willing to do as Captain Walpole had asked. She was willing to give him time. Patience gazed out the window at Richard who was riding alongside the carriage. *So proper! He would not be seen sitting inside the same carriage with her, even with Delphi along for the ride.*

"Everything must be seen to be done with a care for your reputation as a lady," he had told her.

Patience didn't think of herself as a 'lady'. She had been told often enough how unladylike her behaviour was. Richard, however, (and James and Michael for that matter) didn't seem to mind her unladylike ways. It didn't bother him that she painted in oils or played billiards or engaged with unbridled enthusiasm during their little trysts. The only thing that seemed to bother him was her safety. She could be whoever she wanted to be with him. And if they disagreed

A Soldier and his Rules

on something, well then, that was its own excitement, wasn't it? She closed her eyes to see the flash of orange anger in his when she pushed him too close to the edge. She could feel his rough hands on her body, and she could hear him growling for her, a sound that resonated deep in her own chest, sending a shimmer of need down into her very core.

"Miss. Miss. We've arrived."

Patience opened her eyes as the carriage door swung open. She took Richard's hand to step down.

"Patience!" It was Molly running across the gravel drive, brown ringlets bouncing. She was of an age with Grace and precocious as they come. "I have a niece!" she said delightedly. "She's fairly useless for the time being, but she's very sweet . . . when she's not screaming," she added.

Patience looked up to the house, but neither John nor Serafina had shown themselves at the front door. Just the housekeeper and a footman.

"Molly, I'd like you to meet Lord Winter," she said. "Miss Molly Thornton."

She could see that Richard was looking at the little girl with some apprehension. But then his face broke into an awkward smile.

"Pleased to meet you," he said with a gentle bow.

"Here we go," said Molly to herself. Then to Lord Winter, "I've been practising my curtsies for just such an occasion." She held her skirts and gave a delicate bob up and down.

"Nicely done," said Richard.

"Are you a marquess?" asked Molly.

"A viscount," said Richard.

"Oh good," said Molly, "I'm not sure if I curtsied low enough for a marquess. We don't have many peers visiting . . . apart

Touché

from Lord Pemberton, but he doesn't really count, does he?" She put her hand up to her mouth and whispered, "He's only a baron."

Patience watched with some amusement as Richard struggled to respond to Molly's commentary.

"Come with me," said the little girl taking Richard's hand and pulling him towards the house.

Patience could see Richard try to politely extricate himself, but to no avail. She followed the two of them, nodding to the housekeeper and footman as they entered the house. John met them in the foyer looking bedraggled but dapper in shirtsleeves, his pale blue eyes darting from Patience to Richard and then down to his sister Molly holding Richard's hand.

Richard was struck by the tall lean gentleman who had entered the foyer. He was wearing a black mask over his brow and half his face, and Richard assumed this was due to some disfigurement as he could see some serious scarring extend itself down the man's neck. Richard immediately felt pierced through with the hard stare of Mr. Thornton's pale blue eyes. He recognised the wariness of this man's look. He had clearly encountered Richard's father at some point in time, and such encounters were not to be forgotten. Richard was reminded yet again of his uncomfortable resemblance to his father.

"John," said Patience running up to him and giving him a hug. "I can't believe I missed it! Is Serafina alright? How did she manage? I'm so sorry I wasn't here for her—we were waylaid by the storm."

"We?" asked John, looking to Richard from within Patience's embrace.

"John," said Patience, "this is Richard . . . Lord Winter. He was so kind as to escort me for the second leg of my trip."

"He's a viscount!" added Molly cheerfully.

"I know who he is," said John who looked to Patience once more as if to explain the situation.

"Lord Winter," said Patience, "may I introduce Mr. John Thornton, my dear friend."

"I won't be staying," said Richard quickly. "It was my intention to see Miss Pemberton safely to her destination. I found her nearly unconscious in that storm. It gave me a fright, so . . ."

Richard watched the masked man shake himself, a subtle movement, a bit like a dog's.

"I'm sorry," said Mr. Thornton coming forward to grasp his hand. "Where are my manners? Please allow me to thank you for your service to King and country. We are in no small debt." Mr. Thornton looked to Patience then back to Richard. "You are more than welcome to stay and refresh yourself even if you were planning on returning shortly." He looked down at his sister. "Molly, take Lord Winter to the small drawing room. Call for tea." To Lord Winter, "I'll be with you in a moment, once I've deposited Patience with my wife."

Richard watched as John placed a hand to Patience's back to guide her from the room.

"So," said Molly, "you're a soldier as well as a viscount."

"Used to be a soldier," said Richard. "No more."

Molly led Richard to a large drawing room decked out in cream and gold with cherry wood furniture. She pulled a red cord to ring a bell and then took a seat, gesturing for him to

Touché

do the same. Richard had not had much (any) experience with children, but he thought that if they all behaved like this one, he wouldn't particularly mind.

"How many people have you killed?" asked Molly leaning forward with interest.

The direct nature of the question threw Richard slightly off kilter, but he quickly recovered himself.

"Too many," said Richard.

"Good answer!" replied Molly as if she were a school mistress and he were one of her students.

"What would be a bad answer?" asked Richard.

"Not enough," said Molly quickly. Richard smiled. *She was very sharp!*

"Touché," he said.

"Do you speak French?" asked Molly.

"Not if I can help it," said Richard.

"Touché," said Molly brightly, and they both actually laughed.

Richard felt oddly unencumbered sitting and chatting with Molly. He could have done so all day and not begrudged her the time at all, so when the tea arrived with Mr. Thornton, he was strangely disappointed.

One look from her brother, and Molly quickly excused herself and made for the door. Before she left, she turned and said, "Be nice to him, John. I think Patience likes him."

Richard could feel the heat slide up his neck to warm his face.

When Molly had left, Mr. Thornton said, "I think 'like' does not suffice to describe the situation. Apparently, she has agreed to marry you."

"She told you?" asked Richard with some surprise.

A Soldier and his Rules

"She told my wife as soon as she entered the room," said Mr. Thornton. "I just happened to be there."

"Her family does not know yet," said Richard. "I will approach them when I return to London."

"Hm."

"They probably will not like it," added Richard.

"Are you talking about her family, or are you talking about George?" asked John astutely.

Richard stared at Mr. Thornton. The man was as sharp as his sister.

"Mr. Pemberton would like to see me dead," he said matter-of-factly. "And that was before I proposed."

"Yes, I can see how that could be the case," said Mr. Thornton with some mirth in his eyes. "He can be a little overprotective at times."

"I don't think so," said Richard. "He has every right. And I'm not exactly . . . not exactly . . ."

"Prince Charming?" asked Mr. Thornton. "No, you are not. And I've had occasion to interact with your late father . . ."

"I look like him," said Richard.

"But you are *not* him," said Mr. Thornton. "I'm sorry if I was rude earlier. These impressions are difficult to shake off. If I may," said John shifting forward in his seat. "It is my opinion that a lady can make these decisions for herself. If Patience has chosen you, then she has done so with good reason. It's not as if she puts up with much." Here he chuckled.

"Her brother will not see things this way," said Richard.

"No," said John. "You will have to prove yourself. May I suggest, as a tactical manoeuvre, that you attempt to bring Lord Pemberton into agreement first. George worships his father, and he will have a more difficult time killing you if he

Touché

knows it would upset Lord Pemberton."

"I would prefer it if he didn't want to kill me at all," said Richard. "But I appreciate the advice."

The two men looked to the door as Patience cleared her throat. Richard stood immediately, and Mr. Thornton followed suit. *How long had she been there?*

"I will stay the week," said Patience as if answering a question Richard had already posed.

"I'll be back then. To escort you to London," he said. To Mr. Thornton, "Thank you for the talk. And congratulations on your new daughter. I hope to meet Mrs. Thornton one day when she is fully recovered."

Mr. Thornton reached out his hand to shake Richard's.

"It was good to meet you," he said.

"I'll walk you out," said Patience taking his arm.

Richard couldn't believe he was going to leave her here and ride off. It felt as if he were contemplating leaving one of his own limbs behind.

"Patience," he said once they were outside. He took both her hands, but he didn't know what else to say. His heart was over-flowing.

"If I didn't know better, I'd say you're going to miss me," said Patience cocking her head to one side to take him in.

Richard pulled her into a rough embrace, clutching her tightly to his chest. He was suddenly struck with an overwhelming feeling that something bad would happen . . . to her . . . for the simple reason that he loved her. The sound of a pistol shot through his mind. The weight of a horse collapsing to the ground. The sheer devastation of that loss.

"Don't do anything foolish while I'm away," he said.

"I'll try my best," said Patience sliding her hands up his back and tipping her face up to his.

Richard took a quick glance around to make sure there were no servants watching before he touched his lips tenderly to hers. It was as chaste a kiss as he could manage. He knew anything more might light a fire within him that would be in danger of burning out of control. Patience seemed to understand. She smoothed down the lapels of his coat and brushed some dust from his sleeve. When she returned her eyes to his, her face was solemn.

"When I am your wife, I don't think we shall do this often, if at all," she said.

"What's that?" asked Richard.

"Part ways," she said.

Thirteen

Such Fantastical Dreams

Patience had missed the birth of little Kate by only one day. The baby was beautiful—the tiniest hands, long dark lashes, and a little pink mouth. Serafina herself, on the other hand, looked quite ravaged. Patience noticed that Serafina's smile was not as bright as she had imagined it would be, and as Patience sat on the side of her bed asking after her and John and Molly and regaling her with her own stories, she noticed Serafina's attention flagging.

"Perhaps visitors are not what a new mother needs most," said Patience. "You should try to sleep."

"It's not that," said Serafina. "I'm glad you're here. It's just . . ." she looked off to the side of the room away from the baby sleeping in her little cot. When she turned back to Patience, her eyes were filled with tears.

"Serafina, what is it?"

The tears started to fall then.

A Soldier and his Rules

"I don't think I can do it," she said bringing her hands to hide her face. "I'm not a very good mother." She was wracked with a round of sobs that tore at Patience's heart.

"You can't say that," said Patience sliding up to Serafina in the bed and putting her arm around her. "It's only been a day."

"She hates me," said Serafina through her tears. Hiccuping now. "I can't even feed her. It hurts so much. The midwife says I'll need a wet nurse if she doesn't latch on properly soon."

"Well, first of all, babies don't hate anybody. And second of all, no one was expecting you to feed your own baby anyway. I had a wet nurse, and I imagine you did as well. We turned out alright." Patience stroked a piece of Serafina's hair from her face.

"I thought I'd be able to do it. Every woman in the village seems to manage feeding her own infant. John and I had promised each other that we would raise our own children, that they wouldn't be left to a nurse. I feel as if I'm failing my husband *and* my daughter." Another round of sobs that left Serafina looking exhausted and pink around the eyes.

"Now, now," said Patience. "Hush." She pulled her friend into a tight embrace. "We will figure this out together, alright? Have you told John how you're feeling?"

"I can't," said Serafina dabbing at her eyes with the bedspread. "He keeps looking at me with such concern. His nerves are quite frayed as it is."

"I see," said Patience.

Just then, little Kate began to fidget and whimper. Her complaint became a cry and then an all-out wail, her tiny face red with the effort. Serafina started to make her way out of the bed towards the cot, but Patience put a hand on her shoulder and pressed her back down onto the bed.

"I want you to rest now," she said.

"But the baby . . ." said Serafina weakly, face still damp with tears.

"I've got her," said Patience picking Kate up in her swaddling clothes. "I'll see to her now, and you rest."

Serafina appeared too weak to argue, and as she lay back down in the bed and turned over onto her side, Patience stepped gingerly from the room hoping that she was holding the baby properly and wondering what she was going to do. She found John walking towards her down the hall with a stricken look on his face.

"Is she alright?" he asked.

"Just awake and crying," said Patience.

"I meant Serafina," said John taking the baby from her and bobbing up and down to calm her.

"Then no, Serafina is not alright." Patience took a breath. "John, you have to talk to her. She needs help."

"The midwife should be here soon to pay her and the baby a visit." The wail had become a quiet whimper as the baby drowsed back to sleep in her father's arms.

"She believes she is failing you and little Kate," said Patience quietly as they walked down the hall. "She is quite distraught."

"Failing us?" asked John incredulously.

"She needs a wet nurse, John. And she needs to know that it's alright by you."

"Of course it's alright by me! Serafina is the one who's been insisting on doing everything by herself."

"You have to talk to her. She feels as if she is a terrible mother. I'm sure it's just the excess emotion of the situation, but she's very weepy, John."

"She cried?" John handed the sleeping baby back to Patience.

A Soldier and his Rules

"When the midwife arrives, tell her to send for the wet nurse," said John. "Tell her to send for two of them. Now!"

He turned and strode off back down the hall towards Serafina's bed chamber.

By the time the first wet nurse arrived, Serafina was sitting up in bed with a blank expression on her face. The nurse took one look at her, then John who was sitting by the bed holding her hand, then the baby who had just begun to cry again in her cot. The nurse locked eyes with Patience who tried to convey everyone's distress in one pleading look.

Having assessed the situation, she bustled into the room without so much as an introduction, picked up the baby, and took her to a chair in the far corner to feed her. When little Kate was quiet and sated, she brought the baby back and placed her in Serafina's arms.

"If you'll excuse me for being so bold, Mrs. Thornton, but you mustn't despair. I have six of my own at home, and the first one was awful challenging to deal with. I couldn't feed him properly myself. My sister had to come and stay to feed the baby for me—she had a four month old herself, you see. Brought her own baby along as well. It was a full house, although I suppose not so full as it is now."

Serafina tore her gaze from the middle distance in front of her and up to the nurse's face, then down to little Kate.

"Really?" she asked quietly.

The nurse nodded.

"It's alright to have some help. It doesn't make you less her mother."

Serafina wiped a tear away from her cheek. Patience was having a hard time not crying herself.

The nurse continued. "I'll not be taking the baby from you.

I'll just be feeding her and bringing her right back to your arms, alright? And if you decide you want to have a go at feeding her yourself, I can help you with that. But it's not necessary."

Serafina appeared to consider this. John reached a hand up to her cheek.

"We'll do this together," he said. "That was the promise we made. Together."

Serafina leaned her cheek into his hand and gazed into his eyes silently for a very long time. Patience gave a little lift of her chin to the nurse, and the two of them stole out of the room unnoticed by John and Serafina.

John was true to his word. He initially hired two wet nurses so that there would be plenty of rest all around. Normally, the baby would go to live with a wet nurse in her own home, but John informed everyone that that was out of the question. If he had to hire several more nurses so that they could take it in turns to come to the house, then so be it. The baby would stay with Serafina.

Patience took over the management of the house for the week, coordinating her efforts with Miss Browning, the housekeeper, and she also took it upon herself to spend some concentrated time with Molly so that John could be with Serafina and Kate. By the end of the week, Serafina was out of bed and actually smiling. Occasionally, Patience would catch John looking at his wife as she held little Kate or as she sat reading a book. It was a look of such warm admiration and love that it squeezed painfully at her heart.

Was this the way Richard looked at her when she was drawing or reading? Did he love her? Or did he simply want her? Was there a difference?

A Soldier and his Rules

On the morning that Richard was due to come and fetch her, Patience sat with Serafina in the drawing room after breakfast.

"I have to say, that is a lovely dress," said Patience.

Serafina was wearing a gauzy cream and yellow muslin gown that set off her dark brown hair and eyes. She smiled.

"I thought you didn't like yellow," she said.

Patience gave her a look of mock affront. "Moi?" she asked, pretending confusion.

"Yes, toi," said Serafina, laughing now.

Patience broke into a grin. "I like yellow. I just can't wear it because then no one would be able to find me in Mother's drawing room. I'd be like one of those tropical lizards that blend into the scenery to evade their predators. Seriously, though, your dress is divine—it fits you like a glove!"

"John surprised me with a whole closet full of dresses in varying sizes," said Serafina with some embarrassment in her voice. "He knew I wouldn't be as I was before the baby, and he didn't want me to feel . . . unsatisfied with my appearance."

Some colour rose in Serafina's cheeks as she said this, and Patience couldn't help but wonder what her conversation with John had been like when he presented her with such a thoughtful wardrobe.

Serafina considered her friend for a moment.

"Thank you," she said.

Patience brushed off her thanks with a wave of the hand.

"No seriously," said Serafina. "I'm not sure how things would have been without you here."

"They would have been fine. John would have sorted it all out eventually."

"Accept my thank you, Patience," said Serafina in a firm tone. "I don't offer it lightly."

"Fine," said Patience. "You're welcome."

"There," said Serafina with a satisfied grin. "That wasn't so hard, was it? The week has flown by. Now you're leaving, and I haven't had the wherewithal to ask you about your viscount. He'll be here shortly."

"What would you like to know?" asked Patience cautiously.

"Everything," said Serafina leaning forward in her seat.

"Well, I can't tell you *everything*," said Patience suggestively.

"Patience?! Have you engaged in . . . activities related to our lessons?" asked Serafina with some excitement. Then more seriously, "Are you absolutely sure he is trustworthy?"

Patience considered her friend. She was so methodical, so logical in the way she approached everything. So at odds with Patience's own impulsive and passionate embrace of each and every opportunity that came her way, no matter the messy outcomes, the disappointment, the regret. She decided to put Lord Winter in terms Serafina could understand.

"If Richard were a maths problem," she said, "he would be a difficult one. You might struggle for weeks and weeks to work him out, but when you finally did, you'd find the answer to be very simple. It would be a nice round number: one hundred percent."

Serafina smiled at her friend and shook her head.

"Patience, are you in love?"

"I . . . ah . . ." Patience was thankfully interrupted by the footman announcing Lord Winter's arrival.

When Richard stepped into the room, he blocked most of the doorway, like a mountain crowding out the sun. His midnight blue coat was dusty from the journey, and the dark circles beneath his eyes seemed somewhat more pronounced than usual. Patience felt her heart skip up in tempo as he locked

A Soldier and his Rules

his hazel eyes with hers.

Serafina cleared her throat which brought Patience's attention back to the fact that there were three of them in the room.

"Richard," said Patience, "This is my friend Mrs. Serafina Thornton."

Richard stepped forward to take her hand. "Please don't stand on my account. I imagine you need your rest."

"Will you take tea?" asked Serafina.

Richard looked to Patience as if to ask her whether he would take tea.

"Yes, that would be nice. Thank you," said Richard sitting down. He looked around. "Is Miss Thornton not about?"

"Molly?" asked Serafina with some amusement. "She is at her lessons right now."

"Oh." Richard sounded disappointed. "And Mr. Thornton?"

"He had some business to manage this morning, unfortunately," said Serafina. "It's just us girls I'm afraid."

"I wouldn't call either of you girls," said Richard quite seriously. Serafina gave Patience a wide-eyed look accompanied by an amused smile.

Serafina called for tea, and the three of them chatted about portrait painting and Greece and, of course, because they lived in England, the weather. Richard looked embarrassed as Patience told the story of how he had found her frozen in the storm. She watched as he lifted his delicate teacup in one enormous hand. *Sweet mercy, his hands.* Her mind trailed off as Serafina spoke at length about something or other. Patience looked to Richard's lips as he sipped his tea, then wondered at his sunken eyes. *Had he not been sleeping?*

"It's possible," said Serafina, eyeing her friend, "that I have kept you both too long. I'm sure you will want to make an early start on such a long journey. I'll inform the servants to fetch your things," she said to Patience. And with that, she stood and left Patience and Richard alone in the drawing room.

Richard and Patience looked at each other in silence for a few moments.

"Have you not been sleeping?" asked Patience.

"I couldn't," said Richard. "You were too far away."

Patience stood up and walked over to him. He glanced to the door which Serafina had thoughtfully closed behind her and then gently pulled Patience down into his lap.

"I thought we were going to do things properly now," said Patience. She hoped her playful tone would disguise the heavy need that was blossoming down at the root of her being.

"We will," he said. "I just need to hold you. Make sure you're real. That I didn't dream it all."

"I've never had such fantastical dreams," said Patience kissing his ear.

Richard stroked the back of her neck and held her close.

"When we are in London, I shall seek your parents' permission to court you," said Richard. "I do not think your family will be amenable to marriage right away. It will seem too abrupt to them. It will raise suspicions of how we might know each other when we've only been together a scant handful of times."

"Whatever you say, my lord," said Patience into his neck. "So long as we *are* going to marry."

He kissed the top of her head.

"I hope you will not be too disappointed with me as a husband," he said.

Patience pulled her face from his chest and looked him in the eye.

A Soldier and his Rules

"What makes you say that? It's much more likely that it will be *me* disappointing *you*. I have a proven record in that regard. Just ask Mother or George."

Richard kissed her then full on the mouth, and as she felt the heat of him sink through her, she knew that she would do anything for this man—this difficult problem of a man with his sunken eyes and his guarded past.

There was a knock on the door, and Patience leapt from Richard's lap. After a moment, Serafina entered.

"The carriage is all set," she said. "It was my great pleasure to meet you Lord Winter. I hope all goes well in London."

Patience took three quick steps forward and threw her arms around Serafina's neck.

"Write to me," she said.

"Of course."

"Don't keep anything from John," added Patience. "That man loves you."

"I won't," said Serafina holding Patience close.

As Richard rode out beside the Pemberton carriage, Patience's last words to Mrs. Thornton were ringing in his head: "Don't keep anything from John. That man loves you."

Richard thought about what he had been keeping from Patience—the bottomless terror that struck without warning rendering him insensible, turning him into a completely useless human being. *Perhaps it would be simpler if she loved him. Would he be able to tell her then? It was a foolish thing to think about. How could she possibly love him? It should be enough that she wanted him. He certainly couldn't ask for more . . . and he wouldn't.*

By the time they arrived in London and pulled up at the Pemberton house, Richard was weary from riding, but he dismounted his horse and helped Patience from the carriage. As he followed her up the steps to the front door, she turned.

"You're coming in?!"

"It's only proper. I did just now escort you all the way from the countryside."

"Well, then," said Patience with a genuine smile that cracked Richard's tired heart right open.

Lady Pemberton and Grace were there to greet Patience as they entered. When Lady Pemberton saw Richard looming behind her daughter, she let out an involuntary sound somewhere between a gasp and a squeak. She quickly recovered her composure.

"Lord Winter, to what do we owe the pleasure?"

"This is Lord Winter?" asked Grace who was studiously ignored by Lady Pemberton.

Richard looked down at Patience's sister. She was a perfect blonde version of Miss Molly Thornton, right down to the blue eyes and ringlets.

"Miss Pemberton's carriage had a mishap in the storm," he said. "I thought to escort her back to London to be sure of her safety."

"Well that is kind of you," said Lady Pemberton. "Come in, come in. You must sit and have some refreshment."

"That's quite alright," said Richard. "It has been a long ride, and I'm sure Miss Pemberton would like to rest." He took the opportunity to look at Patience.

"Yes, thank you, my lord," she said, and Richard smiled inwardly as he noticed her attempt to sound both dainty and

A Soldier and his Rules

demure for the benefit of her mother. She even dipped into a curtsy!

Lady Pemberton was watching the scene with a calculated look on her face.

"May I call on Miss Pemberton tomorrow?" asked Richard. "To see that she is recovered from her trip?"

"By all means," said Lady Pemberton looking at her daughter with some astonishment. "By all means."

"Thank you. Good day, then," said Richard taking his leave.

As the footman opened the door for him, he walked right into George Pemberton who had alighted at the top of the steps in front of the house.

"What the hell are you doing here?!" asked George craning his neck to look past Richard's wide shoulders and into the house. Patience gave her brother an apologetic smile and a small wave from the foyer.

"Mr. Pemberton, I think we got off on the wrong foot," said Richard.

"No," said George. "We got off on exactly the right foot, the one where I shoot you in the head for compromising my sister."

"I only want to see her safe," said Richard. "Just as you do."

"That is a load of—"

Lady Pemberton appeared in the doorway, and George did not finish his sentence.

"This is not over, Winter," he said through gritted teeth.

Lady Pemberton called out from the doorway in a strained voice: "George, Lord Winter was kind enough to escort your sister's carriage home. It seems there was an accident. George!"

George glared at Richard before leaving him to enter the

Such Fantastical Dreams

house. The front door was slammed shut, and Richard could only assume that it hadn't been the footman doing the slamming.

That didn't go so badly at all, thought Richard as he stepped nimbly down the stairs.

Inside the Pemberton house, Patience had six eyes trained on her.

"Well?" said Lady Pemberton.

"Well what?" asked Patience.

"The viscount escorted your carriage all the way from the countryside, and you have nothing to say about it?"

"We became stuck in the mud in the storm. An axle was broken. We were passing near Lord Winter's house, and he happened to come upon us and helped us on our way. He escorted us to Bosworth Manor." *She didn't need to go into details about her brush with death, her unchaperoned stay at Avery House.* "He insisted on returning to escort me home. He rode the entire way."

"Well!" said Lady Pemberton reaching up to fix a hairpin. "Well!" She smoothed down her skirts.

George was looking at Patience suspiciously.

"A broken axle wouldn't have been easy to fix," he said. "Certainly not in a storm."

"He doesn't look as furious as he did in his portrait," interrupted Grace. Everyone looked down at her. "Or as sad. And he's coming back tomorrow—I can barely wait!" She turned and ran up the stairs.

"Tomorrow?!" George's head swung sharply over to his

mother.

"He asked for permission, George," she said.

"And you should not have given it."

"He's hardly done anything wrong."

"What about the rumours, Mother? Are you not concerned?"

"It's different if he's actually courting her," said Lady Pemberton pertly.

"Courting her!" George was tugging at his hair in exasperation.

"He's a viscount," said Lady Pemberton in her defence. "A former Major in the army. A war hero."

"Neither of you may have noticed," said Patience as she grew increasingly annoyed, "but I happen to be standing right here. I also happen to be twenty-seven years old—a fully grown woman! The only people who should actually be discussing this situation are myself and Lord Winter." She turned the full force of her gaze on George. "I like him, George, and being the gentleman that he is, he has already sought *my* permission to court *me*. I said yes, and that should be enough for you."

George actually staggered back a step as Patience spat out her words. His hands were still in his hair. Patience advanced on her brother.

"George, if you so much as touch Lord Winter, I will never *ever* forgive you. You made me a promise."

"What's this?" asked Lady Pemberton darting her eyes from her daughter to her son. "George?"

"Nothing, Mother," said Patience with her eyes on her brother.

Whatever reason George had for visiting the family house, he did not consider it sufficient to stay. He turned to leave.

Such Fantastical Dreams

As the footman opened the door for him, Patience said, "Just so you know, *John* has met Lord Winter." George paused in the doorway, his back to his sister. "I wonder what he would have to say on the subject."

George stepped through the door without looking back.

"My dear," said Lady Pemberton, looking to her daughter, "you do cause a lot of fuss."

Fourteen

An Improper Fraction

When Richard arrived back at his London house, everyone was waiting for him in the drawing room. James had travelled on his own by carriage. He must have only just arrived. Tea and sandwiches had been served on a low table, and Thomas was munching away contentedly while Richard's mother and brother eyed each other with some reserve. Thomas noticed him first.

"Richard!" he said standing and brushing his hands off on his trousers so that he could reach out and grip Richard by the face. "James tells us you are courting Miss Pemberton."

James gave Richard a dazzling lop-sided grin as Richard ducked out of Thomas's hold.

"He says he's here to make you look good," said Thomas with amusement. "I thought *I* was here to make you look good. Don't tell me you're passing me over for this poor specimen." Thomas gestured to James who sat in an armchair looking

An Improper Fraction

like a sun god perched upon a throne. 'Handsome' did not begin to describe him.

"Is it true, Richard?" asked his mother. She placed her teacup and saucer onto the table in front of her. "You've never shown an interest in a woman before." Here she gave James a look. "I had given up hope of grandchildren."

Thomas lifted his eyebrows at him.

"I need to take a bath," said Richard. Having everyone look at him the way they were doing was a bit too much. "It was a long ride."

As he walked away down the hall, he heard Thomas's voice recede as he spoke: "Richard has shown plenty of interest in women, Lady Winter, but this is the first *lady*."

He could imagine the way his mother would swat playfully at Thomas for such a lewd (though accurate) statement.

"Richard!" It was James chasing him down the hall. He trotted up to his brother. "Don't worry. We're going to do our best. It's all going to work out."

Richard gave a grunt. He was too anxious and too tired to speak.

The next day, Richard prepared to call on Patience at home. He was courting her! The thought itself seemed quite unbelievable to him. Not because she didn't deserve to be courted but because he simply wasn't the courting type. And if he was being quite honest, neither was she.

I should have taken her on the table in the middle of the dishes. Then a quick dash up to Scotland to make things official. Patience would not have minded at all.

A Soldier and his Rules

But Richard knew she would have regretted it eventually. She had a family she clearly loved. To ignore them, to not even attempt to seek their blessing—it would have driven a wedge between them, and he couldn't be responsible for that. Eventually, no matter what she may say to his face, it would have made her unhappy in her secret heart. That was something he could not allow.

Flowers, he thought. *Courting gentlemen bring flowers.* But when he arrived at the flower shop, he was overwhelmed with the sheer abundance of choice. The lady shop attendant seemed intent on offering him a bundle of something homogeneous—lily of the valley or tulips (exceptionally expensive) or roses.

"If it's a lady you're courting, then roses," she said. "Red."

Richard looked about not knowing quite what to do, and then an idea came to him.

"May I choose my own bouquet?" he asked.

He arrived at the Pemberton house with an enormous bouquet held in one large fist. The footman showed him into the drawing room where Patience and her mother were seated quite primly upon a couch. He could see that Patience was trying her best to play her role—a proper lady being properly courted. But when she saw the flowers in his hand, she sprang to her feet and flew across the room to him.

"Oh, Lord Winter," she said quite breathlessly as he handed the bouquet over. "They look like a Mary Moser painting!"

"I thought you might like to paint them yourself," he said.

The flowers themselves were a riotous jumble of roses and poppies, tulips, and cornflowers. Pink, and yellow, blue, white, and lavender, with green ivy trailing round about.

"Mother," said Patience turning with a bright smile. "We

An Improper Fraction

need a clear glass vase. So that the stems are visible." To Richard, "Thank you, my lord. This is possibly the most thoughtful present anyone has ever given me."

Her words were genuine and pure. She was not pretending to be properly courted. She was *being* properly courted, and Richard's heart warmed in a way he had not experienced before. It made him want to do more. To give her more. He thought briefly of throwing a net over the sky to fetch her a tumble of fluffy white clouds and a hot yellow sun.

Patience looked as if she might kiss him, so he stepped back a half pace just in case.

"You'll have to be timely about painting the flowers," he said. "The lady at the shop told me the poppies will not last long at all."

"I shall make several paintings," said Patience coming forward to take his arm and lead him into the room. "I shall paint them as they fade, just like the Dutch masters. A reminder that rich or poor, strong or weak, beautiful or ugly, death comes to us all."

"Patience!" said Lady Pemberton. She laughed nervously. "Don't be so morbid."

Patience looked at her mother with some surprise. "It's not morbid, Mother. It's a reminder to live."

Lady Pemberton made a small strangled sound, then called for a maid to fetch a vase. She would not be leaving the courting couple unattended to fetch one herself.

"Lady Pemberton," said Richard. "You look well today."

"As do you, Lord Winter. You certainly have an eye for what will please my daughter." She gave him an appraising look.

"Mother, would it be alright if we went walking?" asked Patience as she clung to Richard's arm completely ignoring

A Soldier and his Rules

any etiquette there might be for who should be inviting whom to do what.

Lady Pemberton looked to Richard quizzically.

"I would be quite amenable to a walk," he said smoothly.

Anything to keep Patience in physical contact with him would be preferable to sitting in a drawing room making awkward conversation.

As they promenaded along the path at Hyde Park, Richard couldn't help looking back fondly to their encounter there on that morning not so long ago. The sun was bright and the park was crowded now, but that morning had been made for just the two of them. A misty, pale light. Cool air, and all the world awash in green and blue.

Richard leaned his head down to Patience as they walked some distance in front of Lady Pemberton and one of her maids.

"When we are wed," he said, "I shall bring you to the park early in the morning whenever you wish to come."

"Early enough to greet the Dawn?" asked Patience looking up at him tenderly.

"And her rosy fingers," said Richard. He placed his free hand over hers where she held his upper arm.

"How long do you think this whole courting business will take?" asked Patience. "You should know that my name does not suit my disposition. I wish to be with you *now*. In your house. At your table. In your bed."

Richard took a breath to steady himself. *In his bed? For some reason, he had not even imagined her there. Drifting off to sleep with her head on his pillow. Waking beside him. He would be able to reach for her at any time, hold her close. What madness would that be? How could he even contemplate such happiness?*

An Improper Fraction

Richard's father had beaten the hope clean out of him. He had been purified in that way, turning into a man who behaved much as a machine might. Drill and strategise and fight. Drill some more. No thought for himself, for what he might want or need. But Patience had broken through the high wall that surrounded him. She had raised it to the ground with one ridiculous curtsy across a ballroom.

"Patience," said Richard. "Why did you curtsy to me?" He needed to know.

"So Mother would think this is all above board," she said.

"No, not yesterday's curtsy. The other one."

"You mean on the evening we first met?" asked Patience with a smile.

Richard nodded.

"It was impulsive of me," she said. "I'd never done something like that before with a gentleman. I imagine you thought me quite mad."

"Not at all," said Richard.

"You left right away," countered Patience.

Richard said nothing, so Patience continued. "I suppose I did it because I found you interesting. You weren't like any other gentleman I'd met. It was your face. I knew it was guarding something, and I wanted to see behind that shield wall you had erected."

"Did you see anything?" asked Richard.

"Oh yes," said Patience looking up at him. Her eyes were more violet than ever, pupils shrunk to pinpricks in the bright afternoon sunshine. "And it made me want to see more." Richard had to look away from her. He found himself feeling . . . feeling . . . however he felt, his instincts told him quite clearly that it was something to avoid at all costs.

A Soldier and his Rules

After their walk, Richard saw Patience and her mother home. Leaving them in the drawing room once more with many pleasantries and a promise to be in attendance at Almack's later that week, he was escorted by a footman to the front door.

Grace Pemberton appeared like a tiny apparition in the foyer just as he was collecting his gloves.

"Hello," she said.

"Hello, Miss Pemberton," said Richard as he put on his gloves and made to leave.

"Grace," said the little girl. "Miss Pemberton is my sister."

"Well, it is nice to meet you, Grace. I'm sorry, but I'm just leaving."

"You have two out of three points," said Grace as if he should know what she was talking about.

She proceeded to list them off on her fingers. "One, you are a war hero so no need for a duel. Two, you've read Homer. There's only one more point to go," said Grace.

Richard didn't know what she was speaking about, but he didn't mind playing along. He felt much the same way he had when speaking to Molly Thornton—relaxed and amused at the same time.

"How do I acquire the third point?" he asked.

"Do you believe in true love?" asked Grace.

Richard's heart stopped in his chest, a hesitation as if he were frozen momentarily in time. No longer relaxed. No longer amused.

"Lord Winter?"

"Why would you ask me that?" he whispered.

"For the third point," said Grace as if it were obvious. "You have to answer, or I won't be able to recommend you to my

An Improper Fraction

sister."

"In that case," said Richard, slowly recovering himself, "my answer is . . . yes, I believe in true love . . . but to be honest, I'm not entirely certain it believes in me."

Grace stared at him for a moment.

"Oh dear," she said. "I think you just managed to gain a bonus point. So that's four out of three possible marks. My friend Molly would point out that's an improper fraction." Grace screwed up her face. "Because Molly likes to point out irrelevant details."

Richard smiled. "I hope to see you again sometime soon, Miss Pemberton."

"Grace," she corrected.

Patience was wearing her least horrible dress that featured an empire waistline. The ladies at Almack's were not much for forward fashion, so if she wanted to be permitted in, this dress would have to do. She would wear anything to see Richard that evening, although she imagined he wouldn't think much of her figure in this dress. At least it was blue—the same blue as the cornflowers in the bouquet Richard had given her. She contemplated the flowers that were sitting in a globular glass vase on a table in her bed chamber. It had been two days since he'd given them to her, and the poppies were now most definitely spent—drooping and bedraggled. The vase of flowers remained in her studio during the day so that she might paint them as they faded, and each night she carried them to her bed chamber so that they would be the first thing she saw upon waking. The maids had been instructed not to

A Soldier and his Rules

touch them else they would be pulling out the faded flowers and redoing the arrangement each day so that it looked all fresh and new.

Patience imagined Richard in the flower shop choosing the flowers himself with an image of a Mary Moser painting in his mind. Everyone kept reminding her (and him) that he was a soldier—a war hero—but he was so much more than that. Whatever horror and death he had witnessed, it had not destroyed his ability to see the beauty in the world, and that was a magic all itself.

Aside from Grace, the entire Pemberton family was present at Almack's that evening which reminded Patience uncomfortably of the evening she had been introduced to Mr. Ruteledge. George was silent on the carriage ride there, a grim look upon his face and a tightness in his movements. He was clearly displeased with the situation, but to his credit, he had not accosted Richard nor had he challenged him to another duel. When they arrived, Patience spotted Richard right away. He was standing at the far end of the room looking strong and handsome in an understated black jacket that was stretched wide across his broad shoulders. James and Captain Walpole were with him. As soon as he noticed her, he crossed the room with James at his side. Any other woman's eyes would have been drawn to his brother, the Adonis in cobalt blue, but Patience could not tear her gaze from the dark and haunted soldier that approached her.

"Lord Pemberton," he said. "Lady Pemberton." Then a look to George, "Mr. Pemberton, may I introduce my brother Mr. James Winter?"

Lady Pemberton tittered as James bent his golden head over her hand. Then James shook hands with Lord Pemberton and

An Improper Fraction

George in turn, lingering with George.

"My brother tells me you like to shoot, Mr. Pemberton," he said with a radiant smile full of good humour. "I myself am a terrible shot, though, as a gentleman, I should probably not admit to it." He leaned in as if it were a confidence, and Patience could see George's face soften ever so slightly. "You must come and hear the story Captain Walpole has been telling. Did you know he has been taking care of our mother while Richard and I were away? How Richard managed to attract such a loyal friend, I will never know."

Lady Pemberton brought her hand to her mouth to hide a smile, but George's face remained impassive. He did, however, look across the room to where Captain Walpole was entertaining a mixed group of gentlemen and ladies who were all hanging on his every word.

Well done, James, thought Patience. *It's a start.*

"Lord Pemberton," said Richard. "May I have a word with you sometime later this evening?"

"Of course, of course," said Lord Pemberton smiling genially and clapping him on the back.

Patience watched George who was himself watching his father with narrowed eyes, but she lost her train of thought when Richard turned his darkened gaze on her.

"Miss Pemberton, may I add my name to your dance card?"

"Of course," she said, trying not to sound too eager. The entire family watched as Richard bent his large frame over hers to write his name on the card that dangled from her wrist.

"Well if we're claiming dances . . ." said James taking the pencil from Richard. Patience laughed as he reserved his own dance with her.

The orchestra struck up a tune.

A Soldier and his Rules

"Lady Pemberton," said James offering her his hand. "Lord Pemberton, would you mind?"

"Not at all," said Lord Pemberton. "I'm not much of a dancer myself."

Patience could hear her mother chatting animatedly with James as he led her out onto the dance floor.

"Perhaps now rather than later for that conversation," said Lord Pemberton to Richard. The two of them walked off to find a quiet corner.

"It doesn't take a genius to see what Winter is up to," said George to Patience.

"And what's that?" asked Patience.

"Is that man even his real brother?" asked George ignoring her question. "They don't look or act anything alike."

"James takes after their mother," said Patience, leaving silent the second portion of the statement which was that Richard takes after their father. "George," she said, turning to look him full in the face. "Thank you."

"I haven't done anything," said George gruffly.

"Exactly," said Patience. "And I thank you for it."

They both looked out across the dance floor.

"What do you see in him?" asked George. "How can you assume he is any different from his father? Of course he will court you with pretty words and pretty gestures, but they may mean nothing. You can't know him—not really."

"George," said Patience in order to get her brother's full attention (he was now watching Richard speak quietly in the corner with their father).

George looked at her, but she could see his face was guarded against anything she might say.

"Do you remember when we were all so worried about

An Improper Fraction

Serafina living as a governess in John's house? Mother kept insisting he was a dangerous man and that she should leave her position and come to live with us. And then, of course, there were all the not-unfounded rumours about his past, the kind of person he had been?"

George gave a noncommittal grunt. He could see where this was going.

"Serafina was the one who saw through it all. She could see John for who he actually was, and she was no more afraid of him than a fly. What I'm trying to say, George, is that it is very nice that you want to protect me, and I appreciate it, but it has to be my decision. You have to trust *me* at some point."

George looked away from his sister.

"I need a drink," he said, and he strode off, leaving her standing like a wallflower all alone at the edge of the dance floor.

Patience stood there for some time watching the couples dance. Her mother appeared to be having a marvellous time with James.

"Champagne?" It was Richard offering her a glass.

"Thank you," said Patience, startled from her reverie. "I didn't realise you were standing there."

"You look good enough to eat in that dress," said Richard in a low growl.

Patience, having taken a sip of champagne, had to spit it back into the flute lest she choke on it.

"Really?" she asked, eyes twinkling. "I honestly don't think this dress does me any favours."

"I don't know," he said. "Cornflower blue suits you quite well. Have you ever noticed that the centre of a cornflower shifts hue from blue to violet—just like your eyes?"

A Soldier and his Rules

"Is this courting talk?" asked Patience with suspicion.

"No. It's talk talk," said Richard taking the glass from her and placing it on a nearby table. "I believe it's my turn to dance with the most beautiful lady in the room."

"Well, now I *know* you jest," said Patience laughing. "No one wearing this sack of a dress could be considered the most beautiful lady in the room."

"Ah," said Richard smiling and taking her hand, "But I've seen what's *under* that dress."

Patience never blushed, but she could feel her face grow warm at the thought of that night she had spent with him, the way their physical altercation had turned to something significantly more amorous. As he led her out onto the dance floor, Richard's gaze made her feel as if they were both in danger of catching fire. The orange light in his eyes burned as bright as a tiger as he circled her waist and pulled her gently towards him.

"It's a waltz," he said sternly. "No shrieking with laughter this time, Miss Pemberton. We must maintain some decorum."

Patience bit her bottom lip as she slid her hand up the length of his upper arm to his shoulder.

"I'll try my best," she said. "My lord," she added.

If Patience had been on the other side of the room standing at the refreshments table, she would have heard James say to her mother, "Richard would do absolutely anything for your daughter's happiness. He is quite overcome . . . and with good reason. She is an altogether extraordinary young lady."

Lady Pemberton tilted her head to one side as she watched them dance. "They do make a lovely couple, don't they?"

Just then, the baron approached his wife and offered up his open hand.

An Improper Fraction

"What's this?" Lady Pemberton asked her husband.

"Care to dance?" he asked.

Lady Pemberton looked perplexed.

"Edward?" she said with some astonishment.

"Will my wife not dance with me?" asked the baron with a nervous smile.

"Forgive me, of course," she said taking his hand.

As he walked her out onto the floor, she said, "I can't remember the last time we danced together."

Lord Pemberton looked at his wife carefully. "I'm not the jealous type, Agnes, but seeing you with that James Winter set my blood boiling for some illogical reason."

Lady Pemberton laughed. "He is rather outrageously handsome, isn't he?"

"And altogether too amiable," said Lord Pemberton with a smile. "I rather like him, don't you?"

"Yes," she said stepping in closer to her husband. "Yes, I do." A pause. "Did you have a nice chat with Lord Winter?"

"Mm." said Lord Pemberton. "Parliament sits next week. He has some ideas for how we might proceed. Not for nothing they promoted him to Major. He definitely has a strong head on his shoulders. Quite the strategist—a trait he shares with his late father."

As she danced, Patience took her eyes from Richard for only a moment and was surprised to see her parents waltzing around the room like a pair of young lovers, a huge smile lighting up her mother's face.

"Your mother isn't here," said Patience to Richard, suddenly aware of Lady Winter's absence.

"She had a headache," said Richard. "She'll be coming to Vauxhall on Saturday. You can see her then."

A Soldier and his Rules

"The fireworks are quite a show," said Patience.

"You should bring Grace as well," suggested Richard.

Patience looked at him curiously. "Since when do you think about Grace?" she asked.

"Since she is to be my sister soon," said Richard with a dip of his dark head towards hers.

"And James will be my brother," said Patience grinning. "Richard . . ." There was something she wanted to ask him. "James and Michael . . ." she said, "They love each other, don't they?"

To his credit, Richard did not even miss a step.

"Yes," he said stiffly, almost bracingly. She could feel him tense.

Patience smiled. "I thought so," she said. As Richard registered her smile, she could feel his hand relax against her waist.

"Mother likes to remind James that it is a hanging offence," said Richard quietly as they stepped in time to the music. The tempo had slowed.

"I imagine she worries for him," said Patience.

"Yes, but she could do it silently," said Richard. "Her little comments do nothing to help."

"You are remarkably accepting of the situation," said Patience.

She looked up into Richard's face curiously, and he met her open gaze. This man continued to surprise her. Despite all his talk of 'rules', he had a very particular code of conduct in mind that was not exactly conventional. Her heart felt as if it were expanding to take him in, to hold him in all his startling complexity.

"What is it?" asked Richard, noting the look on her face.

An Improper Fraction

"Nothing," said Patience. "You're just . . . I don't know . . . more than I ever expected."

"What did you expect?" asked Richard.

"Oh, you know," said Patience, "a taciturn and brutish soldier with a penchant for giving orders."

"I'm that as well, Miss Pemberton," he said, leaning in to give her a wolfish smile that sent a tiny thrill rippling through her.

Fifteen

Fireworks

It was late morning on Friday, and Patience could hear her brother speaking loudly with her father in his study. Lord Pemberton's voice was low, nearly a murmur, so Patience could only hear George's side of the conversation as she slowed her step at the study door. She halted just past the door feeling a bit bad about eavesdropping but obviously (as is most often the case with eavesdroppers) not bad enough to actually stop.

"It is a likely sham," said George, to which Lord Pemberton made a sound of disagreement.

"I don't mean to tell you your business, Father, but I would be more wary if I were you. What that man wants has nothing to do with any of your causes in Parliament. What he wants is our Patience. I don't doubt that once he has her, he will pull the rug out from under your feet."

Lord Pemberton's low drone countered with something or

Fireworks

other that Patience couldn't quite make out. He never rose to the bait—always so logical and calm.

"He is playing a game with us," said George. "You yourself pointed out that he is a master strategist . . . just like his father." Lord Pemberton maintained his silence, and George continued.

"Just look at him. They are two peas in a pod. You cannot tell me that he inherited only his father's appearance and nothing else."

Patience could hear her father slide back in his chair, and she hurried down the hall.

"There you are!" said Lady Pemberton from the yellow drawing room as Patience passed by. "Come here, my dear."

"Yes, Mother?" asked Patience coming to stand in the drawing room doorway.

"Come in and close the door," said Lady Pemberton.

"I have flowers I need to paint," said Patience.

"They must be quite dead by now," said Lady Pemberton pulling her face into a look of distaste.

"Quite," said Patience. It didn't change the fact that she would be painting them again.

Patience could see that her mother would not let her leave so easily, so she closed the door behind her and took a seat.

"Is there anything you'd like to tell me?" asked her mother.

"About . . . ?"

"About you and Lord Winter," clarified Lady Pemberton.

Patience wasn't entirely sure what was meant by this, so she shook her head.

"My dear, you certainly do not need to tell me if the initial rumours were true—it doesn't matter now anyway since he is courting you and clearly intent upon a permanent outcome."

A Soldier and his Rules

"You refer to marriage?" asked Patience.

"Yes."

"Would that make you happy, Mother?"

"The question is," said Lady Pemberton, "would it make *you* happy?"

Patience thought about how it would make her feel to have Richard as her husband.

"That's answer enough for me," said Lady Pemberton watching her daughter's face carefully.

"Do you approve? Does Father?" asked Patience, her heart beating faster now, pounding against her chest like the hooves of a horse against the earth.

"We will always approve a love match," said Lady Pemberton with a smile.

Patience did not know what to say to that. *A love match? Is that what she had with Richard? He had never said the words.*

"Granted, Lord Winter is not exactly the man I had envisioned for you. He is rather . . . a lot, isn't he? Knowing his father, I was worried about what sort of man he might be. But he does appear to care for you . . . and he does appear to *know* you somehow."

"Lord Winter doesn't mind what I'm like, Mother," said Patience smiling. "I can be myself."

"Yes, I can see that," said Lady Pemberton. "Your father is pleased about that as well, in addition to the fact that Lord Winter is willing to support the more worthy endeavours of Parliament. He does not appear to be following in his father's political footsteps which is heartening."

"George does not like Lord Winter at all," said Patience thinking about what she had just overheard at the study door.

"George does not like a lot of things," said Lady Pemberton.

Fireworks

"That boy—I suppose I should call him a man now—cannot see the light for the darkness. Always so gloomy and so cynical. I cannot understand what has made him so. He takes tea in a yellow drawing room for Heaven's sake! If that does not cheer a person's soul, I cannot imagine what will."

"Perhaps he needs to fall in love." It was Grace who had quietly poked her nose and a few of her ringlets in through the drawing room door.

"Grace! We are having a private conversation," scolded Lady Pemberton.

"Could you even imagine George in love?" asked Grace, ignoring her mother and stepping into the room. "He's as grim as the hooded boatman who ferries the dead across the River Styx. He would have to find a lady who likes that sort of thing—a lot of ominous foreboding and quiet rowing in the dark."

Patience looked at her mother, and they both started to laugh.

"Well, I'm glad I could entertain you this morning," said Grace with some annoyance.

"We're not laughing at you," said Patience. "It's the thought of George in a hooded cloak rowing the dead across a river. The job does suit him."

"You shouldn't laugh," said Grace seriously. "There's a reason he never smiles. We just don't know what it is."

Her words brought the room to a standstill. Patience considered her brother. She knew there was always more to a person than met the eye, but she had never thought that to be the case with George. He was just George—annoying, overprotective, humourless George.

"Grace," said Patience to change the subject, "you're invited to come with us to Vauxhall Gardens tomorrow night."

"Really?!" said both Grace and Lady Pemberton in unison.

"Richard, I mean, Lord Winter thinks you will like the fireworks. He suggested I bring you along."

Grace was grinning from ear to ear.

"I like your viscount, Patience. I interviewed him the other day, and he has full marks as far as I'm concerned."

"I think I will sit this one out," said Thomas as Richard and James joined him and Lady Winter in the drawing room that Saturday evening. The Winters were all dressed up for their evening at Vauxhall Gardens. "Do me proud," he said to Richard patting him on the shoulder. Then he took Lady Winter's two hands dramatically in his. "I shall be counting the minutes until you return, my lady."

James rolled his eyes as his mother's laughter tinkled about the room like chimes caught in the wind.

"And I have a score to settle with you tomorrow," said Thomas narrowing his eyes at James.

"I don't think so," said James smiling. "You shouldn't wager money you don't want to lose."

"No one ever wagers money they *want* to lose," said Thomas with a grin. "Enjoy yourselves tonight."

"What will you be up to?" asked Richard.

"This and that," said Thomas with a wink. "This and that."

As they settled themselves into the waiting carriage, Lady Winter said, "I suspect Thomas has a lady friend."

"I thought *you* were his lady friend," said James which provoked a playful swat from his mother.

Fireworks

"I am perfectly aware that he is simply trying to make an old lady feel appreciated," she said. "I'm not completely senile, you know?"

"I'm glad the senility is only partial," said James in a complete deadpan. His mother laughed.

Richard noticed that the frostiness between James and his mother had been melting over the last few days. James was teasing her—something that never would have happened if their father had been alive. If their father had been sitting in the carriage with them, the air would have been thick with tension. Their mother would be sneaking glances at her husband's face to monitor his mood and adjust her behaviour accordingly. No one would speak unless spoken to.

With his death, everything had changed. James could go travelling with Michael and not fear being actually murdered when he returned. Their mother, despite her periodic bouts of melancholy, had climbed further and further out of the protective shell she had built around herself. And Richard was able to marry a woman of his choosing without the risk that his father might seek to harm her in order to teach Richard himself some sort of perverse life lesson.

Richard would ask for Lord Pemberton's permission to marry Patience tomorrow morning. *She would be his wife!* Richard could barely contain the joy that promised. As the carriage trundled through the London evening, he said a silent prayer committing himself to her happiness, her welfare, and her safety. He had no idea how it was that Patience had come to care for him, but he would do everything in his power to deserve at least a fraction of the warmth she directed his way.

By the time they arrived at the pleasure gardens, the place was abuzz with Londoners out for a night of entertainment

A Soldier and his Rules

and socialising. The tree-lined walkways were hung with lanterns in the twilight, lending the park a romantic fairytale atmosphere that was only enhanced by the distant sound of musicians playing a familiar heart-warming tune.

"There they are!" said Lady Winter spying the Pembertons by one of the pavilions.

Richard's breath caught in his chest as Patience turned her open face away from her parents and towards him. She looked like a dream beneath the many hanging lamps that hovered like enormous fireflies above her. She was wearing a pelisse of some iridescent fabric that shifted from violet to green as she moved under the lights. *Like the wing of a pigeon*, thought Richard. She was holding her little sister's hand, but as soon as Grace saw him, she broke away from the group and came running to meet him.

"Lord Winter!" she said scrambling to a stop and then dipping into a curtsy. "Thank you for inviting me."

Richard introduced Grace to James and his mother as Patience approached them and took his arm possessively. As the company strolled the gardens, Lady Pemberton and Lady Winter made fast friends, commenting on the garden, discussing mutual acquaintances, and complimenting each other's fashion sense. Grace ran on ahead distracted by the scattered attractions, the people, and the lights, while James and Lord Pemberton became engrossed in a discussion of the complexities involved with transportation along the Thames.

Patience slowed her step as she clung to Richard's arm. Their families moved on up ahead blending into the crowd.

Fireworks

The minute Patience laid eyes on Richard that evening, she knew she was lost. He stood there before her like some hulking colossus of a man—harsh and tender, stern and welcoming, all at the same time. They had been promenading and dancing and politely conversing for the past week or so, and she thought she might die if he continued to court her properly and with so much respect for her person. She wanted to feel the way she had when he approached the edge of his restraint, when he growled into their kisses and his hands came roughly around her body. She wanted to see the lick of fire at the edges of his green-gold eyes and to know that it burned for her alone.

As Patience slowed her step to separate her and Richard from the group, she tugged him from the lamplit path and into the darkness of the trees. Richard hesitated, but Patience pulled him by the hand deeper into the shadows.

"Patience, what are you doing?"

"I need to have you to myself for a moment," she said turning. "I'm not sure I can do this much longer."

"Do what?"

"All this courting and promenading," she said. Then pleadingly, quietly, "Richard, I need you."

She did not have to say another word. She felt Richard's large hand at the back of her neck move to gently tilt her head to one side. His mouth came to her ear, and she gasped as the sensation shot down through her body causing her knees to buckle. He caught her in his arms and brought his mouth to her clavicle, then her breast above her neckline. She tangled her fingers in his hair as he pressed her up against a tree, gathering and bunching her skirts in one hand until he could press his palm between her bare thighs.

A Soldier and his Rules

"Is this the sort of thing you're after?" he asked, his voice low and irresistibly seductive.

She could smell the spicy scent of him, feel his hot breath on her ear, the scratch of his beard against her face.

"Yes," panted Patience. Now was not the time to mince words. Her heart was racing and her breath was coming fast. She needed his attention in a way that felt so incredibly urgent, so necessary.

He pressed his palm to her mound and rubbed her in circles, hard and rough, but as far as Patience was concerned, nowhere near hard enough. His mouth came to hers, and the simple taste of him brought her precipitously close to the edge. She pressed her body against his hand as if she might be able to take what she needed in that way.

"Easy," he whispered into her ear. She could hear the smile in his voice.

Then his hand shifted, fingers parting the delicate petals between her legs, pressing themselves to her little bud as they moved rhythmically against her. Patience could feel her body vibrate against him like the soft thrum of a cello string once it has been plucked. As the urgent sensation hummed and surged within her, Patience lost herself on a wave of sensation. She felt herself lifted up, and then as the tension became too much to bear, she finally came apart, muffling a cry with her own hand as she clung desperately to Richard's shoulder with the other.

Richard held her for a moment, kissed her gently, then bent down to smooth her skirts.

"Better?" he asked, standing up to his full height.

Patience couldn't help but feel a little embarrassed.

"Yes," she said, her eyes to the ground.

Fireworks

When she did glance up at him, he had laughter in his eyes.

"Don't!" she said.

"I haven't said anything," protested Richard with a smile.

"But you're thinking it," she said.

"I was merely thinking how lucky I am to have such a hot little bundle of fireworks for a bride."

Patience gave him a playful shove with both hands.

"Come on," she said. "They'll be missing us."

"You'll have to wait a few moments before I'm presentable," said Richard glancing down at the tent he had made of his trousers.

It turned out that no one had missed them at all. Lord and Lady Pemberton were too engrossed in conversation with James and Lady Winter, and Grace had come to a standstill in front of a troop of acrobats who were throwing and spinning and eating fire.

Richard marvelled at the manner in which Patience sparked at his touch. It did not take long at all to bring her to climax, and he imagined doing so again and again, watching her face take on that expression which was both agony and ecstasy at once. He could spend an entire night tending to her in that way, taking his time, exploring every inch of her soft body with his fingers and tongue and . . .

Patience squeezed Richard's arm as they joined the group from behind, and Richard shook the thoughts from his head.

"Your brother didn't come?" he asked.

"He did," said Patience, "but when we entered at the gates, we came across a few gentlemen who encouraged him to join them. He said he would find us for the fireworks."

The rest of the evening was spent walking and conversing in between entertainments—both musical and dramatic. As the evening twilight turned to ink, and the stars made themselves known, they joined the crowd that had begun to gather for the fireworks display. George Pemberton finally made an appearance, sidling up beside Richard.

"Good evening, Mr. Pemberton," said Richard.

"For you maybe," said George. "I'd like to have a word."

Patience twisted herself around from where she held Richard's arm on the far side of him so that she might see her brother.

"Leave it, George. You promised."

"It's nothing to do with that," said George. "I have some parliamentary matters to discuss with Lord Winter."

"It's fine," said Richard in a placating tone. "He's your brother. I should talk to him." Richard untangled her arm from his. "I'll be right back."

George led Richard away from the crowd to a darkened, private corner by one of the pavilions.

"What can I do for you?" asked Richard.

"If you think you can waltz into my family and take over . . ." started George in a voice that shook with emotion.

"Hold on, hold on," said Richard placing both palms forward. "I have no intention of taking over your family. I only want to take care of Patience."

George stepped close, pointing a menacing finger into Richard's face.

"I see what you're doing with my father," said George. "Of all the duplicitous, scheming—"

Just then an eruption of fireworks broke overhead shower-

Fireworks

ing little golden sparks down from the heavens. Richard was looking at George, so he didn't see the display of lights in the night sky. He only heard them. The sound stopped his heart, like an unexpected round of gunfire. George continued to talk, but Richard could no longer hear him. He was kneeling in a dusty street. There was a dead Spanish boy on the ground a few paces from him. Women were screaming. He could hear doors being kicked in.

"Charlie Montgomery," he said looking down at the blood blooming against his jacket.

He watched Charlie drag a young Spanish woman with him across the street. Richard could feel his heart beating hard up into his throat. He yelled after Charlie until he was hoarse—he heard himself screaming something about being his commanding officer, something about a gallows pole. When Charlie disappeared from view, Richard tried to staunch the flow of blood from his belly, but his hands wouldn't move. He couldn't feel them. He was overcome with the kind of fear you feel when you slip on a patch of ice and begin to fall backwards. Only Richard never hit the ground. He just kept falling into the abyss, heart racing, unable to breathe, unable to think. He could taste dirt in his mouth.

"Winter! Winter! What the hell, Winter?"

Richard was lying on his side on the ground trembling while George Pemberton crouched over him and shook him by the shoulder. He pressed himself shakily up to seated and leaned against one of the pillars that supported the pavilion. He still couldn't quite grasp where he was or what he was doing.

"Does Patience know about this?" asked George looking with some concern behind him towards the crowd in the distance. The fireworks were still cracking overhead. "Holy

A Soldier and his Rules

hell, you thought I was someone named Charlie. Nothing you said made any sense. Winter?! Winter, I'm talking to you! Can you hear me?"

Richard could hear George now. He knew exactly where he was. He knew exactly what had happened. There was only the matter of what would happen next. He had never had an episode quite like this one. He had actually hallucinated! He wasn't even sure he could stand on his own now that he was lucid. He forced himself to look George Pemberton in the eye. A wash of shame spread over him like a thick and viscous liquid, weighing him down, slowing his movements. Shame for being the useless and broken man that he was. Shame for believing he could be someone who deserved to have Patience as his wife. Shame for ever thinking he could protect her as her husband. She was too precious to be handed into his care. He could see that now. He could see it written all over George Pemberton's face.

"Help me to the carriage," said Richard weakly.

With George's help, he struggled to his feet as a bright white fountain of flames lit up the night sky. All eyes were turned to the fireworks, so no one saw the two men make their slow way to the park entrance. When George handed Richard up into the carriage, they locked eyes. George pierced Richard with a look of cold judgment that had Richard flushing with shame and guilt and humiliation.

Dear Lord, what had he been thinking? How selfish can one man be?

"Don't tell Patience," said Richard. He couldn't bear for her to know him like this. "In return, I promise not to burden you with my presence in your family. I do not deserve your sister."

George simply stared at him with an unreadable look before

Fireworks

shutting the carriage door. Richard slumped down upon the red velvet seat and brought the heels of his hands to his eyes to press back the tears that were building there. When he arrived home, he dismissed the footman who greeted him at the door and pulled himself bodily up the stairs with one hand to the bannister. He locked himself in his bed chamber, and throwing himself fully clothed upon the bed, he fell asleep and did not wake until noon the next day.

When Richard and George did not return in a timely fashion, Patience went looking for them. She came upon George stumbling back along the path with a glazed look upon his face, his hair completely dishevelled.

"Where is Lord Winter?" she asked as she looked past him.

"He went home early," said George.

Patience didn't understand. It didn't make any sense.

"What? Why?"

George was looking at her as if he had something to say, but he remained silent.

"What did you say to him, George?!" asked Patience.

"Nothing," said George. "He wasn't feeling well, so he went home."

"I don't believe you!" she yelled. "What did you do?!"

When George didn't respond, Patience launched herself at him in a mad fury. George caught her arms, holding her as she struggled, then pulling her to him in a tight embrace that had the effect of pinning her down so that she could not attack him properly.

"Let me go, George!"

"You have to believe me," said George quietly as he held her. "He didn't feel well."

Needless to say, Patience did not believe her brother for a moment. *What could have happened? What could George have said to send Richard off like that without so much as a goodbye?* Patience decided that instead of making a scene at the gardens, she would do well to ask Richard himself. If she could not visit him tonight, she would do so the next morning.

Richard awoke with a sour taste in his mouth at noon the next day. James was calling to him from the other side of his bed chamber door.

"She's been waiting for hours!" said James, his voice muffled by the wooden door between them.

Richard rolled over.

"She says she won't leave until you see her."

Richard felt as if he had been run over by a cart. He was weak, and his legs did not seem to want to move without a great deal of personal resolve to push them forward. He made his way slowly to the door and fumbled with the lock. When he opened it, James stepped back to consider his brother.

"Are you alright, Richard? You look terrible. Mr. Pemberton said that you were unwell, but . . . is there something going on?"

"Is Patience here?" asked Richard.

"Since before breakfast," said James. "We had a devil of a time waking you up. She said that if you weren't up by noon, she would take down the door herself with an axe, so I thought I'd better give it one more try. Richard, I think she was absolutely

Fireworks

serious—about the axe."

Richard pushed passed his brother, and made his way to the drawing room where Patience was sitting with his mother.

"Give us a moment, Mother," said Richard without taking his eyes from Patience.

"I don't think that would be proper," said his mother with a nervous titter.

"Mother!" boomed Richard. And then more quietly, "You will give us a moment."

"No need to be rude," said Lady Winter as she vacated the room in a swish of silk skirts.

As soon as they were alone, Patience ran to him, and he had to hold her back by the shoulders.

"What has happened?" she asked him, genuine concern lacing her voice. "Whatever George has said, whatever George has threatened, it is nothing, Richard. Do you hear me? It is nothing. It has no bearing on our marriage. That is a decision for us and us alone."

Richard swallowed a lump that was building in his throat.

"There's not going to be a marriage, Patience," he said. "I can't marry you."

"What?" She whispered the word, and he thought his heart might shatter right there under that one small word.

"I wouldn't make you happy," he continued. "I couldn't care for you properly. I had fooled myself into thinking it was possible, but it's not. I'm so sorry."

Patience shrugged his hands from her shoulders.

"You're so sorry? What are you even saying, Richard? I don't understand any of this. It doesn't make any sense." Her face was flushed and her eyes were shining. "What did George say to you?"

A Soldier and his Rules

"George didn't say anything," said Richard trying his best to hold himself together, to make it through to the other side of the conversation. "This is my own decision."

"Your own decision?" repeated Patience as a tear rolled down her cheek. She stepped away from him. "Why are you hurting me like this? Have I done something? Is it me?"

Richard had to resist the urge to reach for her and pull her to him.

"The problem lies entirely with me," he said attempting to take all the emotion from his voice. He clasped his hands together to keep them from trembling. "I think you should leave now."

Sixteen

The Way these Stories End

Patience left the Winter residence on shaky legs. She felt cold and completely numb, as if someone had submerged her in a bath of ice water and then left her to stand in a breeze. She walked mechanically back to her carriage.

"Patience!" called James as he ran down the front steps of the house. "What has happened?"

She looked at James from the carriage, but she couldn't answer. Her mouth didn't work. That, or she simply couldn't bring herself to say the words. Saying them would make them real, and they couldn't be real.

Her carriage left James standing at the side of the street glancing back up to the house behind him. Patience had thought to go home, but she couldn't go home. If she did, what then? So she banged for the driver who stopped the carriage.

A Soldier and his Rules

"Mr. Pemberton's apartments," she said.

When she arrived at George's bachelor apartments, the driver helped her up the stairs. She was unsteady on her feet. Her arms were beginning to tingle. She was shown into George's study by a footman.

"Patience?" said George standing from his desk. "You look pale. Are you alright?"

"You," she said weakly, "did something. You said something to Richard." She wanted to point an accusing finger at him, but her arm felt as if she were dragging it through molasses. Her vision of George became obscured by large black spots surrounded by halos of light. "He won't marry me," she said as her vision left her entirely. Her legs gave way, and she crumpled to the floor.

Patience awoke on a couch with George leaning over her.

"Have a sip of water," he said offering her a glass.

Patience sat up and knocked the glass angrily from his hand. It thumped to the carpet, spilling its contents under the couch.

"Are you happy, George?"

"No," said George quite honestly. "But that doesn't mean it isn't for the best."

Patience glared at him.

"It's not because of me, Patience. Winter made the decision himself. I'm as surprised as you are."

"Something happened," countered Patience. "Something you're not telling me."

George picked the glass up from the carpet and set it on the table.

"I've sent for Mother. She will fetch you home," he said dispassionately. "We all want the best for you, Patience. This is a good outcome. It's not a happy outcome, but it's still a

The Way these Stories End

good one. In time, I think you will see that."

"In time?" said Patience feeling the blood return to her head. "I love him, George! Do you even know what that means? Time will not change that. I love him, and you took him from me!"

"You can't *love* him," said George clearly taken aback by her outburst. He tugged his fingers through his sandy hair standing it on end. "Mother will be here soon."

At home, Patience was given a cup of tea and put to bed. She did not join her family for dinner, and she left the plate of food her mother brought up for her untouched. She stared blankly up at the white curtains that were tied to the posts of her bed, and she refused to speak with anyone who entered the room. Patience felt entirely adrift, as if her bed were floating in some nowhere place as she lay on top.

The following afternoon, George came to call, and she could hear him and her mother whispering loudly about her outside her door.

"She hasn't eaten," said Lady Pemberton.

"It will pass," said George.

"By the time it passes, she will be skin and bones," countered her mother. "I'll not stand for it, George."

"I'm afraid you'll have to stand for it, Mother," said George firmly, "because this is the way it's going. There's nothing any of us can do except be by her side, offer her our support."

Lady Pemberton made a familiar strangled sound, and Patience could hear their carpet-padded footsteps retreat down the hall.

That evening after Patience had left her supper plate uneaten on her bedside table, Grace crept quietly into her room. She took off her shoes and pulling back the covers, climbed into bed with her sister. Patience lay motionless staring up at the bed curtains the way she had done all day as Grace curled into her and wrapped an arm around her waist. Her breath was cool and smelled of lemon. Patience imagined she had been eating lemon ice for dessert.

"This is not the way these stories end," said Grace giving her sister a sticky lemony kiss on the cheek. "None of them end this way."

Patience said nothing.

"There is always some obstacle or other," said Grace. "It might be a mad former wife hidden in the attic, or it could be that the hero is just a little too arrogant and condescending. Sometimes, especially if the hero has money troubles, he finds himself contemplating a loveless marriage in order to secure his family's finances. What I'm trying to say is that there is always something to overcome. It's not a proper love story without a struggle."

Patience could feel her sister squeeze her closer.

"Sometimes," said Grace, "the circumstances work themselves out. But more often than not it is either the hero or the heroine who has to do something about it."

Grace sat up and walked across the room in her stockinged feet. She returned with a hairbrush and pushing Patience over onto her side, began to brush out her hair.

"Tomorrow is a new day," said Grace gently tugging the brush through the tangles of her sister's hair. "You can start fresh in the morning. If it helps, I may have a clue for you. I once asked Lord Winter if he believed in true love. Do you know what he said?"

Patience twisted towards her sister. She needed to hear this.

"He said, 'I do believe in true love, but I'm not entirely certain

The Way these Stories End

it believes in me.'"

"He said that?" whispered Patience with tears welling in her eyes.

Grace nodded. "I gave him a bonus point."

Patience sat up and pulled her little sister into an embrace.

"You do talk a lot of nonsense," said Patience, "but sometimes it's very wise nonsense."

Grace laughed. "Does this mean you're going to eat something?"

"Pass me the plate," said Patience gesturing to the side table. Her stomach was suddenly feeling very empty.

Patience did not leave her room to join her family that evening, but she did eat. And when she slept she dreamed that she did so in front of a fire, in Richard's warm lap with his strong arms wrapped around her. She burrowed her face deeper into the pillow dreaming as she did so that she was snuggling closer into his embrace. She awoke early, dressed quietly, and stole from the her room and out to the mews. Before long, she was riding through Hyde Park in the early opalescent light that preceded the break of dawn. This early in the morning, there was absolutely no one at the park, so when she heard hooves behind her on the path, she turned to see who it might be. It was a gentleman unknown to her riding a dappled grey gelding. He lifted one hand from his reins to tip his hat to her.

She turned away from him, and remembering Richard's warning all those weeks ago, she spurred her horse to a canter. She could hear the gentleman's horse following suit, so she proceeded to a gallop. The gentleman's horse matched her pace once more.

She heard the man call out to her: "Is it a race you're looking

A Soldier and his Rules

for, young lady? I would be happy to oblige."

She didn't look back. He may be harmless, but his tone was oily, and his behaviour was inappropriate at best. She squeezed her horse between her thighs urging him on, turning from the path and down through the trees towards the Serpentine. She could hear the gentleman follow, and panic rose in her chest. *Stay calm. Think.* Patience mapped out a route in her head that would see her exiting the park by a side entrance. Once she was back on the street, there would be at least a few people wandering about in the early morning. She could call out for help if the man followed or attempted to accost her.

She galloped through the trees, weaving her way deftly between the trunks that stood like so many sentries blocking her path. Eventually she broke out into the open. An expanse of green lawn spread out ahead of her stretching downhill to the Serpentine that lay like a sheet of glass in the early morning. A hint of pink was breaking above the trees on the far shore, and down by the water was another gentleman on horseback staring out into the mist. Changing her plan, she did not turn in an effort to exit the park but instead, rode at speed down towards the Serpentine with the gentleman behind her now in hot pursuit.

Richard had come to the Serpentine for peace and quiet. To watch the rosy Dawn and to make amends in his heart for leading Patience on, for hurting her, for failing her, for imagining he deserved her. *How had it all gone so wrong?* When Richard heard the quick beat of horses' hooves approaching

The Way these Stories End

him across the grass, he turned to yell at whomever it was to take their race to Rotten Row.

He could hardly believe it was Patience galloping towards him, her green hood fallen back, hair streaming out behind her. Richard registered the panicked look on her face, saw the man on horseback behind her, and as Patience reined in her horse beside him, he instinctively placed himself between her and the gentleman on her heels.

"We were just having a little race," said the gentleman to Richard. "I do so like a chase, don't you?"

Richard could feel his hackles rising at the back of his neck.

"If you don't remove yourself from the park this instant," said Richard in a tone dripping with menace, "I shall crack your head open on that rock over there."

The gentleman laughed nervously, and his horse, sensing his change in mood, stamped agitatedly at the ground. When the man didn't move, Richard spurred his horse forward.

"Come, come," said the man. "It was just a bit of fun."

Richard was at his side in an instant, wrestling the reins from his hands.

"I've changed my mind," said Richard, shoving the man from his horse so that his body hit the ground with a hard smack. "You can leave the park *on foot,* or I can crack your head open on that rock over there. The choice is yours."

The man scrambled across the ground on all fours before getting to his feet and fleeing back up the hill.

Richard turned furiously on Patience. *Sweet Lord, she was beautiful in the morning light.*

"What the *hell* are you doing here all on your own?! Did I not warn you?! Do you understand what could have happened?!"

Patience gave him a small smile. "I don't take well to

instruction," she said apologetically. "It might be different if it were my husband giving the orders, but as it is, you are neither my husband nor my husband-to-be. Anyway, I risked coming because I thought you might be here."

She was so beautiful and so infuriating. Richard knew he had to remove himself from her company before she weakened his resolve, but if he did that, she would be alone at the park. He realised he was trapped until he could return her home.

"Come along then," he said. "Let's get you home."

Patience didn't so much as budge. She held his hazel eyes in her blue. Richard watched as Dawn reached her pink fingers over the Serpentine, through the mist, to bathe Patience's face in her light.

"I love you," said Patience. "I thought you should know."

Richard felt as if he might fall from the horse. The words hit him like an unexpected gust of wind, sending him sideways. He righted himself atop his steed, gripping the reins so tightly, he soon lost all circulation in his fingers.

She continued, "I don't need you to be perfect, Richard. I just need you to return my love. It will be enough—more than enough."

Richard stared at her for sometime. He wanted so much to be able to give her what she asked, but he knew it was a fool's hope that tugged at his heart.

"It won't be enough," he said, forming the words with some effort. "Promise me you won't blame George. He is quite innocent in all this."

"I'll blame George if I want to blame George," said Patience defiantly as Richard turned his horse to lead her home. "I know you love me, so why are you doing this?" She spurred her horse forward to follow his.

The Way these Stories End

Of course I love you. Heavens above, I wouldn't be putting myself through this torture if I didn't love you, thought Richard. But he said nothing. He simply led her home in silence. They passed through the park and along the cobbled street until he saw her safe to the mews behind the house. Patience dismounted her horse and looked to him, but Richard turned and left her there without a word of farewell.

As he made his way home, he couldn't help but feel glad to have seen her. The very sight of her lifted his soul up from the murky depths. But he knew it was useless to let his mind linger, so he dragged his thoughts to matters of Parliament. The House would be sitting this afternoon, and he would see Lord Pemberton there. He hoped that the baron would be able to forgive him for hurting his daughter. Richard suspected the man would actually be quite relieved that the marriage was not taking place. It had been kind of him to keep his doubts to himself—Richard could not imagine that he did not have at least some misgivings after what he had witnessed at the musicale.

Patience was still somewhat shaken by the time she returned home. Thank goodness Richard had been exactly where she had expected him to be that morning.

At least she had said her piece. It was not lost on Patience that her little declaration of love had nearly knocked him to the ground. *Why would he be so surprised? It's not as if I have ever hidden my attraction to him.*

That morning, Patience took breakfast with her family. She wasn't yet talking to anyone, but she was eating, and Lord

253

A Soldier and his Rules

and Lady Pemberton exchanged looks of relief when they saw their eldest daughter sit down at the table. Grace offered her sister a smile.

"We shall put it about that it was you who broke off the courtship," said Lady Pemberton. "That way we will keep your reputation somewhat in tact."

Patience couldn't believe how quickly her mother was swooping in to tidy up the mess. Soon she would have it all swept under the carpet as if nothing had ever happened. As if Patience had never been in love and never had her heart broken. Patience couldn't care less if her reputation remained 'in tact' or not. It's not as if she would ever agree to marry anyone but Richard, so to her the subject was moot. At least her father was not offering her any aggravating platitudes. He watched his daughter as he ate his own breakfast, and then he pushed back his chair.

"Parliament sits this afternoon. I think I shall head over to Westminster a bit early, see who is knocking about. You never know what can come of a conversation."

"That's nice dear," said Lady Pemberton who did not appear to be listening at all. Patience imagined she was already plotting her reputation damage control right there at the table.

"I'll be teaching Potato how to sit today," said Grace passing her pug a small piece of bacon under the table.

"Grace! You know that dog is not permitted to eat at the table," said Lady Pemberton. She gestured to a footman who scooped up the little tan pug and took her from the room.

Grace shook her head. "It's so sad you treat Potato this way," she said. "It hurts her feelings."

Lady Pemberton rolled her eyes and made no response.

The Way these Stories End

Richard strode down the wide halls of Westminster. He hoped he would be able to make some sort of difference in Parliament.

Let this be the silver lining, he thought. *Let my life have some purpose without Patience.*

Several members of the House of Lords had appeared early that day. They were talking in low voices, banding together in little enclaves scattered throughout the building. When he passed by one small huddle of such lords, one man broke away from the group and followed Richard down the hall.

"Lord Winter," the man called out hesitantly.

Richard turned to see a small elderly man with a pleasant face and strangely fearful eyes.

"Yes," said Richard.

"Derby," said the man. "I'm sure your father mentioned me."

"The Earl of Derby?" asked Richard.

"The same," said the man. "I wanted you to know that my agreement with your father—it's important to me that it still stands." The earl was darting his eyes about as if to assess their relative privacy.

"Agreement?"

"I can pay monthly as always," said the earl quietly. "But you must let me know how you would like me to vote."

"How I would like you to vote in the House?" asked Richard incredulously. The light of realisation slowly descended upon him bringing with it a wave of nausea.

Dear God, this earl is one of Father's puppets! He thinks I mean to continue whatever blackmail Father has threatened.

Richard reached out to shake the man's hand, and the earl actually flinched before hesitantly placing his hand in Richard's.

A Soldier and his Rules

"Earl of Derby, is it?" asked Richard.

The man nodded.

"I know I resemble my father in the most uncanny of ways, but it is only an appearance. I do not need your monthly payments, nor do I need to tell you how to vote in the House. Consider yourself released from whatever blackmail it is that has you shackled."

The man's eyes went wide.

"Oh. My. Well. Thank you, Lord Winter," said the earl, bowing his head several times.

"I apologise on behalf of my entire family," said Richard sincerely. "He was a truly despicable man."

Derby seemed to be having trouble processing this unlikely turn of events as he looked up into the face of his former tormentor.

"Thank you," he said again. "I'll not forget this."

"Please do," said Richard.

Derby turned to leave, then turned back, his mouth open like a fish. It took him a few seconds to spit out the words, but they finally did come: "Lord Winter, you should know, there are others."

"I don't doubt it," said Richard. "If you know any, send them along, and I'll set them straight."

"Right," said the earl. "Right. I'll do that."

He scurried off down the hall as if Richard might withdraw his offer if he lingered too long.

Before Parliament was actually in session, Richard had spoken to a half dozen lords— two marquesses, an earl, a viscount, two barons—and even a duke as well. His father had been holding them all hostage, if not for their votes (because a couple of them actually agreed with his father's

The Way these Stories End

brand of politics), then for their money but most often for both. Richard knew it would take some time to cleanse the Winter name of the stain his father had placed upon it, but at least this was a start.

As the last baron left him standing alone in the hallway, Richard looked up to see Lord Pemberton approaching. The two men greeted each other with a handshake.

"It is likely you will have a few more voting with you this year," said Richard to Lord Pemberton. "My father was not one to keep a secret if a favour was not exchanged for the service, and it turns out he was keeping a lot of secrets."

"I see," said Lord Pemberton assessing Richard carefully. "I suppose we shall see which way the wind blows as the week progresses."

Richard gave a grunt of acknowledgment, and Lord Pemberton continued.

"I am not one to meddle in the affairs of my children." he said. "They have their own lives and minds. But it would be remiss of me if I did not express my sincere disappointment that your courtship of Patience has come to an end."

Richard felt winded by the statement, as if he'd taken a swift punch to the gut. He knew Lord Pemberton was not the kind of father who wielded his power over his children, and he had assumed the man had been assenting to Patience's preference of husband despite his own misgivings.

"Come," said Lord Pemberton looking over to where the lords were filing into the chamber. "It begins."

He doesn't know. Not really, thought Richard. *What he witnessed at the musicale was nothing—a small attack of the nerves. He would not be speaking this way if he knew the true madness that lurks within me. George knows, and his judgment was written all over his face: Patience is not safe in my care.*

Parliament, it turned out, was an extraordinarily tedious affair. Long rambling speeches were given by various lords who seemed more intent on listening to their own voices than in making any discernible point. Richard watched Lord Pemberton sitting attentively in his seat as if he were watching a boxing match. He was always listening. The afternoon dragged into evening, and despite the fact that there were still votes to be taken, members of the House began to trickle out, heading for home—for supper, a glass of whiskey, and bed. As the hour drew late, Richard noticed that among those that remained were his father's former hostages.

At the very end of the evening, he shook hands with Lord Pemberton before they parted ways.

"A good start!" said the baron. "Thanks to you, we've made some unexpected allies."

When Richard arrived home, he found James had held supper for him.

"Mother ate at the usual time," he said. "She's already in bed."

"Where's Thomas?" asked Richard.

"Gone home," said James. "He thinks that three gentlemen looking after our mother is one too many."

"He deserves a break," said Richard.

"How did it go?" asked James.

"Well," said Richard. He didn't feel like elaborating.

As they ate their supper, Richard could feel the weight of James's unspoken words upon him.

"I had to let her go," said Richard to the unasked question. "She would not be safe with me."

"Of course not," said James with annoyance. "No one is safe

with you. You can't protect anyone. Not me from Father. Not England from Bonaparte. You're an utter disgrace of a man."

James was only sarcastic when he was angry, and Richard could tell that he was very angry.

"It's not the same," he said to James as he placed his cutlery down on his plate.

"Isn't it?" asked James fixing him with an icy glare.

Seventeen

One More Rule

As the week slid inevitably towards its end, Patience knew she would have to throw out the flowers that sat beside her bed. They were beginning to putrefy, and the odour was not exactly pleasant. Each time she set her mind to the task, however, she simply couldn't do it. For some reason, she felt that if she disposed of the flowers, then it would all be over. Completely over.

She had spent the week painting those flowers as they had continued to decay. Losing herself in her art was the only way Patience could contemplate passing the cold hours that loomed in front of her. She would dissolve herself into the process, emerging only to eat and then, at the end of the day, to sleep. The next morning, she would begin the cycle all over again.

Lord Pemberton was attending at Westminster most evenings, so she often did not see him for supper as he tended to stay late. George was a conspicuous absence all week. Patience imagined he was avoiding her and her accusations. *He probably thinks I will attack him physically if he visits*, thought Patience. *And he wouldn't be wrong.* She knew her brother had something to do with all this, and she would not forgive him. Not now. Not ever.

She had not had any word from Richard, but James had written her a letter expressing his warmest regards and his sincere sorrow that things had ended the way that they had. He was returning to Avery House in the countryside with Lady Winter who was in need of some quiet and fresh air. He hoped Patience would write, but he understood if she didn't.

At one point in the letter, James wrote, *I never did show you the orangery, and I doubt very much that Richard took you there when you were visiting. When our father was alive, it was an aviary—fruit trees and dozens of birds flying to and fro under the glass roof. Those birds were my father's pride and joy. It wasn't so much that he thought they were beautiful. Rather (as with everything else in his life) he liked the fact that he owned them. After Richard returned from the continent to find our father was dead and he the new viscount, he dragged his wounded body across the house to the aviary, threw open all of the windows, and promptly collapsed on the floor with the considerable effort it had cost him. The birds left, and now it is just an orangery. Honestly, I'm not entirely sure why I'm telling you this. Just as before, I suppose I feel as if it is something you should know. A piece of the puzzle that is Richard.*

Saturday morning at breakfast, Lady Pemberton looked surreptitiously across the table at Patience as she sipped her tea.

"Lady Hartlebury is hosting a ball tonight," she said. "Perhaps it would cheer you."

"Balls never cheer me, Mother," said Patience. "I don't care to socialise, and I don't care to dance."

"I said we would attend."

"Then you should go, but I will be staying home."

"You can't stay home forever, my dear. Life moves on."

Patience looked down at her plate. A piece of half-eaten buttered toast, a moon-shaped slice of melon.

"No," she said quietly to her plate. "It doesn't."

She pressed herself back in her seat.

"Excuse me," she said before leaving the breakfast room to paint her dead flowers once more.

The morning passed in swift strokes of the paintbrush. The originally luminous colours of the flowers had faded, and Patience found herself mixing a lot of varying shades of brown. A green slime had coated the stems beneath the water on whose surface floated a few small dead insects among the fallen petals.

There was a knock at her door sometime late in the morning. George opened the door slowly and peered into the room. When Patience saw him, she threw her paintbrush at him. He dodged, and it hit the white wall beside him, spattering brown paint before it hit the floor.

"Patience," said George using the door as a shield. "I need to talk to you."

"I *don't* need to talk to *you*," said Patience rummaging around her art supplies for another paintbrush.

"There is something you should know," he said. "Something I didn't tell you before."

"Why, pray tell, are you telling me now?" asked Patience as she dabbed at her flower painting.

One More Rule

"I just now spoke with Father," said George creeping into the room. "He says that this season of Parliament holds much promise. Apparently, Lord Winter has managed to shift the tides as it were."

"Of course he did," said Patience. "He and Father are of one mind on many issues."

"I did not believe Lord Winter would follow through," said George sheepishly. He pulled a hand through his hair so that it stood on end. "I thought it was a ruse to see you wedded to him. I had imagined he would shift allegiances once Father had handed you over."

"Well, he doesn't want me anymore, so you've nothing to worry about," said Patience striking at her painting angrily with the brush.

George walked up to her and took the brush from her hands.

"Sit down," he said gesturing to a chair.

"Why?"

"I need to say some things," said George. "Patience, don't make this any harder than it already is."

Patience was moved to silence by her brother's demeanour. He seemed . . . contrite. Patience shook her head. That couldn't be it. George was never contrite.

"Well?" said Patience impatiently sitting down. "Go on then."

George took a deep breath. His face flushed crimson. "I was wrong," he said.

"Excuse me?"

"I was wrong about Winter. He would make a good husband for you," said George.

"You're so full of yourself, George," said Patience rising from her seat with annoyance. "In case you hadn't noticed, it's not up to you! Richard has called it off."

George tugged at his hair with one hand as if he might pull it out by the roots.

"You said you *loved* him."

"I say lots of things," said Patience.

"Do you love him or don't you?!" asked George grabbing her by the shoulders. His grey gaze was more intense than ever, and Patience felt herself growing quiet inside herself.

"Yes," she whispered. "More than you can know."

"Sit down," said George, pressing her gently back down to the chair. He crouched low in front of her.

"Winter is not well," he said. And then he proceeded to tell her everything that had happened that night at Vauxhall Gardens.

"He was ashamed, Patience. He saw me looking at him. I don't know how I was looking at him, but I can imagine it wasn't in a particularly nice way. I hated him in that moment. I realise now that what he's most afraid of is the same thing I'm most afraid of—not being able to care for and protect you properly. That's why he called it off. It's not for lack of caring for you. Quite the opposite."

Patience thought of all the times Richard had protected her. He had actually danced with her to save her from conversing with Mr. Ruteledge, and then he had stood up to the very same gentleman when he had taken her shawl. He had rescued her in the storm and seen off her pursuer in the park. And now here he was trying to protect her from himself even if it came at the cost of his own happiness.

You have to hand it to him, thought Patience, *he is nothing if not consistent.* She looked at her brother. *These men and their ideas of manhood.* Patience bristled. *As if I cannot take a decision*

One More Rule

for myself!

"What are you doing?" asked Grace walking into Patience's bed chamber.

Every drawer was open, and the entire contents of her closet lay in a heap upon her bed.

"Tell me," said Patience as she handed a dress to Delphi who was carefully packing one of a number of trunks and cases that lay open on the floor, "how do your romance stories usually end?"

Grace's face lit up at the question. "There's often an emotional scene in which some misunderstanding or other is set to rights. Sometimes there's a big dramatic gesture that demonstrates one person's love for the other. The two people finally realise they cannot be apart. I imagine there's some kissing, but I've yet to read a novel that describes that sort of thing properly."

Delphi coughed. Patience smiled at her sister.

"But you still haven't answered my question," said Grace. "What are you doing?"

"A big dramatic gesture," said Patience. She tried to sound confident, but she was more anxious than she had ever been in her life.

"Does Mother know?" asked Grace wide-eyed.

"No, and you mustn't say a word until I'm gone," said Patience. "She will think it quite scandalous."

"It will be if it doesn't work," said Grace as if she had seen this sort of thing before.

What if it doesn't work? thought Patience in a momentary

panic. *No. I can't think like that. I will take this one decision for myself.*

Grace put her hand on Patience's arm. "If there's one thing you're good at," she said, "it's big dramatic gestures."

"Thank you," said Patience with a weak smile.

Richard was working in his study when a footman knocked at the door.

"Miss Pemberton is here to see you, my lord. She's in the drawing room."

Richard felt her name like a knife to the heart. He wished she would just leave it alone, and he thought to send her away without seeing her. It might be better for the both of them.

"She's brought several trunks with her, my lord. They are piled up in the foyer. Is there somewhere you would like me to put them?"

"What?! No. I'm coming," he said rising from his desk. *What in the hell was she playing at?* A familiar feeling rose inside him—a shiver of anticipation coupled with the stomach-roiling sensation of not knowing what she was about. That he would have to push her away again was almost too much to bear. As Richard walked down the hall, he felt himself heating uncomfortably and had to remove his jacket. He arrived in the drawing room to find Patience seated on a couch in front of the fireplace. Sandy blonde tendrils framed her bright flower of a face which was looking at him in that way she had. No, not looking *at* him—looking *through* him. She was wearing an extraordinary lilac dress that cinched at the waist. Though the dress was cut in a modest fashion, the fabric hugged her body

One More Rule

to reveal every plump curve. She did not appear to be wearing anything beneath it—no stay or corset or chemise. Richard's hands twitched with the effort of not reaching out to stroke and squeeze her body through that ridiculously alluring dress. He distracted himself by tossing his jacket to a chair.

"My lord," she said standing.

"Miss Pemberton, what can I do for you?"

"You can grant me the freedom to make my own decisions," she said. Richard couldn't help but detect a tinge of anger in her tone.

"George told me about your . . . affliction," she said as she stepped towards him.

"He what?!"

"He thinks you would make a good husband."

"I wouldn't," said Richard reflexively. Then, "George said that?"

"Yes," said Patience. "And if George says it, it must be true, mustn't it?" She paused. "Richard," she continued. Her voice had lost its anger. Her tone was tender now. "I know you're quite accustomed to suffering in order to protect those that you love, but you don't have to do this for me. I don't want you to. A marriage isn't all one-way—it's a partnership. We will support and care for each other." She took another step towards him. "I may be just a weak and feeble woman, but—"

"—I've never thought of you as weak and feeble," interrupted Richard.

"Your actions suggest otherwise," said Patience, closer now. He could reach out and touch her if he were not so terrified. "Do you not think me strong enough to support you through your own troubles? Do you think me so frail that I cannot, even occasionally, be the one protecting you?"

Richard felt her questions burn through him. He didn't want to answer.

"Why have you brought all those trunks?" asked Richard. His heart was starting to beat a little harder in anticipation of her answer.

"Because I'm not leaving," said Patience matter-of-factly. "I love you, and I'm not leaving."

"Patience, you can't—"

"—just move in?" she asked, finishing the question for him. "Do you want me to leave? If you can tell me you don't love me and that you wish me to leave, I will do so. But you *will* have to say you don't love me."

Patience was so close to him now. She was looking down at his hand as if she might reach for it, but she thought better of it and lifted her eyes back to his.

"Patience," said Richard. He was feeling more than a little overwhelmed, like a dam beginning to crack under the pressure. He placed the heels of his hands to his eyes. When he removed them, he could feel the swell of tears. "I'm worried I can't do it," he said. "I can't be the husband that you need, that you deserve."

"I've told you," said Patience reaching up to wipe a tear from his cheek, "I only need you to love me. And you don't even have to do so perfectly. Everything else is extra."

Patience was holding her breath as if any sound or movement might frighten Richard away. She could see him weigh her words.

"You haven't seen me when it happens," he said. "It will scare you. It's possible I should be for the mad house."

"The only thing that scares me, Richard, is contemplating my life without you. And there will be no talk of the mad house. George told me he spoke with Father, and he says that this sort of thing is very common among soldiers returning from war. It can get better."

"And if it doesn't?" asked Richard.

"If it doesn't, I will be there beside you. Holding your hand. Loving you in sickness and in health. Till death do us part. Please, Richard. Let me make this decision for myself. I'm a grown woman."

She reached her hand out, and her heart leapt as he took it in his own. He tugged her into an embrace, and they stood like that quietly breathing against each other for what felt like a moment and an eternity all at once.

"Patience," said Richard eventually, "does this mean you're staying the night?"

"This night and every other night," said Patience looking up into his solemn face. "My home is with you."

"It will cause a scandal," said Richard softly.

"Then you'd better marry me soon," she said with a smile.

"Martin!" called Richard as he held Patience to him. "Martin!"

The footman soon appeared at the door.

"Have my wife's things taken up to the master bed chamber," said Richard over Patience's head which was nestled beneath his chin.

"Your wife?" said the footman taking in the scene. He did not wait for an explanation. "Yes, my lord. Right away."

"Have you eaten luncheon?" asked Richard.

Patience laughed. "I thought you'd never ask. I didn't have

time to eat what with all the packing."

Richard watched as Patience ate her lunch. He had dismissed the staff from the dining room so that they may speak privately . . . and so that he might gaze upon her openly. He hadn't kissed her yet and with good reason. *Sweet Mercy, that dress she was wearing would be the end of him.* If he touched her lips or heard her gasp or make any of those tiny little noises she made as he kissed her neck, he might lose all sense of restraint.

It is broad daylight. There are servants about. It would be unseemly.

"I should pay your father a visit," said Richard. "Ask him properly for your hand."

Patience dabbed at her lush little mouth with a pale blue linen napkin.

"It would be the right thing to do," she said. "I think I'll stay here."

She locked eyes with him, and it was all Richard could do to keep himself from leaping across the table at her like a wolf. He imagined himself growling and snarling and sniffing at her in the most ungentlemanly way. He would shred that dress with his teeth, and then . . .

Patience interrupted his thoughts by rising from her seat. She stepped around the table to him, and he stood.

"I believe we have some unfinished business," she said.

"I don't know what you m—" started Richard, but he found himself quite speechless as she tugged her gauzy lilac dress down to reveal one soft creamy shoulder.

Richard's hands went to her waist, then slid down over her

round bottom. He pulled her to him—hard. The movement was sudden, and she let slip a small sound that sent Richard quite mad with desire. He leaned down and bit her shoulder, inhaled the scent of her neck. It wasn't enough. The wolf inside him wanted more.

I should leave now and speak with her father, thought Richard.

Instead, he turned her around and undid the buttons at the back of her dress. She turned back to face him, and he peeled her dress down to release her breasts to the gaze of his greedy eyes. She was looking at him with anticipation, her pink lips parted.

"Are you not going to touch me?" asked Patience, her voice thick with desire.

Richard grazed the tip of one nipple with his palm, then cupped her breast in his hand and groaned. He had to talk to her father, and he'd better do it now before he took Lord Pemberton's daughter in broad daylight in every room of the house.

"If we start this," said Richard in a low gravely voice, "we won't want to stop."

He gently pulled her dress up to cover her and turned her around to do up her buttons.

"And I *have* to speak with your father."

"Is that a rule in your head?" asked Patience with amusement. "Check with young lady's father before engaging in amorous congress out of wedlock?"

"Yes," said Richard. "I'm afraid it is." He took her chin in his hand. "But I object to the term 'amorous congress'. It is far too polite a designation for what I plan on doing with you."

Patience gave a short sharp exhale through her mouth.

"I shall hold you to that, Lord Winter."

A Soldier and his Rules

After Richard left, Patience wandered the house with a tail of servants following a few steps behind her. Word had spread quickly through the house that she was Lord Winter's new wife, and they were already calling her Lady Winter. The housekeeper finally made herself known—a Miss Rowling whose pinched mouth and severe expression reminded Patience of Serafina's own housekeeper. She looked Patience up and down, and while her demeanour was polite, Patience suspected that she did not approve of whatever it was she thought was going on.

When Miss Rowling had nearly finished giving Patience a proper tour of the house—the bits she hadn't seen yet—she opened the door to Richard's bedroom where Patience's trunks had been stored.

"I'm not sure why your trunks were delivered here," she said apologetically. "The viscountess has her own quarters."

"There should be space in Richard's closet for my things as well," said Patience poking through the room. It was an enormous bed chamber decorated in moss green and cream with gold accents. "I shall be sleeping here anyway," said Patience turning brightly to Miss Rowling. "I doubt very much that Richard will countenance any other arrangement."

The housekeeper flushed pink, and Patience realised she had been entirely too forward. *Well, how am I supposed to say these things and not be forward?* Patience took the arm of the housekeeper as they strode from the room. She could feel the woman stiffen at her touch.

"It's clear you are doing an admirable job managing this household," said Patience. "I shall be happy to receive any suggestions you might make. And if you wouldn't mind, Miss Rowling, I should very much like to paint your portrait.

One More Rule

Perhaps, one day, if you have a few minutes to spare."

The housekeeper stopped walking and turned to her with an open mouth.

"I'm sorry, my lady. Did you say you would like to paint my portrait?"

"Yes," said Patience. "It shall be a gift if you like."

"That would be . . . yes . . . thank you, my lady." Miss Rowling actually smiled, and Patience was able to glimpse the girl she had once been so many years ago. *That is how I shall paint her*, thought Patience. *As she is right now with that youthful light shining through her.*

When the tour was over, Richard had still not returned from the Pembertons'. Patience sat in the drawing room with a charcoal and paper making sketches and listening carefully for any sound from the front door. When she heard Richard finally entering into the foyer one floor below her, she flew out of the drawing room and to the top of the stairs. He glanced up at her as he handed his coat to Martin.

"Your father is a very reasonable man," said Richard. "But your mother—"

"Did she give you an earful?" asked Patience grinning down at him from the railing above.

"And then some," said Richard. He took the stairs three at a time to land in front of her at the top. "She said I must return you to her at once."

"What did you say?"

"I said that I cannot order my wife around. I'm not that sort of man," said Richard shifting a stray tendril of hair behind her ear and smiling mischievously. "I told her you were a grown woman and capable of making your own decisions."

Patience laughed. "Did she believe it?"

"No," said Richard.

"Do you believe it?" asked Patience quietly. Richard looked at her quizzically.

"Of course," he said.

"Richard," said Patience, trying to find the right words so that she didn't sound too . . . contradictory. "I hope you know that I don't mind being ordered around *sometimes.*"

She gave him a look hoping he would take her meaning.

"Oh really?" he asked as his eyes darkened leaving only that ring of orange fire at the edges.

Patience felt his gaze upon her like an electric storm. She held her breath.

Eighteen

Caught in the Blaze

Richard had to concentrate to slow his breathing. *The things this woman says to me!*

"Right," he said. If she wanted him to take control, then he certainly would. Richard was not one to disappoint his wife.

He took her chin in his hand and brushed his thumb along her bottom lip. Her lips parted in a pant, and she tilted her face up to his, lifting herself up on her toes ever-so-slightly. He brought his lips a hair's breadth from hers, holding himself just out of reach. He tilted his head to skim his lips lightly along her jaw and up to her ear with the lightest touch imaginable. He could feel his pulse throbbing like a heavy beat through his body.

"Lady Winter," he whispered, breath hot on her ear. "Is it a kiss you're after?"

"Yes," she whispered. "Please," she added.

A Soldier and his Rules

It was the 'please' that sent Richard's eyes rolling back in his head. He could hear the wolf inside him howling to be let out. He shifted his hand from her chin to the back of her head and took her luscious mouth in his. *Merciful heavens, she tasted exquisite.* A low guttural sound emerged from deep in his throat as he found himself trying to drink her all up—every last drop of her sweet lips, her warm liquid tongue. His hands slid down the gauzy lilac length of her back to rest on her wide hips, and he could feel her reach around him. As he leaned into her to take his fill, she staggered backwards, and he had to brace them both with a hand against the wall.

He lifted his face from hers and leaned over her.

"Will you do as you're told?" he asked.

She pressed her lips together to hide a smile.

"Yes, my lord," she answered with lowered eyes.

"You will look at me when I'm talking to you," he said, trying to keep his tone firm.

When Patience lifted her blue gaze to his, the look in her eyes was so carnal, so sensual that Richard nearly lost his balance. Steadying himself on his feet, he scooped her up into his arms, and cradling her to his chest, he carried her down the hall to their bed chamber.

"Richard," she whispered as he carried her, "I know we're playing, and I know I sometimes behave like a hot little bundle of fireworks, but I should probably tell you that I'm just a tiny bit nervous."

Her words hit him like an arrow. *Of course she was nervous. Just because she had some idea about what was going to happen didn't make her any less a virgin.* He kissed the top of her head as he carried her into the bed chamber closing the door with a backward kick of his foot.

Caught in the Blaze

"It might be best," he said laying her down on his enormous bed, "if we save our little game for another time. I don't want you to feel as if you must follow my orders." He looked at her carefully, with concern. "Always be honest with me, Patience. If you don't like something, tell me. If you want me to stop, say so."

Patience scooted herself to seated. She nodded and smiled gratefully.

"Now," he said, crawling towards her on the bed like a tiger stalking his prey, "How attached are you to this dress? Because I should very much like to rip it from your body."

Patience bit her lip. She looked pleased.

"I don't particularly care for this dress," she said with a giggle.

Richard growled and lunged for her as she fell backwards on the bed with a small shriek of delight. He nuzzled and snarled his way up from her soft belly to the large swell of her breasts where he spent some time working her nipples into hard little peaks using his mouth overtop the thin muslin. She writhed and gasped beneath him, her hands in his hair, as he made his way to her neck, then licking his way up to her mouth like an animal. Her hands still in his hair, she pulled his mouth forcefully to hers, pressing her sweet tongue inside him, taking as much as he could give. He rose up above her on his knees and gripped the low neckline of her dress in both hands.

"Ready?" he asked.

Patience smiled. "Release me, my lord."

Richard rent her dress apart with one quick movement, spilling her breasts out into the open. He plunged down to her bosom once more with a growl, lifting and kneading her breasts in his hands. She became quite breathless as he

A Soldier and his Rules

licked and sucked at her until she was arching up into him with pleasure. He continued to rip her dress apart as he slid down her body, kissing and licking and biting. When his face reached her thighs, he rose up once more.

"It needs to come off," he said of the dress.

She shimmied out of it, and he tossed it to the floor. He was straddling her with his knees and the sight of her so completely naked and vulnerable beneath him gave him pause. *How was it possible she was in his bed? And gazing at him with such desire?*

"Richard," said Patience quietly sitting up to his kneeling form.

She pulled at his belt. As she undid his trousers, he threw off his jacket, tugged loose his cravat, and drew his shirt up over his head. He stepped from the bed to remove his trousers and drawers, and when he looked up, Patience was staring at him with her plump lips parted.

"You are rather larger than I had expected," she said softly, reaching out a hand to touch him as he stepped forward to stand at the side of the bed.

She gripped his shaft lightly with fluttery fingers, and Richard groaned with pleasure at her inexperienced touch. She explored him with one hand. The other slid around to his buttocks to pull him in towards her. Gripping tighter she moved her hand along him, sliding it up and down, her head tipped to one side as if his member were some new species she was examining. And then, without warning, she dropped her face forward and took him in her mouth.

Holy hell!

For several long delicious seconds as Patience ran her hot little mouth over his now fully engorged member, Richard found he could not speak.

"Patience," said Richard when he finally found his voice. He tugged gently at her head. She pulled her lips from him, and he sucked in his breath.

"You don't like it?" she asked. "I just thought . . ."

"No. No. I like it," said Richard groaning inwardly. "A little too much," he added. "I'm afraid I won't last very long if you continue."

"Oh."

"Let me take care of *you*," he said, pressing her back down to the bed.

Patience smiled. "Whatever you say, my lord."

As Patience lay back down on the bed, she could feel the swollen heavy need between her thighs. Richard climbed on top of her, the muscles in his arms twisting and tensing as they took his weight.

He dropped down to his elbows, and she felt the pleasant tickle of his chest hairs against her breasts. He pressed his lips to hers for a kiss so tender, tears began to gather behind her eyes.

"I don't think I've said this properly, Patience, but you should know that I love you with every useless scrap of my body and soul. I will do anything for you."

"I know," whispered Patience.

Richard placed a knee between her legs and spread them apart.

"Are you going to . . . ?" Patience thought perhaps she should brace herself. Serafina had said it might hurt a little at first.

A Soldier and his Rules

Richard put a hand up to stroke her hair from her face.

"Not yet," he said. "I need to make sure you're ready first."

Patience gave a small nervous laugh as Richard moved down her body, stopping to lick at her nipples, kiss her belly. And then his face was between her thighs! Patience could barely contain the coiled need within her as his beard scratched and tickled its way deeper into the delta of her outspread legs. And then his tongue was licking up and along her outer petals, a slow and lazy caress that had her place a hand across her own mouth as she arched up into him. He worked his way up to her little bud of pleasure, licking and sucking at it in a way that sent an electric current right through her. Patience was writhing and moaning with complete abandon now. She felt so thoroughly lost to his touch, so completely out of control as her breath was let loose in short bursts from her mouth. She heard him growl between her thighs as she spread her legs wider in an effort to find some release. When her release finally did come, it felt like an explosion of radiant sparks cascading through every inch of her body.

Richard slid up along her with a smile. As he kissed her lips gently, he placed his fingers between her legs, slipping one softly inside her.

"You seem quite wet and ready now," he said. "What do you think?"

"I think," said Patience trying to slow her breathing. "I think you're going to have to give me a second to recover."

"I can do that," said Richard.

He stroked her body slowly with a light touch—across her collar bone, circling both breasts, swirling down to her belly, then back up along the inside of her arm. He touched two fingers to her lips and she lifted her head slightly to take them in her mouth.

"I think I'm ready now," she said when he had pulled his fingers from her lips.

"Would you like to be in charge?" asked Richard. "So that you can control what's happening?"

She liked the sound of that.

"How would that work?" asked Patience.

"I'll be underneath," he said sitting up against a few pillows at the headboard.

Sweet Lord, with his beard and his wide chiselled torso, he looked like Neptune waiting for her at the top of the bed.

Patience crawled up the bed and straddled him. He placed a hand to each of her luxuriously thick thighs and squeezed gently as she shifted herself over his still swollen member. He tilted his face up to hers, and she pressed a very hot breathy kiss to his lips. And then she reached down to angle him in place. As she lowered herself, she felt him pressing into her, soft and hard at the same time. Gently, gently, she lifted herself up slightly, then lowered a little further down onto him. He took one of her breasts in his mouth.

"Oh Richard," she said when he was halfway inside her. "It feels so . . . so . . . full."

"Good or bad?" he asked reaching up to stroke her face.

"Good," she said sliding even further down with a gasp. "So good."

When she realised she had taken him entirely within her, she looked at him with some amazement.

"It didn't hurt," she said.

"Might be all that horseback riding did the job for me," he suggested with a smile.

Patience continued to ride him, clinging to his shoulders

as she chased after something just out of reach. His hands slid up to stroke her back as he gazed hungrily up into her eyes. When she felt as if she might collapse with her efforts, Richard tumbled her to the bed so that he was on top. The tiger was back now, groaning as he took several long smooth strokes inside her. Patience could feel her climax building with each of his thrusts. Her body craved more. She wrapped her legs around his hips and placed her hands to either side of his head.

"Harder, Richard. I need it harder."

Richard looked at her with some surprise, and Patience worried that he would decide she was in need of a gentler approach. He paused to kiss her neck and mouth.

"Tell me if it becomes too much," he said, his voice hoarse in her ear.

Then he proceeded to give her exactly what she had asked for. Patience thrilled with pleasure. As Richard landed with force at the end of each thrust, she could feel her body begin to lose itself with the vibrations set loose inside her until she was quivering and trembling against him. She heard herself cry out like an animal as she erupted in a fountain of fire. Richard practically roared on top of her as he found his own release before lowering himself beside her on the bed.

"You'll be the death of me," he said, drawing her close and wrapping his strong arms about her. "That was . . . something else."

"Is it not usually like that?" she asked snuggling into him, listening to the thud of his heart.

"No," he laughed as he held her tight and kissed her head. "No, it is not."

They lay together in that embrace, their heartbeats becom-

Caught in the Blaze

ing slow, relaxing into a synchronised rhythm. Patience drifted off in Richard's arms, and when she woke, it was early evening. She was lying naked by herself in the bed, and Richard was standing nearby wearing a pair of trousers and pulling a white linen shirt over his head.

"If you don't feel like getting dressed to go down for supper, I can bring supper up for you. For both of us," he said shrugging into his shirt and crawling over her on the bed.

He gave her a quick hungry kiss on the mouth, and Patience laughed.

"I wouldn't be opposed to supper in bed," she said, "but what will the servants think?"

"They'll think," said Richard, kissing her lips once more, then her neck, her breasts, "that we are making the most of our honeymoon."

Richard could not quite believe that George Pemberton was paying him a visit the following afternoon. Richard wished that Patience were there to greet her brother alongside him. Her presence would have been a kind of buffer against the necessary awkwardness such a meeting would entail. After Patience's success at the Royal Academy exhibit, she had acquired several portrait commissions, and today she had an appointment to discuss one such commission with (of all people) the Earl of Derby's wife. So Richard was on his own.

George Pemberton stood in the doorway to Richard's drawing room as if he were hesitating to step fully inside. The last time he had been in that room, he had attacked Richard—twice—and threatened to kill him with a convincing degree

A Soldier and his Rules

of hostility. George did not look particularly hostile this afternoon however. He pulled a hand through his sandy hair and cleared his throat.

"Come in," said Richard. "Please take a seat."

George walked into the room slowly and sat down in a chair opposite Richard. He looked to a table on his left where a lamp had once sat.

"Sorry for smashing your lamp," he said, his face as serious as ever.

"That's quite alright," said Richard remembering that day. George had smashed in more than the lamp. "I'm sure I deserved every punch you landed."

"Maybe," said George, his face softening slightly.

"Patience tells me," said Richard, "that you think I would make a good husband. Are those her words or yours?"

"Unfortunately, they're mine," said George twitching at the corners of his mouth as if he were holding back a smile. "It seems we are of one mind when it comes to Patience. I trust you will look after her."

"I'll do my best," said Richard, "but I think that perhaps we might underestimate how capable she is of taking care of herself."

"No, Winter," said George, quickly correcting him, "I don't think that we do. She is impetuous and stubborn. She takes unnecessary risks. She speaks without thinking." George shifted forward in his seat and leaned in towards Richard. "You must keep an eye on her. The world does not expect to have her in it."

Richard smiled. George certainly knew his sister.

"Alright," he said. "I take your meaning. You can rest assured that Patience's welfare and happiness are my chief concerns in this life."

George sat back as he appeared to breathe a sigh of relief. He pulled a piece of paper from inside his jacket.

"I have secured a special licence for you," he said as he handed it over. "Mother is currently suffering a fit of the vapours over all this, and the sooner your union is blessed by God the better."

Blessed by God. The words burrowed themselves down into the centre of Richard's heart. He knew he had already been blessed by God for no good reason that he could discern. For the first time in his life, he realised he was surrounded by love—Patience of course, but also James and Michael, and Thomas whose unwavering support had seen him through the most difficult times. And here was George Pemberton apologising! Richard felt a weight being lifted from his soul. He felt happy to be alive.

"Yes, thank you," he said taking the licence from George. "I would have secured one myself, but—"

"—but it's only been one day, and you've been busy," said George with no hint of malice. "I had a feeling." He stood to shake Richard's hand. "I should be off. Tell Patience I said hello."

"I will," said Richard gripping his new brother's hand warmly. "I will."

A week or so later, Patience clung possessively to Richard's arm as they entered the ballroom at Almack's. They had been married in a simple ceremony with only her family and Thomas present. The less fuss made about the wedding, the better, according to Lady Pemberton (who had miraculously recovered from her fit of the vapours once a wedding day had been set). If no one actually knew the precise date of their marriage, then it was entirely possible that a scandal could be avoided. That Richard had instinctively referred to Patience as his wife from the very beginning, even when speaking to his servants, had done well to advertise the fact that she was a legitimate presence in his house. Now that they were actually wed, it was necessary to make that fact known to the ton. So here they were at Almack's being presented as Lord and Lady Winter.

"Richard!" said Thomas, striding up to clap him on the back. "And you've brought your engaging wife with you as well! The evening is looking up, if I do say so myself."

"Hello Thomas," said Richard. Patience could see the affection in his eyes as he shook his friend's hand.

"Now," said Thomas dramatically scanning the room. "If only you could find *me* a wife—not a girl mind you. I don't take kindly to any sort of conversation involving ribbons and gossip." He winked at Patience, and she laughed.

"I do believe Miss Fernside is in need of a dance partner," said Patience glancing across the room to where her friend was standing by the wall sipping a cordial. She had said the words without thinking and winced inwardly. Abigail would not be pleased with her if she knew. When Patience looked back at Thomas, his expression had shifted—those grey clouds again, clustering low on the horizon.

"I . . . uh . . . I think I have monopolised Miss Fernside's time enough this Season. She must be growing tired of my antics by now." He cast about the room as if looking for an escape. "Ah! There is your brother, Lady Winter. I've been

Caught in the Blaze

meaning to speak with him." He strode off across the room.

Patience looked at Richard who returned her curious gaze.

"Thomas has been meaning to speak with George?" she asked. "Somehow that doesn't ring true. Is there something I'm missing?"

"With Thomas, there is always something we're missing," said Richard.

The orchestra struck up a lively waltz.

"They're playing our song," said Richard offering Patience his hand. She looked up into his grassy, fiery eyes before taking his hand and allowing him to lead her out onto the dance floor.

"One dance is appropriate," he said placing his large hand on her waist and pulling her indecently close to him. His eyes were sparkling. "Two dances will land us in the gossip sheets. I shudder to think what will happen when I take a third and a fourth dance with you this evening."

Patience gave a joyful shriek as he took control of her body with his powerful arms and swung her into the music.

As they danced the night away, George watched them from the corner of the room. Thomas had tried to engage him earlier, but George had been as taciturn as ever. His inability to smile at Thomas's quick wit had left the poor captain with no proper foothold on the conversation. Eventually, he had made his excuses and wandered off in search of a more receptive audience.

Later in the evening, Patience caught sight of George knocking back a drink at the refreshment table. He looked like a handsome shadow lurking at the edges of the lively room. He was there with them, but he was somehow separate from them, as if he existed on the other side of a transparent curtain.

A Soldier and his Rules

She could not recall seeing him dance with anyone all night.

Why would he not dance? she asked herself. There were any number of young ladies there who would have swooned had he approached them. Patience examined her brother as if for the first time. He was handsome. He was clever. He had a certain aloof charm that so many ladies found appealing. Not least of all, he was the first—the only—son of a baron, so he would inherit a title, not to mention money and land. He was possibly the most eligible bachelor in the room. Yet there he stood, alone, looking as if he carried the weight of the world on his shoulders. *At least I am no longer a burden to him*, thought Patience. *He always seems to have so much on his mind.*

She would never truly know how her brother actually saw her—not as a burden at all, but as his great privilege. That he mourned the loss of his sister as he tossed back his drink would be entirely unthinkable to Patience. But he did. He felt the loss of her quite keenly, a chasm in his life that he did not know how to fill.

Patience's gaze shifted across the ballroom to land on Thomas standing uncharacteristically by himself in one corner holding an empty glass. He was watching Abigail dancing with another gentleman, and the look on his face was one of pure torment. Patience saw Abigail turn her head in his direction, and Thomas dropped his eyes quickly to stare at the glass in his hands.

Well, thought Patience, *there is definitely something I'm missing there.*

Patience was distracted from her thoughts by Richard who had placed his hand in hers and was leading her from the ballroom.

"Where are we going?" she asked.

Caught in the Blaze

"I'm not sure," he said in a low voice.

He tugged her down the hall and around a corner, then turned and pressed her into a recessed portion of the wall. He darted a look down the hall to make sure they were alone.

"Lord Winter," she said, eyes glistening, "this is highly inappropriate."

"I haven't begun to show you inappropriate," responded Richard, eyes flickering with fire.

It had been over a week since she had arrived at his house, but Patience still found her breath coming fast as Richard reached for her. His hands roamed the curves of her body, and he breathed in the scent at her neck tickling her with his beard. He knew what he was doing—teasing and tormenting her until Patience was quite desperate to feel his mouth on hers, to have his hands delve deeper.

"Richard," she said pleadingly.

"I like to hear you say it," he said, his eyes growing dark.

"I need you," said Patience pressing herself against him. "Now."

She could hear him growl softly against her.

We need each other, thought Patience. *Like this, and in so many other ways.*

"The carriage is waiting for us outside," said Richard before taking her mouth in a ravenous kiss.

Hand-in-hand, they made their way outside into the cool night air where they were greeted by a multitude of twinkling stars gazing down at them from an inky sky. Patience looked over and up at her husband's profile in the faint light cast out from the building. He turned to look down at her, and she found herself caught in the blaze of his eyes.

"I love you, Lady Winter," he said.

Epilogue

Three Months Later

Patience lay sideways curled around Richard on their enormous bed. They were both fully clothed. His back was to her, and she was holding him in a fierce embrace. She could feel his heart beating as if it wanted to escape his chest, and she tried her best to slow her own heart to a pace that would soothe him as she pressed her chest against his back. She kissed the clammy nape of his neck and felt him take the hand of the arm she had draped around him. He pulled her hand to his lips—just a touch, simple contact. He was in no state to kiss her properly.

They lay there like that for over an hour. Patience could feel the attack come in waves. His heart would be galloping along for some time before it became steadily slower, softer. There would be barely a few moments of respite before it would start up again, like a terrified horse taking off across a field. Sometimes Patience would count his breaths with him in a slow even pace. Sometimes she would murmur soft words of love, but more often than not, she simply held him until

Epilogue

it was over. When his breathing came more easily, he would roll onto his back, and Patience would stroke his face and the palms of his hands. He would reach for her and hold her close as he fell into sleep, his body so completely and utterly spent that it would take hours before he could rise from the bed again.

The first time it had happened, Patience knew right away that something was wrong. She had stepped out of her studio to find Richard walking shakily along the hallway with one hand to the wall. He had given her a wobbly smile, and she had taken his arm and led him to their bedroom where she locked the door against the servants. Everyone was so used to them spending extended periods of time in their bedroom during all hours of the day that no one batted an eye if they did not emerge until evening.

"I'm sorry," he said sitting down on the bed. "I didn't want you to have to see this."

"I want to see all of you," said Patience removing his jacket and untying his cravat. "I'm your wife."

Richard gave her a weak smile. "You are, aren't you?" He shook his head gently. "What kind of miracle is that?"

Patience lay him down and climbed into bed with him.

"I'd say it's an everyday miracle."

It was July now, and both Patience and Richard were firmly ensconced at Avery House in the countryside. Richard's mother had moved herself into a dower house on the property, and James and Michael had taken themselves off to a cottage by the seaside. It was thoughtful of everyone to give Richard

A Soldier and his Rules

and Patience time to adjust to their life together, but Patience would not have minded a fuller house. While Richard's mother had insisted on moving out of the main building, Patience made certain that she joined them for dinner every evening.

"I don't think she should be alone in that house, Richard," Patience had said.

"Let Mother do as she wishes for now," said Richard, pulling Patience to him. "Once James and Michael return, she will feel less like she is intruding if she moves back in."

As much as Patience loved Richard, she did miss her family at times, especially Grace. After much discussion (and no small amount of pestering from Grace), Lady Pemberton had agreed that Grace could come to stay with Patience and Richard for several weeks in August.

"Does she like to ride? Or would she enjoy learning to fence?" asked Richard looking up from buttering his toast at the breakfast table one morning.

"Who?" asked Patience stabbing at a piece of ham on her plate.

"Grace."

Patience looked at him curiously. "Yes, I suppose she does like to ride. Why?"

"I was just thinking about how we should amuse her while she is here."

Patience grinned across the table at her husband.

"Really?" she said.

"Why is that so hard to believe?" asked Richard taking a bite of his toast.

"I suppose it's not," said Patience. "I'd just imagined that the viscount had more important things to do than plan a recreational itinerary for a little girl."

Epilogue

"I've never had a sister before," said Richard. "I don't want to let her down."

"You can't let her down, Richard. She already thinks the world of you."

"Oh."

"She would probably die of excitement if you taught her to fence," offered Patience.

Richard's face lit up. "Do you think so?"

"I know so," said Patience standing and coming around the table to give him a kiss on the forehead.

Richard was never content with one kiss, especially one so chaste. He dropped his toast on his plate and shifted himself back in his chair as he pulled Patience down to his lap. The footman standing in the corner of the breakfast room cleared his throat. Richard gave him a look, and the man left the room, closing the door behind him.

"Martin must be quite fed up with us," giggled Patience.

"Martin is paid well for his service," said Richard with amusement as he tugged her dress down from her shoulder, "but I should probably increase his salary to compensate him for all the awkward moments he must endure in our company."

"That would be a nice gesture." said Patience, "Most commendable of you."

She pulled her own dress down even further to expose one of her breasts to Richard's gaze, and Patience felt his desire for her begin to strain against his trousers.

"Mm," said Richard as he kissed her neck. He reached behind her to sweep the dishes to the side of the table with a clatter. "But first," he said standing and lifting her with him to place her up onto the breakfast table, "there is something that requires my more immediate attention."

Richard had hoped and prayed that his happiness upon marrying Patience would be some sort of magical cure to his affliction. He knew she had accepted him as he was, but he wished in his darker moments that he was someone else for her, someone who would be less of a burden.

He had imagined that his attacks would frighten her, that he would warn her off if he felt one coming on, and that she would give him his space until it had passed. But Patience was stronger and braver than he had ever imagined. She spoke in a calm and even voice to remind him that she was there, and she would touch him the way only she could. It was her voice and her touch that would draw him back from the abyss again and again. She never—*never*—left him on his own when he was weakened, curling up with him for hours until he could rise again from the bed. He had not hallucinated again the way he had done at Vauxhall Gardens, but he knew that if it came to it, Patience would be able to manage that as well.

Occasionally, Richard would wake in the night and prop himself up on an elbow to watch his wife's sleeping face in the silver light of the moon. He would follow the lines of her face with his eyes, imagining how he might paint her if he had such a talent. As he watched the gentle rise and fall of her breast with her breath, Richard wondered how this had come to be, how he could be so loved. One night, Patience stirred and woke. She saw him watching her.

She rolled into his body, nuzzling her face into his neck, breathing him in.

"Sometimes," she whispered. "I wake at night, and I watch you too." She kissed his neck, his jaw. "Thank you for sharing yourself with me."

That *she* was thanking *him* was almost too much. His life was

Epilogue

now full of precious moments like these—too many to count. They were like the tiny sparkling drops of dew that decorated the grass in the morning, each one a perfect memory that overwhelmed his heart.

Richard pulled his wife close and stroked her down the length of her bare back as she drifted off against his chest. They would wake early in the morning as they always did, and they would ride out to greet the rosy Dawn together.

Thank You!

Thank you for reading *A Soldier and his Rules.* This book was truly a pleasure to write, and I hope you enjoyed your time with Richard and Patience as much as I did!

- Receive a free subscribers-only steamy novella called *The Bull of Bow Street Meets his Match* when you sign up for my mailing list at oliviaelliottromance.com. This is Book 3.5 in *The Pemberton Series*.
- Reviews help other readers decide if a book would suit them. I appreciate all reviews, both positive and negative, so please think about leaving a star-rating or, if you have the time, a few thoughts about my book.
- *A Soldier and his Rules* is the second book in *The Pemberton Series*, and I am currently working on the fourth, so stay tuned!

Also by Olivia Elliott

You may also enjoy these books in *The Pemberton Series*.

A Dangerous Man to Trust?
Bridgerton meets *Jane Eyre* in this spicy, slow-burn Regency romance written with humour and wit. A strong yet vulnerable hero who feels he's unworthy of love, a feisty governess who has sworn off marriage, and a world of heartache and longing between them.

A Baron's Son is Undone
He is the uptight son of a baron. She is the banished daughter of . . . a pirate? Each guards their own terrible truth that threatens the blossoming intimacy between them in this emotional—and steamy—Regency romance.

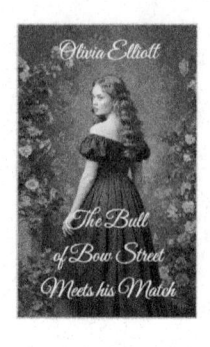

The Bull of Bow Street Meets his Match

She is a devastating beauty with a sense of social justice. He is a Bow Street runner with blood on his hands. As the first hesitant sparks kindle a blaze of fire, these two must eventually decide if love is worth the risk.

Receive a free copy of this book by joining the author's mailing list at oliviaelliottromance.com.

Printed in Dunstable, United Kingdom